Kendra Leighton was born in 1983 and spent most of her childhood absorbed in books. After completing a degree in English Literature and a post-graduate in Education, she taught English in China, Spain and in UK middle-schools. She rediscovered her love for Noyes's 'The Highwayman' while teaching the poem to thirteen-year-olds, and for YA fiction while browsing the school library. In 2008 she left teaching to co-found a chocolate company, giving her the time to indulge in her true passion: books. While making chocolate she listens to audio books. The rest of the time, she can usually be found writing YA or studying the writing craft.

KENDRA
LEIGHTON

Much-in-Little

Constable & Robinson Ltd.
55–56 Russell Square
London WC1B 4HP
www.constablerobinson.com

First published in the UK by Much-in-Little,
an imprint of Constable & Robinson Ltd., 2014

A copy of the British Library Cataloguing in
Publication Data is available from the British Library

ISBN: 978-1-4721-1034-3 (paperback)
ISBN: 978-1-4721-1044-2 (ebook)

Printed and bound in the UK

1 3 5 7 9 10 8 6 4 2

For my dad, whose story ended as this one began

The Highwayman

PART ONE

I

The wind was a torrent of darkness among the gusty trees,
The moon was a ghostly galleon tossed upon cloudy seas,
The road was a ribbon of moonlight over the purple moor,
And the highwayman came riding –
     Riding – riding –
The highwayman came riding, up to the old inn-door.

II

He'd a French cocked-hat on his forehead, a bunch of lace at his
    chin,
A coat of the claret velvet, and breeches of brown doe-skin;
They fitted with never a wrinkle: his boots were up to the
    thigh!
And he rode with a jewelled twinkle,
     His pistol butts a-twinkle,
His rapier hilt a-twinkle, under the jewelled sky.

III

Over the cobbles he clattered and clashed in the dark inn-yard,
And he tapped with his whip on the shutters, but all was locked
    and barred;
He whistled a tune to the window, and who should be waiting
    there
But the landlord's black-eyed daughter,
        Bess, the landlord's daughter,
Plaiting a dark red love-knot into her long black hair.

IV

And dark in the dark old inn-yard a stable-wicket creaked
Where Tim the ostler listened; his face was white and peaked;
His eyes were hollows of madness, his hair like mouldy
    hay,
But he loved the landlord's daughter,
        The landlord's red-lipped daughter,
Dumb as a dog he listened, and he heard the robber say –

V

'One kiss, my bonny sweetheart, I'm after a prize to-night,
But I shall be back with the yellow gold before the morning light;
Yet, if they press me sharply, and harry me through the day,
Then look for me by moonlight,
        Watch for me by moonlight,
I'll come to thee by moonlight, though hell should bar the way.'

VI

He rose upright in the stirrups; he scarce could reach her hand,
But she loosened her hair i' the casement! His face burnt like a
    brand

As the black cascade of perfume came tumbling over his breast;
And he kissed its waves in the moonlight,

    (Oh, sweet, black waves in the moonlight!)

Then he tugged at his rein in the moonlight, and galloped away to
    the West.

PART TWO

I

He did not come in the dawning; he did not come at noon;
And out o' the tawny sunset, before the rise o' the moon,
When the road was a gypsy's ribbon, looping the purple moor,
A red-coat troop came marching –

    Marching – marching –

King George's men came marching, up to the old inn-door.

II

They said no word to the landlord, they drank his ale instead,
But they gagged his daughter and bound her to the foot of her
    narrow bed;
Two of them knelt at her casement, with muskets at their
    side!
There was death at every window;

    And hell at one dark window;

For Bess could see, through her casement, the road that he would
    ride.

III

They had tied her up to attention, with many a sniggering jest;
They had bound a musket beside her, with the barrel beneath her
    breast!

'Now, keep good watch!' and they kissed her.

　　She heard the dead man say –

Look for me by moonlight;

　　Watch for me by moonlight;

I'll come to thee by moonlight, though hell should bar the way!

IV

She twisted her hands behind her; but all the knots held good!

She writhed her hands till her fingers were wet with sweat or
　　blood!

They stretched and strained in the darkness, and the hours crawled
　　by like years,

Till, now, on the stroke of midnight,

　　Cold, on the stroke of midnight,

The tip of one finger touched it! The trigger at least was hers!

V

The tip of one finger touched it; she strove no more for the rest!

Up, she stood up to attention, with the barrel beneath her breast,

She would not risk their hearing; she would not strive again;

For the road lay bare in the moonlight;

　　Blank and bare in the moonlight;

And the blood of her veins in the moonlight throbbed to her love's
　　refrain.

VI

Tlot-tlot; tlot-tlot! Had they heard it? The horse-hoofs ringing
　　clear;

Tlot-tlot, tlot-tlot, in the distance? Were they deaf that they did not
　　hear?

Down the ribbon of moonlight, over the brow of the hill,

The highwayman came riding,
    Riding, riding!
The red-coats looked to their priming! She stood up, straight and
    still!

VII

Tlot-tlot, in the frosty silence! *Tlot-tlot*, in the echoing night!
Nearer he came and nearer! Her face was like a light!
Her eyes grew wide for a moment; she drew one last deep
    breath,
Then her finger moved in the moonlight,
    Her musket shattered the moonlight,
Shattered her breast in the moonlight and warned him – with her
    death.

VIII

He turned; he spurred to the West; he did not know who
    stood
Bowed, with her head o'er the musket, drenched with her
    own red blood!
Not till the dawn he heard it, his face grew grey to hear
How Bess, the landlord's daughter,
    The landlord's black-eyed daughter,
Had watched for her love in the moonlight, and died in the
    darkness there.

IX

Back, he spurred like a madman, shrieking a curse to the sky,
With the white road smoking behind him and his rapier
    brandished high!
Blood-red were his spurs i' the golden noon; wine-red was his
    velvet coat,

When they shot him down on the highway,

    Down like a dog on the highway,

And he lay in his blood on the highway, with the bunch of lace at

    his throat.

X

And still of a winter's night, they say, when the wind is in the trees,
When the moon is a ghostly galleon tossed upon cloudy seas,
When the road is a ribbon of moonlight over the purple moor,
A highwayman comes riding –

    Riding – riding –

A highwayman comes riding, up to the old inn-door.

XI

Over the cobbles he clatters and clangs in the dark inn-yard;
He taps with his whip on the shutters, but all is locked and barred;
He whistles a tune to the window, and who should be waiting there
But the landlord's black-eyed daughter,

    Bess, the landlord's daughter,

Plaiting a dark red love-knot into her long black hair.

Alfred Noyes, 1906

Chapter One

GOALS (HOW TO BECOME NORMAL)
NO NIGHTMARES
NO GLIMPSES
STOP WORRYING DAD
GET FRIENDS

I scrutinized Miss Mahoney's face as she read. Her eyebrows had been raised for a few minutes now. I ran through each of the four points in my head. She must have read them ten times. I wished I knew what she was thinking.

She lay the paper face down on the desk and spread her hands over it as though it might fly up and hit her in the face.

'Liz,' she began.

My stomach tensed. She didn't like it. I'd learnt early on in our year of meetings that her 'I'm being serious now' voice was not a good sign.

'This list . . .'

She fixed her gaze on a point somewhere over my left shoulder instead of meeting my eye. She really didn't like it.

'This list . . . Now, it goes without saying that I am happy for you. Delighted for you. I wouldn't normally advise students to move schools at this point in their studies, but I know being at Jameson Secondary has not been easy. I can understand why you're itching to get away.' She finally turned her gaze to me and I made an effort to stop fidgeting in my chair. 'However, this whole obsession with being normal . . .'

I folded my arms around me.

'"Normal" is meaningless, Liz. You are only as normal as you feel inside.'

I sighed. 'That's the point,' I said, picking my satchel off the floor and resting it on my knee.

'I'm pleased you've written down some goals like I asked you to, but I was thinking of something more achievable. More . . .' She waved her hands as if trying to pull the right words to her.

'These are achievable, miss. Well, the first three anyway.'

The corners of her mouth drooped. 'How?'

'I'll be gone from this school. I'll be living in a different house.'

'And the nightmares will stop, just like that? Your "Glimpses"—' she made quotation marks in the air with her fingers '—will stop?'

'Yes.' My heart was pounding, the way it always did when someone tried to talk to me about my Glimpses. I glanced pointedly towards the door.

Miss Mahoney sighed and leaned back in her chair. She looked at me for a long moment. I wrapped the lace hem of my dress around my finger and tried to keep my face calm.

'I know you don't want to hear this again,' she said, 'but I need to remind you that you can't expect to run from your problems, as if they're separate from you. I'm concerned that you're setting yourself up for disappointment—'

I stood up, cutting her short with the squeak of my chair on the tiles. I pressed my satchel to my chest like a shield. 'Well, you can stop worrying about me now, miss.' I pursed my lips together and stared at an ink stain on her desk, not wanting to see the sympathy I knew would be in her eyes.

She held my 'Normality List' out to me. 'I just don't want you to have unrealistic expectations.'

I took the paper and pushed it into the outside pocket of my bag. 'I'm going to be fine.'

'I hope so, Liz.'

The lunch bell rang, punctuating the end of her sentence. The corridor outside her office exploded with the noise of classroom doors banging open, the pound and squeak of feet racing to join the lunch queue, 'No running!' yelled by a teacher.

My stomach clenched. But then I remembered – this was my last lunchtime here; my very last – and my tension eased. I reached for the door handle. 'Bye, then. And thanks.'

Miss Mahoney's raised voice followed me as I stepped into the flow of bodies in the corridor. 'Bye, Liz. I'm only an email away if you need me.'

I gave her a last smile as the door swung shut behind me. I won't be emailing, I thought. Four hours from now, the nightmare of my school life here would be over. Five weeks from now I'd be leaving this town for good. Things could only get better.

I looked down, held my satchel to my chest like a battering ram, and headed through the corridors. The crowd thinned as I moved away from the dining hall. By the time

I'd reached my locker, I was as alone as I ever was at Jameson Secondary.

Finally breathing easy, I put my satchel on the floor, opened my locker, and pulled out my lunchbox.

'What have you got for me today, freakazoid?'

An ink-stained hand plucked the box from my fingers. I slammed my locker door shut to reveal Derek, busy examining the contents of my lunchbox through its transparent lid. His friends – his usual gang, three boys and two girls – grinned over at me from behind him. One of the girls, Danielle, waved; a sarcastic wiggle of her fingertips.

'Give that back!' I lunged for the lunchbox, tripping over my satchel and sending it spinning towards Danielle. Danielle squealed and jumped sideways, like my bag was something disgusting, then picked it up and threw it to Leah. Leah echoed Danielle's squeal and let my bag whack to the floor. My books spilled around Derek's feet.

'Stop it!' My voice was small, like my lungs had shrivelled. I balled my fists at my sides.

Derek shook my lunchbox, making peanut butter smear across the plastic. 'What is this?' His tone was bright, like we were having a friendly conversation. 'Diarrhoea sandwiches? Your dad send you to school with diarrhoea sandwiches, did he, loony?'

I wanted to tell him to shut up. I wanted to tell him we weren't twelve any more; that I didn't care what he said, because after today I'd never see him again. But all that came out when I opened my mouth was another weak, 'Give it back.'

Derek held the box towards me, a smile on his round face. 'Go on, then. Take it.'

I hesitated, then reached for it. With a flick of his wrist,

Derek flung my lunchbox past me as if it were a Frisbee. It banged against a wall further down the corridor. There was a rustle, splat and crunch as the contents fell out.

'Oops. Slipped. No shit sandwiches for you today.'

I folded my arms across my chest. My heart pounded against my ribcage. Four more hours, and I'd never have to go through this again, I told myself. One more missed lunch didn't matter.

'You've got what you wanted.' My voice was almost a whisper. 'Please leave me alone.'

'Leave you alone?' Derek's eyebrows shot up, his new eyebrow ring – which had already earned him multiple detentions – glinting in the light. He lowered his voice to a whisper and leaned close enough for me to smell his cheap aftershave. 'But I thought you were never alone.'

I stiffened. Though I knew he was winding me up, the hairs rose on my arms, making my skin tighten. Without warning, the sensation on my skin intensified into full-blown pins and needles. No. Please not now. Not in front of him . . . But it was now. The tingling spread across my skin like flames.

I gasped and stumbled backwards, bashing my heels against the bottom of the lockers. Unable to stop myself, I scanned the corridor, my eyes wide. No, no, no . . .

'Oh my God, she's scaring me!' Danielle shrieked gleefully, grabbing Derek's arm.

'And the freak show begins,' Derek said. 'Luke, get your phone out. I want a video of this. I'm going to miss Loony over the summer.'

I pressed my back against the locker doors. I didn't know which way it was going to come from, but I had to be ready to run.

I saw it. Behind Leah's head. A pair of disembodied hands.

I knew those hands. Of all the Glimpses I'd seen at Jameson Secondary – the booted feet that had run towards me, the eyes that had glared at me, the mouths that had snarled at me, the torsos that had floated behind me – I knew those hands the best. I knew every coarse, black hair sprouting from the pale skin. Knew the exact red of the shiny, stretched nubs where thumbs should be.

They were the hands that had attacked me in year seven, making me scream – the first time Derek noticed me.

They were the hands that had earned me the title Loony Lizzie, when they'd attacked me in a Science lesson in year eight.

And now they were ruining my last day at Jameson Secondary.

I watched, transfixed, barely daring to breathe, as the eight pale fingers tangled in Leah's shoulder-length hair. I couldn't tell whether they were trying to caress her bottle-blonde locks or pull them.

Leah, of course, had no clue. She grinned at me, and made circles next to her ear with her index finger. 'Looooony,' she sing-songed.

One of the hands freed itself from Leah's hair and copied her gesture, circling her other ear. Then, in sickening slow motion, it pointed its long index finger at me.

I shrieked and ducked as the hands flew straight for me, fingers spread. They slashed across my cheek with a sensation light and creepy as moth-wings, then disappeared down the corridor behind me. The tingling on my skin cut off, like my body was a conductor and someone had pulled the plug.

The hysterical laughter of Derek's gang filled my ears.

'Jeez, don't pee yourselves,' Derek told his friends, though he could barely get the words out, he was laughing so much. 'Good show, Loonz.'

He turned away from me, which was the cue for the others to leave. They kicked the contents of my bag – my school books, my pencil case, my purse – halfway down the corridor with them, before they finally got bored.

'Watch out for men in white coats over the summer,' Derek called over his shoulder, before they rounded the corner. 'Though even a straitjacket would be an improvement. At least then your grandma could get her dresses back.'

The peals of Danielle's and Leah's laughter echoed down the corridor towards me.

I hissed every swear word I knew, standing up for myself too late, as always. I looked down at my vintage purple dress – a seventies charity shop find I'd been proud of, until this moment – and tugged angrily at its lace cuffs. I was glad I hadn't told anyone but the teachers I was leaving. I could only imagine the torture Derek would have inflicted if he'd known this was his last chance.

Shaking with adrenaline, I gathered the contents of my bag and the bits of my lunch that were still edible from the floor. I kept an eye out, but the Glimpse-hands had gone, their damage done.

I thought of the creepy way those fingers had tangled in Leah's hair, and shuddered. Miss Mahoney was wrong. I might be the only one who saw Glimpses, but there was no way those horrors came out of my own head. I was messed up, but not that messed up.

No. The Glimpses were real, just like Derek was real; and that was why I was going to be able to leave them behind, just like I was going to leave Derek behind. By the time I got to my next school, my nightmares and the Glimpses and Derek and his stupid cronies would be gone, and no one there would know a thing about me.

Six weeks from now, I was going to seem perfectly normal, for the first time in seven years.

Chapter Two

This isn't happening. Concentrate, and the pins and needles will go away. Concentrate, and there won't be anything there.

I edge towards my bedroom door. With each step the tingling gets worse. Dread churns in my stomach. It's like I'm ten years old again. This should have ended.

Nausea rolls through me and I clamp a hand over my mouth. My fingers burn where they press my teeth into my lips. It's in my room. My new room.

Wait.

Like a compass needle, my focus flips. I freeze, my skin on fire where I'm touching the door handle. It's moved. It's . . .

Behind me.

My back bristles, not with pins and needles, more painful — more like daggers and blades.

Fighting every instinct, I turn. I don't want to see, I don't want to see, I don't want . . .

I see it.

The Glimpse.

★

I slid out of bed and picked the crumpled ball of paper off the floor. I'd almost got it in the bin, not bad for a half-asleep throw.

Smoothing it with one hand, I looked again at the offensive words: '1. No nightmares'.

Okay, so my resolutions hadn't got off to a good start. No big deal. No need to give up so quickly.

I padded across the floorboards to the boxes piled in the corner – I really had to unpack today – rooted for some sticky tack, and fastened the crinkled list to my wardrobe door. White tack, white paper, white wardrobe. Everything in my new room was white. The door, the bed covers, the furniture, the shutters at the window. Even the exposed beams that criss-crossed the walls and ceiling, that were dark brown in the rest of the inn, were painted white here. That's why I'd chosen this room. It was a blank canvas.

Bang bang bang bang bang.

'Liz? Liz! Are you okay in there?'

Bang bang bang bang bang.

'Dad, what's wrong?'

'I heard you shrieking.' His voice was muffled by the thick door, but the worry in it was obvious.

I winced. 'I'm fine.'

I really had to work on 'No nightmares'. It would help a ton with 'Stop worrying Dad'.

'Are you almost ready for school?'

I frowned. School was still hours away. I was up early; my alarm hadn't even gone off yet. My gaze slid to the bedside table, finding the digital display of my alarm clock. The very blank display of my alarm clock. I hadn't plugged it in.

I inhaled sharply. 'Dad, what time is it?' I didn't bother to sound calm this time.

'I'm coming in.' Dad pushed my door open. He stared at me from the threshold, his eyes wide beneath his glasses, his pyjamas rumpled, his hair wild from sleep. 'Liz, you're still in your nightie.'

'What time is it, Dad?'

'Seven forty-five.'

Twenty minutes until my bus. Twenty minutes until my first bus journey, on my first day at the new school.

I yelped, and dived for the pile of clothes I'd laid out yesterday.

'I'll make you breakfast,' Dad said, and speed-stumbled away.

I pulled on my brand-new jeans and shirt and ran down the worn carpet to the nearest bathroom, pulling my unbrushed hair into a ponytail on the way. There was no time to tiptoe through the corridors like I had yesterday, no time to think about the abandoned rooms I passed.

The dank air of the small bathroom filled my mouth. I scrubbed it away with a thirty-second toothbrushing, then ran back to my room for my bag and half fell down the unfamiliarly steep stairs.

Dad stood at the bottom of the staircase, a plate of toast in his hand.

'You eat it,' I said. 'Sorry, no time. Bye, Dad.'

I pushed open the inn's heavy front door and headed into the dull morning. I shivered. I should have brought a jacket. I'd have given anything for one of my comfortable, thick dresses and a pair of tights right then, but I was taking no chances: nobody would call me 'granny girl' again.

Just school, just school, just school.

I crunched across the gravel towards the road, skirting

around the gnarled tree that filled the driveway. I slowed only to slip a compact mirror from my jeans pocket. For a second, the reflection of the Highwayman Inn loomed in the glass, framed by dark clouds that promised rain. The inn looked like an abandoned building from a horror movie.

My face was scarier though. My unwashed curls sucked to my scalp, then exploded out of my ponytail like broken tarantula legs. My eyes were puffy and rimmed with shadows, and my cheeks were pale.

So much for first-day-at-school attractive. Six weeks of summer holiday hair-and-make-up prep wasted because I forgot to plug in my alarm. I looked like a corpse with issues.

At least my outfit – skinny jeans and a fitted white shirt – would pass for 'normal'. I'd chosen it straight from the pages of a magazine, accessories and all, for being just the right blend of fashionable and forgettable. The only things that were 'Liz' about my outfit were my old leather satchel and my gold heart-shaped locket. I tugged the necklace straight under my shirt collar, and rounded the corner out of the inn's driveway.

I could feel them watching as I started down the road towards the bus stop. I scanned the queue as I got closer, passing a row of chocolate-box cottages. I ignored the kids in uniform – they wouldn't be going to my new sixth form, they were no threat. It was the faces of the students in jeans and dresses and logo-ed T-shirts that I scrutinized. A few of them stared at me right back, but seemed nonplussed. I silently congratulated my new clothes – score one for New Liz.

At the edge of the group, a goth couple were latched in an unending kiss. I moved to the other side of the crowd. I held back from speaking to anyone.

Less than a minute after my arrival, the double-decker

pulled up to the kerb. I hadn't taken the bus to school in years, not since Derek had moved to my part of town.

My nerves jittered as I joined the back of the sloppily formed queue. When I got to the front, I flashed my pass at the driver in the nonchalant way I'd seen the other girls do, and took the stairs to the upper deck, where I found an empty pair of seats at the back. Today was all about number four on my list – 'Get friends' – but I wouldn't introduce myself to anyone yet. Not till I'd worked out who they were and how nosey they were likely to be.

'Down the corridor, up the stairs, turn left, and 12G's the third door on your right.' The receptionist circled a room on a map of the school and handed it to me along with a timetable. 'Smile, love. We're all friendly here.'

I shoved my way through the scrum of first-year students and their parents at the reception desk. The school map sprawled across the paper. Noyes College was the only sixth form for miles, and served all the local villages. It must have been at least twice as big as my last sixth form. I couldn't decide if that was a good thing or not. More potential friends, but also more potential enemies.

Right now, it was bad. I twisted the map and frowned.

'Need a hand?'

I recognized the girl instantly as one of the goths from the bus. She was dressed all in black, with New Rock boots, which looked too heavy for her slight frame, and a tutu-like skirt with stiff net layers. Her chin-length bob was black, with a slash of red dye through the fringe. Black eyeshadow ringed her eyes – which were rapidly changing from friendly to 'maybe I shouldn't have asked' the longer I stared at her.

Smile, Liz. I beamed so suddenly that the girl's eyebrows shot up. 'Yes! Thanks. I'm trying to find 12G?'

She smiled, and jerked her chin to the right. 'Easy. I'll show you. I'm Susie, by the way.'

'Liz.'

Susie set off through the teeming corridors, and I followed. For a moment, everything felt incredibly surreal; familiar and alien at the same time. Automatically, my head lowered and my gaze dropped to the floor, but I caught myself in time and pulled both higher. As far as anyone here knew, I was as normal as they were, I reminded myself.

'Did you just move here, or something?' Susie looked back over her shoulder at me as we climbed a flight of stairs.

'Yes, on Saturday.' I picked up my pace to catch up with her.

A boy coming down the stairs the other way nearly barrelled into me. He stopped short with a tsk of annoyance. 'Sorry,' I blustered.

Susie reached back and caught my satchel strap, tugging me to the side. 'Keep to the left. School rule.' She pushed through some double doors at the top of the stairs. We entered a corridor of classrooms. Groups of students chatted by the lockers. Susie wound between them.

'I saw you coming from the Highwayman Inn this morning.' Her voice held an open question.

I grimaced internally. I knew I couldn't keep my new home a secret – not the way I planned to keep some other facts a secret – but it was a definite flaw in my plan to seem normal. The Highwayman Inn was not a normal house. Derek would have loved that.

Susie stopped outside a door with a fresh, white '12G' painted on the wood. She looked at me expectantly.

I felt for the familiar shape of my locket. 'Um, yeah,' I said. 'The inn belonged to my granddad, but he died a few months ago and left it to us.'

Her face lit up with genuine glee. 'Oh my God, you live there? You own it?'

I nodded, and couldn't help beaming back at her in relief.

'That is so cool!' Susie exclaimed. 'We went on an English trip there in year seven. We were studying that highwayman poem, you know?'

I nodded – I knew. Derek would have loved that too; I had moved into an inn famous for inspiring an old poem about ghosts. Derek had always told everyone that I was crazy, that I thought I saw ghosts. I wasn't sure what my Glimpses were, but if they were ghosts (dear God, I hoped not) they definitely weren't romantic spirits like in that poem.

Doesn't matter any more, I reminded myself. I'd left the Glimpses behind.

I tuned back into Susie's gushing.

'You're going to get so much attention from the English teachers,' she was saying. 'You noticed the highwayman statue in the school car park, right?'

I nodded again.

'If you live at the inn, does that mean you've got your own bar? Does your bedroom have chandeliers?'

I nodded. Shook my head. 'There's a bar. But no chandeliers.'

'It's got to be haunted.' She bit her lip with glee.

I stopped smiling. 'No.' The word came out too hard, too serious, but Susie was already turning away, and I hoped she hadn't noticed.

'See you on the bus, yeah?' She disappeared into the crush.

'Thanks!' I called after her, a moment too late.

I tugged hard on my necklace, trying to regain my composure. Susie thought the inn was cool, she knew nothing about me; everything was fine.

Chapter Three

I peered into room 12G through the glass panel in the door. Compared to the first-day-back excitement in the corridors, it looked an oasis of calm. A man with a grey beard – 12G's form teacher, I guessed – pored over a pile of papers at his desk. The rest of the room was empty, chairs stacked neatly behind freshly polished tables. From the few maps and flags pinned to the walls, I guessed 12G was a Geography room.

Teachers were one of the few things about school that didn't bother me – a good thing considering the number of extra classes I'd had to attend over the years – so I tapped on the glass and went in.

The man looked up. Before either of us could speak, the bell rang. The classroom door crashed open behind me. Students burst through the door like sprinters crossing the start line of a race.

'You must be Elizabeth Rathamore,' the teacher called, over the stampeding of feet and the scraping of chairs. 'I'm Mr Scholars. I'll catch up with you at break. I've had some notes through from your old school, from a Miss Mahoney.'

I nodded, my heart sinking. Of course my old school would send my notes through. But I'd still hoped they'd forget.

I joined the rush to find a chair. Most had already been filled. This was a crucial moment – I knew from experience that being stuck in the wrong seat could spell a year's worth of misery, especially when it came to picking partners for group work. At Jameson Secondary I'd had no choice but to sit on my own; I refused to let that happen again.

I made a beeline for a large table at the back of the room that had free spaces. 'Can I sit here?'

The four boys and two girls who'd claimed the rest of the table glanced up at me. One of the girls nodded. I slipped into one of the two empty chairs. I hoped someone would take the empty seat next to me, but when they didn't, I put my bag on it, so it would look like I'd meant it to be that way.

'You moved into that inn, didn't you? I saw you on the bus.'

I looked up to see my nearest neighbour, a girl in a bright pink top, looking at me expectantly. Her words had grabbed the attention of the rest of my table, and suddenly, I had an audience.

I smiled my best my-house-may-be-freaky-but-I'm-not smile. 'That's me.'

'Quiet, 12G!' Mr Scholars roared. I closed my eyes in a brief moment of relief as the gazes at my table slid away from me. 'So Elizabeth – heiress of the Highwayman Inn, no less – come up to the front and introduce yourself.'

A jolt of adrenaline killed my relief.

'Don't worry, I'm not an English teacher. I won't quiz you on the poem.' Mr Scholars grinned beneath his moustache.

I blinked back at him. At least I knew now that he hadn't read Miss Mahoney's notes. He wouldn't be asking me to do this if he had.

I reached down to straighten a dress I wasn't wearing – I still wasn't used to jeans – and squirmed my way up to the front of the room.

I scanned the faces in front of me. No one looked particularly hostile. No one was laughing. No one was sneering at my clothes. Still, it was impossible not to feel a familiar panic.

'Hi.' I lifted a hand in an awkward wave. 'I'm Liz. Short for Elizabeth.' I gave Mr Scholars a pleading look. *Enough?*

'And what subjects are you taking?' he asked, oblivious to my discomfort.

'English, History, Art, General Studies.'

'An arts girl, eh? None of my classes. Who here does some of those subjects and would like to show Liz around?'

Long seconds passed with a distinct lack of hands being raised. The invisible gas ring under my chin started clicking. Any moment now and I'd burn up.

'Sarah, you take History don't you?' Mr Scholars said. He fixed his eyes on a girl in the front row, who started opening and closing her mouth like a fish.

'And James, you take Art?'

A hand shot up at the back of the room. It was the pink top girl from my table. 'I'll show her,' she called.

'Thank you, Katie,' Mr Scholars said.

The classroom door flew open and bounced against the wall with a bang, making me jump. Chair legs scraped against the floor as every student in the room turned round, startled. A frazzled-looking teacher marched into the room towards me and Mr Scholars. I took my chance to dart around her and back to the safety of my seat, glad not to be the centre of attention any more.

'Mr Scholars!' the woman screeched behind me. 'I cannot

do it. I'm sick of him already and the school year's barely started.'

I buried my head in my bag, pretending to retrieve a pen that had fallen from my pencil case, and took a calming breath.

The room fell silent.

'Miss Webb,' said Mr Scholars, trying – unsuccessfully – to be discreet. 'We promised his father we'd give him another chance. There's a procedure. Verbal warnings, then written warnings, then—'

'I don't care!' Miss Webb's voice went up another decibel.

Katie winced and stuck her fingers in her ears.

'I'm not suffering another year of this. He's completely destroyed my seating arrangements already, he causes chaos wherever I put him.'

There were sniggers now, quiet ones. Katie unstuck her fingers, leaned towards me and whispered, 'Miss Webb's one of the History teachers. I'll show you where the History block is later, if you like.'

I sought for my smile muscles and mouthed a grateful, 'Thanks.'

'I'm sending him to you,' Miss Webb continued behind me. 'You can deal with him this year, Mr Scholars. I've had enough!'

The door banged again as she flounced out of the room. Giggles spread around the class.

'Class 12G, settle down.' Mr Scholars sounded tired. 'Apparently, we're going to have two new students this year. Elizabeth Rathamore and Scott Crowley.'

There was a collective groan. Even I wasn't paranoid enough to think it was over me.

I vaguely registered the sound of the classroom door opening again as Katie leaned back towards me, her eyes sparkling. 'Scott, right, he's—'

Thunk. My bag plummeted from the chair next to me and onto the floor.

'Scott Crowley!' Mr Scholars bellowed.

My eyes drew level with a fashionably sagging waistband, then moved up to take in a grin, the silver glint of an eyebrow ring, and white-blond hair. Scott − I assumed − was tipping the chair where my bag had been at a forty-five-degree angle. When I met his eyes his expression twisted in a double-take.

'Kicked out of class before the school year's even started. Disgraceful. Sit down this minute!'

Scott didn't flinch, just smirked down at me, his eyes not leaving mine. 'Oops, was that your bag?' he said, with mock innocence. 'You must be the new girl. Sorry about that.'

Mr Scholars marched over to our table and folded his arms. 'Show over yet, Scott?'

'Carry on, sir.' Scott sat down next to me in a cloud of aftershave. For a moment I was transported right back to my old school, to Derek hanging over me, laughing through a fugue of cheap-smelling chemicals.

Scott made a show of picking my bag off the floor and returning it to me, his leg bumping mine as he did so. I took the bag, my fingers numb. I hoped I was succeeding in keeping my face blank.

This boy wasn't Derek, I told myself. I wasn't the Liz I'd been six weeks ago. And everything was going to fine.

Thunder rolled outside the windows, making the whole class groan again. I kept my face neutral, and turned my eyes on the teacher, away from Scott.

Chapter Four

As Dad was so fond of telling me, there was a time when I hadn't needed to try to be normal. I just was.

Not that he used that word. Adults – teachers, doctors – shied away from saying 'normal' or 'abnormal' around me, like the blunt truth would hurt my feelings. Instead, Dad told me I 'wasn't always so socially troubled'. I think that was a phrase he'd picked up from Dr Roberts.

I had to take his word for it, but the old photos he trundled out now and then – the ones with Mum in their own separate pile, so I wouldn't come across one unexpectedly and get upset (read: so Dad wouldn't get upset) – did seem to back him up.

'You were such a happy child,' he'd say, as though by pointing it out he could magic me back into that grinning little girl who was the exact opposite of everything I was now.

There I was in the photos, surrounded by hordes of friends at my fifth birthday party, taking riding lessons with my then best friend at age eight, winning the egg-and-spoon race at the school sports day at age nine. It was only the last seven years that had been tricky.

Rain poured off my umbrella. I followed the long brick

wall that marked the front boundary of the inn's land, turned at the entrance to the driveway, and took one last look down the road. The Highwayman Inn was the last building before Hulbourn turned to farmland, so the few kids from the bus who'd followed me had already disappeared inside the chocolate-box cottages.

A stream of students walked, or ran, shrieking, if they didn't have raincoats, in the opposite direction from me, towards the village centre. I could just make out Susie, a slim black blob holding hands with a taller, wider black blob. A dark umbrella that made me think of bat wings curved over the top of them.

Susie had smiled at me on the bus journey home. Relief slunk in my belly at the thought of it.

Other than my encounter with Susie, though, my day hadn't been perfect in the 'Get friends' department. After Scott arrived in 12G, Katie and the others had turned subtly away from my end of the table, their noses wrinkling like they'd smelled something sour. Katie had flashed the occasional glance my way, but they'd kept conversation between themselves.

It was more Scott's fault than mine – none of them knew anything about me yet – but it had paved the way for Old Liz to slip back. Countless times I'd had to consciously un-slouch my shoulders, stop chewing the inside of my lips, lift my gaze from the desk, release my locket from my iron grip.

Tomorrow, I'd make more effort. Tomorrow, maybe I'd find a seat that wasn't near Scott.

I crunched through the inn's open metal gates and into the wide driveway. The Highwayman loomed ahead of me, as huge and unfriendly-looking as when I'd first seen it in person two days ago. The dark sky and sheets of rain were the perfect backdrop. I almost forgot about school for a moment as I took in the dark, dripping woods to my left (now mine, I realized with a jolt of disbelief), the wide, sodden lawn to my right (mine), the sprawling inn (mine), with its peeling white paint and countless small dark windows that reminded me of spider eyes; the outbuildings (mine) that sloped from the side of the inn and merged into the woods.

Mine. Such a little word – and either it was one of the most exciting in the dictionary, or one of the most terrifying. The inn wasn't legally mine till I was eighteen, but Granddad had still left it to me. I was like a modern-day Cinderella, Miss Mahoney had said – poor little girl turning rich at the wave of a magic wand. (Or, as I'd thought in silent rebuke, more like the poor little girl benefiting from the heart attack of the grandfather she couldn't remember meeting.)

But this inn was no princess castle. This was a standing stone, a blot of rough-hewn severity. If I was going to restart my life, it could have been somewhere prettier, somewhere more . . . normal.

I sped up as I neared the front door, giving the old tree in the middle of the driveway a wide berth. Huge raindrops fell from the tips of its gnarled branches, hitting my umbrella like bullets.

'I'm back!' I yelled in the hallway. My vision swam green and black as I adjusted to the dimness inside. I kicked off my soaked ballet pumps and propped my umbrella in the metal stand by the door, destroying a dozen spider webs as I did so. The slate tiles were cold under my bare feet. It had been chilly enough outside, but entering the inn was like stepping into a dark fridge. Not exactly comforting.

'Dad, I'm home!' I paused and listened. 'Dad?'

He was sleeping, I guessed. He did that a lot, but I couldn't stop a pang of disappointment. It wasn't like I'd thought he'd be waiting for me with tea and biscuits, but I had hoped he'd at least be waiting for me.

It was a good thing, I told myself. 'Stop worrying Dad' was my number three priority, and if he was asleep, that meant he wasn't panicking about me.

Inclining my head towards the stairs, I listened for the grunts and gasps of Dad's snoring that had welcomed me home from school so often in my old house. But the only sounds breaking the vacuum-still silence were the dry tick, tick, tick of a grandfather clock further down the hall and the patter of rain against the windows.

To my right, a door led into parts of the inn I had yet to explore properly: sitting rooms with ancient furniture under dust sheets; a pantry taken over by mice; a drawing room with a piano that looked like it really should be in a museum. All creepy, dusty rooms, perfect for Derek's version of the Old Liz – not perfect for my hopes for New me.

I padded along the corridor, heading for the one downstairs room Dad and I had so far claimed as our own. I passed a door under the stairs marked 'Library', and a dark-wood sideboard with a dead spider plant on it, before swerving into the main kitchen.

The doorway was an obstacle course of packing boxes brimming with familiar objects. Dad wasn't here, but his faded blue sofa was – it, along with the TV, was one of the few pieces of furniture we'd brought from our old house. Dad had even sold his piano – not that he'd played it much in the last seven years. The rest of the kitchen was unfamiliar, a cold sea of marble and stainless steel, created for serving hotel guests, not heating up microwave meals for Dad and me.

I felt like a trespasser, like at any moment some kitchen
maid in period costume would bustle into the room and ask
me what the hell I was doing. But I couldn't deny that another
part of me felt strangely right about being here. Maybe it was
because I'd spent the summer poring over the photos the
lawyers had given me, but I preferred to hope that, being back
in the place where I'd apparently spent so much time as a child,
I was finally starting to remember.

I wanted to remember.

With a surge of determination, I picked one of the packing
boxes off the floor – cleaning stuff and tea towels – and lugged
it over to the grey marble work surface. Maybe if I banged
around enough while unpacking, Dad would come downstairs
and help me.

Next to the kettle was a note. I grabbed it.

GONE TO TOWN. JOB HUNTING AND SUPER-
MARKET. TEXT IF YOU WANT ANYTHING.

I had to read it twice before I could believe the words. Dad
had gone out?

I crunched the note in my fist, telling myself the sudden
pounding of my heart was surprise, not panic. Dad lived
in pyjamas, he didn't just go out. And especially not on his
daughter's first day at a new school.

I was totally speechless. Dad had left me alone. Alone in
a 500-year-old building. A structure pretty much perfectly
designed for catching Glimpses.

I was halfway to the kitchen door before I could stop myself.
My mind presented a roll-call of all the places where Glimpses
could be hiding. The old hotel dining room, just the other side

38

of that serving hatch, with its red and gold tables under dust sheets. The bar room, with its worm-eaten stools and festering mouse droppings. The safe, a room in itself, big enough to lock a person in. Any one of the six guest bedrooms (or all of them). The outbuildings. The library. The downstairs toilet with the huge spider—

No. No.

No Glimpses, I told myself. I'd left them behind.

I clenched my hands into fists. No more running. I could be home alone now.

Taking a deep breath, I forced my imagination away from the dark corners of the inn. I had to focus on myself now: the new, not frightened Liz, just standing in my new kitchen. With a conscious effort, I dropped Dad's note in the bin.

I looked at all the boxes, still full of our stuff, but didn't feel like unpacking any more. I needed to be somewhere I felt safe.

I tiptoed back into the corridor, which was still damp with my footprints, and up the steep stairs towards my room. No more Glimpses, I repeated in my head like a mantra, no more worrying Dad. A line of closed doors stretched ahead of me down the dimly lit, mildew-tinged corridor. I pushed back thoughts of the creepy four-poster beds and the inches of dust gathered behind them. I couldn't imagine how Mum had grown up here and turned out so happy and normal.

In the safety of my white room, with its clear view of the driveway, I did feel safer. I sat on the white bed for long minutes, my arms held out like antennae, waiting to feel the first pins and needles that always heralded my Glimpses, but there was nothing.

I hadn't seen a Glimpse in over two days, not since leaving

my old house. Even Miss Mahoney would have to agree I was right. The Glimpses had gone.

Breathing more freely, I popped open the window – I loved the sound of rain, when I wasn't standing in it – and riffled through my open suitcase. I pulled out a pair of maroon tights, and my comfiest, if least-flattering, dress – a long-sleeved, brown wool, sixties number. One of the girls at Jameson Secondary had told me it looked like her nan's curtains, but no one was here to see me now. I felt more like myself with the familiar fabric against my skin. I dropped my too-tight jeans and shirt in a damp pile next to the bed.

From downstairs came a soft click and a bang. Dad. I pulled open my door and ran into the corridor with a welcoming smile on my face. From here, I could see all the way down the stairs to the closed front door. No Dad. Whatever I'd heard, it wasn't him.

My smile vanished, and the hairs on my arms became alert. Last night's nightmare lurched from the depths of my mind. I'd been standing right here. Outside my new room.

Hardly breathing, I turned, very slowly, back around. Pins and needles exploded across my body.

Floating level with my head was a face.

Chapter Five

Every muscle in my body froze.

Every muscle on the face opposite me sprang to life. The blue eyes narrowed, the small nose wrinkled, the mouth – oh God, the mouth, with tiny teeth like a child's – opened in a snarl. Around the face was nothing but cold, empty air.

I opened my mouth to shriek. Nothing came out.

Run, run, run, I urged my legs, but then, over the top of my fear, rose a tsunami of wild fury.

The Glimpses were meant to have ended. I was meant to have left them.

Barely knowing what I was doing, I leapt forwards. 'Go away!' I screamed, swinging my arm at the face.

The Glimpse zipped sideways with a rush of air, past my shoulder and into the corridor behind me. I span round, but it had disappeared.

I turned frantic circles, panting, whimpering. The tingling on my skin faded, leaving me with chills.

The Glimpses had followed me here.

I turned to run downstairs – I'd wait for Dad in the rain; anything but wait for that Glimpse to come back – when a voice floated through my open window. 'Are you all right up there?'

A fresh jolt of adrenaline shot around my body, but for a different reason than before. I took a breath, swiped my hands across my face and down the front of my dress – I must look a panicked wreck – and walked on shaky legs to the window.

The caretaker stood near the tree on the gravel below, staring up at me.

'Are you all right?' he called again. 'I heard shouting.'

I cursed inwardly. I had no idea the caretaker would be around. I'd only met him briefly when we first arrived, and I'd half forgotten about him. It was hard to get my head around the idea of living somewhere big enough to need a caretaker.

'I'm fine, Mr Crowley.' My voice wobbled. I tried again, but louder, trying to drown out the wobble. 'Thanks. I saw a spider, that's all.'

Crowley squinted up at me, his eyes almost disappearing inside his fleshy face. He was a big man, and he was standing right under the edge of the tree's canopy, so the branches barely sheltered him. Rain dripped down his thick neck and plastered his thin, blond hair to his head.

'Spider, eh? You'd better get over that one, or you'll be doing a lot of screaming in this house.' He cocked his head to the side. 'Come down, since you're here. I want to introduce you to someone.'

I dredged my brain for a good excuse not to, but, as usual, it deserted me when I needed it most. 'Um. Okay.'

I stepped back from the window with a quiet groan. I'd just seen a Glimpse. I was in no state to meet anyone.

Since Crowley was the only member of Granddad's staff that Dad had kept on, I guessed he just wanted to show me a stable cat or something. There was no one else at the inn left to meet.

I wished Dad would hurry up and get home.

I glanced in the age-spotted mirror over the white dresser. I looked as pale as I felt. My curls were even more of a frizzy mess than they'd been this morning, thanks to the rain.

I stepped into the corridor. When I was sure the Glimpse hadn't hung around, I hurtled down the stairs, slipped my wet ballet pumps back on and grabbed my dripping umbrella.

Crowley watched me crunch across the gravel towards him. The shoulders of his grey T-shirt were black with rain. There was another dark patch on his stomach, which protruded from his body as if he had a cushion shoved up his shirt.

I stopped a couple of metres from him, and shivered. I hoped he didn't expect to share my umbrella.

'What hours do you work here? I thought you'd have left by now.' I knew it was a rude question – at least, my reason for asking it was – but Crowley didn't strike me as the sort of man to get nuances.

'Oh, no. I'm here pretty much all the time. I stay overnight too.' He smiled, like he'd said something I should be happy about. 'Your granddad liked to have me around. I have my own place in the village, but—' he shrugged, and looked back at the outbuildings, which he used as his offices '—I like it here.'

I gave him my best, polite smile. I definitely needed to talk to Dad about that. The last thing I wanted was a stranger hanging around my house when I was home, especially if the Glimpses were back.

'I'm glad I caught you, anyway,' he said. 'Here's who I wanted you to meet.' Crowley gestured over his shoulder as one of the outbuilding's doors opened. 'My son. He helps me out here after school. Maybe you met each other already?'

My smile had vanished even before the boy came into view, but by the time he'd emerged from the gloom of the doorway and raced through the rain towards us, my jaw was practically hanging down to my chest.

No. No, no, no.

'Hey, new girl.' Scott smiled, coming to a halt under the canopy of the tree. He wiped the rain from his forehead with his shirtsleeve.

I snapped my mouth shut. My eyes flicked back and forth between Crowley and Scott. This had to be some awful joke. 'Scott's your son? And he works here?'

Crowley slapped a beefy hand onto Scott's shoulder. 'Keeps me out of mischief.' He grinned.

Scott grinned too, the mirror image of his father's.

I blinked at them, too stunned to say anything back. My whole Normality List depended on my new schoolmates knowing nothing about the real me. Scott being here at my house was not part of the deal.

Oh, God. What if he'd heard me screaming?

As if he could read my mind, Scott blurted, 'Watch out!' and pointed at me. 'Spider on your dress!'

I gasped, and swiped my hand along the fabric. Immediately, Crowley and Scott started laughing.

'He's such a joker,' Crowley said, ruffling Scott's hair. 'Gotta watch out for my Scott.'

I tilted my umbrella over my face so Scott wouldn't see my cheeks burn.

'Nice dress though,' Scott said, his tone more serious. 'Unique.'

I stiffened. 'Thank you.' I allowed a long, silent pause. 'I'm going inside now. Scott, I suppose I'll see you tomorrow.' From the other side of the classroom, I hope.

Before I could make a show of stomping away, Dad appeared at the entrance of the driveway. His arms were weighed down with shopping and his raincoat was dripping wet, but right then he was as good as a knight in shining armour. A knight that turns up an hour after the maiden's been given the fright of her life that is.

'Hey, Liz,' he called. 'Mr Crowley, Scott, hello again.'

'Hey, Dad,' I said.

'Want some help carrying your bags, Mr Rathamore?' Scott asked.

I rolled my eyes, and hurried inside and up the stairs to my room before Scott could follow me. I headed to the open window and peeked down at the driveway from behind the shutters. Crowley stayed alone under the tree, mopping at his streaming wet face with a hanky.

After a moment, Scott's white-blond head emerged from the inn. I stepped closer to the window. He ran through the rain to Crowley, rolling his shoulders back and flexing his biceps like he'd just finished weight training, rather than carrying Dad's shopping.

Crowley's low voice drifted up to me. 'So what do you think?'

A pause. Then: 'I think it's going to be easy.'

A smile appeared on the caretaker's face like a gash in a lump of dough. He and Scott disappeared into the outbuildings.

Chapter Six

Crowley and Scott must have thought they'd won the lottery, swapping their boss from a grumpy old man to a seventeen-year-old girl and her soft-touch dad. They must think we were going to be pushovers.

I folded my arms and glowered at the packing boxes in the corner. I might have been a pushover six weeks ago, but I wasn't any more. I was the girl who attacked Glimpses now.

I was also the girl who still had Glimpses.

My throat tightened like I was going to cry. I scrunched up my face, refusing to let any tears fall.

Grabbing the nearest packing box, I channelled my frustration into unpacking its contents. For ten minutes I was a whirlwind. I flung suitcases onto the bed in the middle of the room, making the wooden headboard bang against the wall. From there, I threw my possessions into semi-organized heaps around the room. The wardrobe was Scott's face as I lobbed my collection of vintage shoes into it. The chest of drawers was Crowley's fat stomach as I punched a pile of biographies down onto it.

I hung up a few of my favourite dresses, and closed the

wardrobe door, revealing my Normality List, where I'd tacked it. I scanned it and frowned. 'No nightmares'. 'No Glimpses'. 'Stop worrying Dad'. 'Get friends'. I'd failed at all of those today.

But it was 'Get friends' that taunted me most. With Scott at the inn as well as at school, I was going to have to be on my best behaviour twenty-four hours a day. Even if he wasn't as bad as Derek, he had only to hear me screaming my head off again, tell his mates at school about it, and I could kiss my dream of 'seeming normal' goodbye.

I had to talk to Dad.

I followed the familiar sound of the TV downstairs to the kitchen. In our old house, the tinny blare had filled every room, every hour of the day that Dad was awake. When I'd lain in my bed above the living room, I could almost follow Dad's shows word for word. But here the sound was smaller, muffled by the inn's thick walls, as if the TV was intimidated by its new surroundings.

A bizarrely familiar scene met me in the kitchen – packed shopping bags standing on a kitchen table, Dad peering at me from over the back of his sofa. But the table was twice the size of the one we'd left behind on Saturday morning; and Dad was over on the other side of the cavernous kitchen instead of in the boxy living room I was used to.

'Liz, how was your day?'

I'd had a dozen things I'd wanted to tell him when I got home – about the two-hour-long assembly the whole school had been subjected to; about the choice of food in the dining hall; about Susie helping me find 12G – but none of those things seemed important now.

'Good.' I shrugged.

'Glad to hear it.' Dad gestured at the TV with the remote. 'This is over in a couple of minutes. I'll help with the shopping then, okay?'

I nodded. I knew the routine. I grabbed one of the shopping bags, wiped the rain off a bag of pasta, and chose a cupboard out of the vast array to put it in.

Everything about this new house was excessive. Not all the rooms were as big as this one, most were quite poky and small, but there was too much of everything – too much dust, too much furniture, too many rooms. I wondered how Mum had coped moving to a normal-sized house when she'd married Dad.

The moment the end credits rolled on the TV, I turned around. 'So,' I said. 'I want to talk to you.'

Dad paused in the process of clambering off the sofa. 'Sounds serious.' He walked over to the table, rubbing his hair, which had dried in thick clumps. 'There's not a problem with school already, is there?'

'School's fine.'

He looked relieved.

I leaned back against the marble counter. It was cold, even through my wool dress. 'I want to talk about the caretaker. Mr Crowley. You know he has his son working here with him?'

'I do.'

'Well, two caretakers is a bit much, don't you think?'

Dad rubbed at one of his eyes under his glasses. 'Crowley told me Scott comes over by choice. We're not paying him anything, if that's what you're worried about. He's not exactly a second caretaker.'

'But . . . he kind of is.' I folded my arms. 'And Crowley said

48

he's here all the time. I'm not comfortable with having two strangers around my home.'

'Scott's nice. And Crowley's not a stranger, Liz. He's been here for years. He was here long before . . . you know. The accident.' Dad looked down at his hands.

I squeezed the locket at my throat.

'You won't remember him,' Dad said, after a pause, 'but he was here. Used to chat with your mum when we visited.'

'Okay,' I said, more gently. 'But maybe you can ask him to stick to regular work hours. Just so he's not here all the time.' And so Scott can't be here at all.

To my surprise, Dad seemed to consider it. 'Well, I suppose that's reasonable.' He shrugged. 'I'll mention it to him tomorrow, see what he says.'

I exhaled. 'Thanks, Dad.'

He smiled. Then he scooped up two shopping bags with sudden enthusiasm and joined me at the kitchen side. 'Are you proud of your old dad, then? Shopping before we even ran out of bread for toast.'

I grinned, and took one of the bags off him. 'Yeah. I am.'

'And I picked up a local newspaper to look at the job section.'

'Wow. Where is my dad and what have you done with him?'

He smiled. 'I was thinking, you know. I'm so proud of you, trying to make a go of things. Maybe this can be a new start for both of us.'

'That would be nice.' I hugged a family-pack of crisps to my chest. 'Really, really nice.'

He smiled back at me, happy and shy as a kid who's been given a gold star for their star chart. My heart ached for him suddenly. It was so rare he looked genuinely happy.

He upended a shopping bag on the counter, scattering

chocolate bars and packets of biscuits and apples across the marble, along with a sorry trickle of rainwater.

I picked a sodden bag of bread rolls out of the mess. 'Maybe next time, take a taxi home. Or, even better, since we're talking about new starts, you could take up driving again?'

My words fell into silence. If they'd been spaghetti, I'd have sucked them back in.

'Ha,' Dad said, a beat too late. His grin strained. 'One step at a time, Liz. One step at a time.' He gestured at the mess on the kitchen side, and sighed, as if he'd only just realized how much work it was. 'Leave this. I'll finish it later, okay?'

He shuffled back to his sofa. I rolled my eyes at my reflection in the microwave door. Good one, Liz.

I finished unpacking as the TV blared with Dad's next show.

One step at a time. That was the trouble – I wanted it now. I'd once been happy, Glimpse-free, with dozens of friends; after seven years of crazy, I wanted normal again. Dad had once played piano and been a full-time sound engineer; after seven years of grieving for Mum, a string of temp jobs and a full-time TV-watching career, I wanted him to be happy.

But maybe he was right. A little more time, maybe that was all we needed. Maybe tomorrow would be the day I made friends. Maybe tomorrow would be the first in a lifetime of Glimpse-free days.

And maybe tomorrow would be the day Dad forgave himself for driving his car into a tree and killing his wife.

Killing my mother.

Automatically, I reached for my locket, and squeezed.

One step at a time.

Chapter Seven

The nightmare starts the same as always. I'm standing on a lawn. The breeze ripples the short grass. Wild rabbits chew the stalks warily. Everything's quiet, but it's not peaceful. There's a tension in the air, inside me, like the moment of silence in a horror movie before the axe falls.

I've been through this a thousand times. I should know what's coming. It's on the edge of my mind. It teeters there, just out of reach.

The axe falls. A screech of metal, the breaking of glass, shatters the silence. Somewhere close by, a child screams. I lift my skirt, and I run.

I see it. The mangled car, forced into the body of a tree; shards of glass, spilt oil and a shower of leaves. Yes, I remember this now.

Without warning, the scene flips. Now I'm inside the car; I am the screaming child. I'm scrunched into the back seat. Something warm and wet is running into my eyes. It doesn't hurt, but it seems like it should.

The passenger door rips open. My mother! She's come to help me! I want to cry out to her, but I can't speak, I can't move. She reaches into the car for me . . .

And then I see her face. Her features are twisted by violence. She's angry as a Halloween witch. She snarls at me, her teeth bared. Her eyes bore into me like she wishes I were dead.

If I could cry now, I would. Big, wracking sobs build in my chest as my mother claws at me, tries to dig her nails into my flesh. She can't get a grip on me. She hauls at me, but I'm a rock. She can't move me, and I can't tell her to stop.

'Get out!' she screams. Her voice is worse than the sound of ripping metal. 'Get out, get out, get out!'

Over and over and over she screams. Each word slices my heart as deeply as the wounds that cover me with blood.

My mother hates me.

I gasped awake. The air juddered through my lungs, releasing the pain in my chest. The nightmare had been no worse than usual – I'd lived through it a thousand times since the crash – but it still bruised me every time.

I propped myself up against the pillows and flicked on the bedside lamp. For a moment, I was disorientated to see white walls, unfamiliar furniture, before I remembered where I was.

Strands of hair were plastered to my face. I wiped them away, my hands clammy. My mother . . .

I shook myself. I had to get the nightmare out of my head, and fast. I reached for the locket on my bedside cabinet, and pressed the gold heart between my fingers, feeling the familiar shape of it. I gently cracked it open.

A tiny, heart-shaped photo looked back at me. I knew every detail of it – it was as familiar as my own face in the mirror – but I brought it close to my eyes anyway, and studied it by the glow of the lamp until the hammering in my chest slowed.

A woman in her late twenties held a smiling girl in front

of a blue screen painted with clouds. This is my mum, I told myself. This woman, with her arms around me and her loving smile, was my mother. That banshee in my nightmare was not.

Dad had given the locket to me shortly after the accident. He'd told me it had been hers; she'd been the one who'd put the picture of us inside it, she'd been the one who'd kept it close to her heart once.

But she'd never have looked at it for the reason I had to – as an antidote to a nightmare.

Looking at the photo didn't stop the dreams, didn't change them – there was no secret hidden in the locket to make my dream-mother love me again – but if I didn't look at it, all I'd remember would be the monster.

The picture dated from the summer before the accident. Look at the way her arms are wrapped around me. Look at how happy I am, snuggled inside her bear hug.

There was no way to make my mum alive again, but I wished there was a way to stop the imposter of my dreams coming back.

My only hope was that, now I was here, in her childhood home – the place Dad told me I'd visited so often as a child – some of my real memories of her would start to come back.

I closed the locket, sealing my mother, and the little girl I'd once been, inside with a click. I put the necklace gently back on top of the cabinet next to me, scooched down under my duvet, and turned off the lamp.

Crunch.

I froze, my hand still on the lamp switch.

Crunch. Crunch.

I shot upright in bed. My eyes strained in the moonlight. The flashing yellow digits of my alarm clock read '02.00'.

I was alert, waiting to hear the sound again. My mind felt like it had been plunged into a bath of cold water, dreamy to red alert in a matter of seconds.

Crunch, crunch, crunch.

Something was definitely on the gravel under my window.

Trying not to panic, I slipped first one foot, then the other, down to the floorboards.

It was probably an animal – the inn was bordered with fields and woods. But it would have to be a very heavy animal. Maybe it was the caretaker. Though that wasn't a good option either.

I stood up. Holding my breath, I inched towards the open shutters, the floorboards cold under my feet.

The old tree filled the night sky, its branches spidering across the moon like black lace. I leaned into the window so I could follow the lines of the vast, black trunk down to the ground.

My heart spasmed with fear.

There was a man there.

A man. Standing under my bedroom window. In the middle of the night.

The figure – yes, it was definitely a man – peeled slowly away from the tree's shadows. Too slim to be Crowley, too tall to be Scott, too everything to be a Glimpse.

In an instant, he darted towards the wall and I lost sight of him. I could see his shadow though, moving back and forth across the moon-striped gravel as if he was looking for a way in. He could be a burglar. A murderer.

My breath came in shallow bursts. Slowly, quietly, I eased the window open, letting in a sigh of damp night air. I leaned out, as far into the darkness as I dared, trying to see better.

The man stepped back into the open.

I froze, exposed in the window. *Please don't look up. Don't look up.*

He looked up.

A gasp built and died in my throat. The man – boy – was young, probably just a bit older than me. His green eyes, the only colour in his white face, widened. He leapt back into the tree's shadows, and was gone.

Vanished.

I slammed the window down and made it to my bed in two leaps, clambering onto it as though it were a life raft on the *Titanic*.

I should get Dad. No. He'd only panic, and not for the reason I'd want him to. It was a bad idea telling him I'd seen something I couldn't prove had ever been there. I knew that from experience.

For long minutes, I crouched on the bedcovers, straining to listen for more footsteps. When all remained quiet, I climbed back under the duvet and eased myself down, trying not to rustle the sheets.

There was never a good reason for a stranger to be creeping under a girl's window at two in the morning. I could only hope, now I'd seen him, that whoever it was wouldn't be back. He was probably one of Scott's friends. The sooner Dad spoke to Crowley about his work hours, the better.

I sighed, turned over in bed and shut my eyes. Tomorrow was a whole new day. Tomorrow, I would see nothing I didn't want to, and everything would be just fine.

Chapter Eight

The next morning, I worked hard on washing every trace of yesterday from my skin. I swapped my long white nightie for a new pair of navy trousers and a cream T-shirt that no one would look twice at. I washed my hair and plaited it, and applied just enough make-up so that when I looked in the mirror I was a vision of understated normality. Not weird, not eye-catching, just normal. New me.

I even made it to the bus on time. The bus, however, was less punctual.

I arrived to registration five minutes late, my back damp from running. When I scanned the classroom, there was only one empty seat – the one next to Scott.

'Sit where you did yesterday, Elizabeth,' Mr Scholars called from the front of the room. 'If we can all keep the same seats this year, it'll make life easier.'

I was glad he started calling the register then, so I didn't have to speak to anyone at my table when I sat down. Smiling was difficult enough.

Doesn't matter, I told myself. Dad would tell Crowley about his new work hours today, Scott would be gone from my home, and then I wouldn't have to worry about him.

'So we've got our own Bess,' Mr Andrews said, as he handed out stacks of orange cards in my first English lesson. 'Elizabeth, you could be straight out of "The Highwayman" poem with those lovely black curls of yours. Pity we're not studying it this year or you could have given us a tour of your inn.'

I smiled weakly, more for the benefit of the twenty heads now craning in my direction than for the teacher.

'Bess, the landlord's black-eyed daughter,' Mr Andrews intoned as he distributed cards to the tables behind mine. 'Bess, the landlord's daughter, plaiting a dark red love-knot into her long black hair.'

Susie prodded me with her elbow. 'See, I told you the English teachers were going to bug you over that poem,' she whispered.

I smiled. Registration had been a flop in terms of seating arrangements, but my first English lesson was making up for it. I thanked the school timetable gods when I discovered that Susie was in two of the same classes as me. I practically dissolved with relief when she remembered who I was, and let me take the seat next to her.

It was the first time I'd spoken to Susie since yesterday. I had planned to say hi while waiting for the bus this morning, but she'd been with her boyfriend again, each totally absorbed in the other.

I hoped to make up for it now – 'Get friends', and all that – but, so far, I'd barely had a chance to say more than 'Can I sit here?' The English teacher was an enthusiastic talker, and he seemed to have picked me as his subject of the day.

'Are you a poet at all, Elizabeth?' Mr Andrews continued his tour of the room, sliding a stack of orange cards onto the table between me and Susie as he passed. 'Can we expect some epic romantic verse from you, since you're living in the building that inspired one of our nation's favourite poems?'

'Um.' I tugged at a curl that had escaped my plait. 'No.'

'What a shame. Maybe you're a budding romance novelist, then? Or maybe you're more of a horror writer?'

'Ha,' I said. 'No, not really.' I tugged at my hair a little harder.

Susie prodded me with her elbow again. I rolled my eyes towards her. *Help.*

'Well, do let us know, Elizabeth, if Bess or the highwayman turn up.'

Romantic, poetic ghosts were one thing; horrific Glimpses were another. I shivered at the memory of that creepy, dis-embodied face.

'Okay, enough chit-chat.' Mr Andrews handed out his last pile of orange cards, and headed back to the front of the room. 'Welcome to A2 English. I commend you all on your terribly good taste in academic subjects. What a delight to see so many familiar faces. On to today's Learning Objective.'

He picked up a pen and wrote on the whiteboard: 'To consider the effect of a character's past on their actions'.

'Write it down. Underline it. Let's start as we mean to go on.'

There was a rustling as twenty sheets of paper were pulled out, twenty pens taken from pencil cases.

Glad the focus had shifted off me, I exhaled and copied down the words. When Mr Andrews turned his back to the class, I whispered to Susie, 'Does everyone here know about my inn?'

'Yup,' she whispered back. 'You don't know how obsessed the teachers are with that poem. I can't count the number of essays and poems and paintings and clay models and dramatic interpretations—'

'Susie—' Mr Andrews' voice was jovial but firm '—don't lead our new girl astray now.'

Susie rolled her eyes and fell quiet. I gave her an apologetic smile.

Mr Andrews turned on the whiteboard projector. I settled back in my seat, ready for a breather after my public grilling. My hopes rose as Mr Andrews flicked off the classroom lights – maybe we were going to watch a film.

My hopes dimmed again as the whiteboard brightened with a display of pictures. Not of books or theatre shows or anything English-related, but images of children and young teens, with their parents and friends, all smiling and happy.

I frowned in the dull glow. They made me think of the photos of my own childhood, the ones Dad dragged out to cheer me up when he thought I looked glum, but that just made me painfully aware of how much I'd changed.

Mr Andrews pointed at the board. 'Believe it or not, I was this age once. You all were. You played in the park like this girl. You picked your nose like this little fellow.'

A few snorted laughs came from the class.

'It may have been a long time ago, and longer for some of us than for others—' Mr Andrews paused for effect '—but the things we did, the things that happened to us in our earlier years, will have affected who we are today.'

'Yeah, James still picks his nose,' someone in the row behind me muttered.

'Today,' Mr Andrews continued, oblivious, 'I want you to

choose a character from one of the texts you read over the summer.' A few moans came from the class. Mr Andrews silenced them with a glare. 'No complaints now, you all got your summer reading lists. Elizabeth, did you?'

I jumped – I'd been staring at the happy kids on the board – and nodded.

'You're going to plan an essay about the effect of one character's past on their present. *The Great Gatsby* would be an excellent choice. Or *Othello*, perhaps. I'm going to assume you've all read both.'

Mr Andrews turned the classroom lights back on. 'But first, a fun activity to get your brains ticking. Each table has a stack of orange cards. Everyone – get into pairs and take turns choosing a card. Ask your partner the question on it, keeping the Learning Objective in mind as you do so. Class discussion in ten minutes.' He checked his watch. 'Go.'

I read the Learning Objective on the board again: 'Consider the effect of a character's past . . .'

This did not bode well.

Susie and I looked at each other. If this had been any other activity, I would have let her go first. But I had a bad feeling about all this, and I slid the pile of orange cards towards me. Finally, all those lunchtimes spent playing Snap with the librarian at my old school instead of going out to the playground had paid off. My reflexes were lightning fast. I took a card and twisted it into my palm so Susie couldn't see. I read the question with a mounting sense of trepidation. It was just what I'd feared. Mr Andrews had designed an activity perfect for digging out the very facts about me that I wanted to keep secret. I tried stalling for time.

'So, Mr Andrews seems nice,' I said.

'He's big on games.' Susie looked around the classroom, which was already buzzing with excited chatter. She was probably regretting she'd let me sit near her. 'So? Shall we start?'

I was New Liz now, I told myself. As long as I kept Old Liz out of this, everything would be fine.

I brushed my locket once with my fingertips, then asked her the question. 'What did you want to be when you were little?'

'Paranormal investigator.'

I looked up. The expression in her black-rimmed eyes was genuine. 'Really?' I couldn't think of anything worse than looking for things that shouldn't be there.

'Yeah. My mum and I used to watch all those shows on TV – *Haunted Mansions* and *Britain's Most Haunted*. If you'd moved here when you were ten, I'd have bugged you so much to let me look for ghosts at your house. I begged my mum for an Ouija board for my birthday every year, but she never let me till last year.'

Susie reached for the next card, so she didn't see my bemused expression. 'Your turn. What is your happiest memory as a child?'

'Um.' I looked down at the desk. I tried – just for a few seconds – to think of the real answer. But there was little point; like always when I tried to think too far into the past, my mind stayed murky as the surface of a polluted lake, its secrets hidden out of reach far beneath.

Just say something. I plucked a random image from my mind: a photo from Dad's collection. 'Riding a donkey with my mum on the beach,' I said.

I looked at Susie, anxious – surely she could tell I was lying – but she just nodded and said, 'My mum did that with me too.'

Really? I wanted to ask. *What was it like? Did your mum hold your hand?* But instead, I just took the next card.

'What were you scared of as a child?'

'The dark.' She shrugged. 'But then everyone's scared of the dark when they're little, right?'

'You were a ghost hunter who was scared of the dark?'

Susie smiled. 'I was going to be a ghost hunter who carried a very big torch.'

I laughed, surprising myself.

'What were you scared of?' she asked.

I stopped laughing. I didn't know the answer. I knew I hadn't had the Glimpses as a child, at least; I wouldn't have smiled so much in all the photos if I had.

'Pick a new question,' I said, sliding the card stack towards her.

'What is your first memory?'

This one, I knew the answer to – lying in a hospital, wondering who I was, how I'd got there, who the snivelling man by my bedside was, and why I could see body parts floating around me.

There were a lot of problems with that memory. The Glimpses being one, not recognizing my dad being another, being ten years old and not able to remember my newly dead mother being the worst.

'Sitting on my dad's knee in front of the TV,' I lied, tapping my pen on the table. 'That is my first memory.'

'Time's up!' Mr Andrews called. I sagged back against my chair, as exhausted as if my brain had run a marathon. 'Cards down. Class discussion.'

'Class discussion' – never my favourite words, but combined with 'childhood memories', I wanted no part in it.

Letting Old Liz take over, I dropped my gaze to the desk and found a bit of old graffiti to stare at. Right now, I needed to work on my invisibility. I'd passed the test with Susie, but I didn't trust myself to come up with something fast enough if Mr Andrews called on me. Having only seven years of memories, and not one of them before the age of ten, was one of my weird traits that I really didn't want to broadcast.

Chapter Nine

I got away without speaking for the rest of English. But even after the class discussion shifted to Jay Gatsby and Othello, my insides were in knots.

I hated that I'd had to lie so soon. It wasn't like I thought Susie would tease me if she knew the truth. It had been beneath even Derek to bully me about the car crash that had wiped my memory, taking with it every image of my mother that wasn't printed on photo paper.

But my amnesia bothered me. It was like knowing my brain was a mansion, but that all the nicest rooms, the rooms I'd played in as a child, the rooms where my mother was, were locked, and the rooms I had to exist in were filled with nightmares and Glimpses.

By the time the bell rang for the end of the lesson, I'd made a decision. When I got home, I was going to add one more line to my Normality List: 'Remember Mum and my past'.

Unrealistic, Miss Mahoney's voice whispered in the back of my mind. And maybe it was. But I had to try.

Feeling a few hundred watts brighter, I shoved my English things into my bag and followed Susie to join the break-time crush out in the corridor. Her boyfriend, Matt – I'd deduced his name from the number of times it was written on her pencil case – was already waiting for her, the jet-black hair of his head towering above everybody else's. Their hands reached for each other automatically, like two magnets. Click.

Time for me to leave.

'So I'll see you in History?' I said to Susie, looking back over my shoulder as I turned away. I was already thinking of my locker, and of finding a quiet place to recover my composure before my next lesson.

'Sure,' she called. Then, 'Hey, look—'

Something large and bony whacked into my chest. I stumbled back, banging into some lockers. 'Sorry!' I gasped, automatically.

I looked up, and wished I hadn't. I hadn't walked into one boy, but a solid block of them.

'Watch it,' snapped the one I'd banged into, a skinny boy with greasy brown hair. He straightened the arm of his black zip-up jacket, glaring at me as if I'd done it on purpose.

I waited for him to move so I could get past, but he didn't. All six boys glared at me.

Then one of them smiled.

'Hey, spider girl.' Scott caught jacket-boy's eye, and jerked his chin towards me. 'She's the one I told you about.'

My heart spasmed as jacket-boy looked at me with renewed interest. *She's the one I told you about . . .?* I could only guess what image Scott had painted – a girl in a granny dress, screaming at spiders.

My cheeks burned. It was only a couple of seconds before jacket-boy grunted and his gang swaggered away, but it felt like an eternity.

Susie materialized by my shoulder. She touched my arm, making me jump. 'Hey, are you okay? You've gone really pale.'

I shook myself. 'I'm fine,' I said, watching the boys retreating down the corridor.

Susie followed my gaze. 'Those guys are bad news. They walk around the school like they own the place, and the village too at weekends. But you're all right as long as you stay out of their way. That's what the rest of us do.'

A memory lurched up in my mind, like a half-remembered dream – the boy under my window last night, with the green eyes and pale face.

Too late, I wished I'd looked more closely at Scott's friends. I was sure I'd recognize the trespasser again.

'Are there more of them? Scott's gang, I mean?'

Susie rolled her eyes at me. 'God knows. I think they hang out with some older guys in the village, but I avoid them when I see them. Why?'

'No reason.' I chewed my lip. If one of Scott's gang had been at the inn last night, Scott was worse than I thought. I really hoped Dad had spoken to Crowley today.

'Seriously, forget about it.' Susie took Matt's hand and looked at me. 'Now, please tell me you're coming with us to the dining hall for break. I've heard a very reliable rumour that there's chocolate crispies.'

I smiled gratefully. 'Best news I've heard all morning.'

The moment I saw the car I had a bad feeling.

It was boxy and red and parked right in front of the out-buildings when I got home from school. It couldn't be anything to do with Dad. When Scott and Crowley emerged from their office brandishing cups of tea and a toolkit, my fears were confirmed.

I scuttled, head down, towards the inn's front door.

'Hey, Liz!' Scott called. 'I got a car! What do you think?'

I lifted my head just long enough to smile and shout, 'Looks great!' before bursting in through the front door like a Tasmanian devil.

Dad practically fell off his sofa with shock when I stomped into the kitchen. 'Liz, what's wrong?'

'I thought you were speaking to Crowley today!'

He exhaled and turned back to the TV. 'Well, I did.'

I dropped my satchel and stood in front of the television, hands on hips. 'And?'

'And I've decided it's not appropriate to tell him what hours he can work here.' Dad didn't meet my gaze.

I sighed and slumped onto the sofa.

'I invited him in for coffee—' I rolled my eyes, but Dad continued, oblivious '—and we got to talking. He lost his wife too, back when Scott was small. It's clear he thinks of the inn as his home. I'm not going to treat him like he's just an employee.'

'Da-ad.' I flopped back against the cushions.

'Tell me what the real problem is here.'

I gave him a sideways glance. He looked back at me steadily. 'It's Scott,' I said. 'He reminds me of Derek.'

Dad's face softened. 'Liz, Derek was a bully. It's natural you'd be wary after what he put you through. But Scott seems nice. Helpful. He carried my shopping the other day, remember?'

'I knew you'd say that.'

Dad sighed and ran a hand through his hair, which was flat at the back from leaning against the sofa all day. 'Give the boy a chance. I thought you'd be happy having someone your own age around. I thought you wanted to make friends.'

'I do, but . . .' I chewed my lip. Nothing I could say was going to sound right. *But the only people who seem to like Scott are his horrible gang. But he's already told his friends about me. But there was a man outside my window last night, and I think Scott had something to do with it.* All based on nothing more credible than a bad feeling, a sixth sense.

I crossed my arms and legs and stared at the wall beyond the TV. There was no point arguing with Dad about this any more, not without making him worry. But he didn't need to think I was happy about it.

If and when my suspicions about Scott were confirmed, I'd talk to Dad again. In the meantime, I'd have to make sure I didn't put on any more displays of weirdness at home that Scott might see.

I thought of my Normality List, and remembered the new line I wanted to add. I shifted my head to look back at Dad. 'Can I have the old photos? The ones with Mum?'

Chapter Ten

Up in my room, I closed the window so I wouldn't have to hear Scott and Crowley tinkering with their car. Dad had given me two dusty shoeboxes of photos: the ones with Mum in them, and the ones without. I changed out of my new school clothes and put on my tattiest dress – a shapeless, grey velvet thing that didn't mind the dirt. Then I sat on my bedroom floor and went through each box, taking out all the photos that showed the inn. I spread them out on the floorboards. The last photograph dated from before the accident.

I'd seen a lot of these photos back when Dad first told me we'd inherited the Highwayman – to show me what it looked like. It was strange, looking at the same pictures again now, sitting right here in Hulbourn. After Mum died, I thought I'd never see this place again.

I picked up a photo of pre-accident Dad and me, eating breakfast at the inn's kitchen table. Dad looked so young and happy, wearing a T-shirt printed with 'Ripe Banana Studios', the music studio he used to work at. Little-me beamed at the camera like always. The staff bustled around us with racks of toast and baskets of boiled eggs for the dining room next door.

The kitchen was almost unrecognizable from today. Back then, it had been so full of life I could practically hear the chatter of voices from below the photo's surface.

I had the absurd urge to reach out and pat my bedroom wall. Poor inn. Granddad had closed down the hotel in his grief, and let seven years of dust and spiders gather in its corners. This place had been scarred by the accident, just like we all had.

But there was nothing I could do about that right now. I needed to concentrate on my own scars.

I scooped the photos up off the floor, and stepped out of my room into the corridor. I paused, listening to the far-off chatter of Dad's TV and the distant revving of Scott's car engine. Then I tiptoed to the furthest end of the corridor from the stairs and pushed open the first door.

A musty smell gushed out. In the middle of a patterned carpet thick with dust stood a four-poster bed with dark-green covers. Dark-wood furniture, with chips and mug rings from its hotel days, crowded the walls.

I flicked through the photos, but none showed this room. There weren't likely to be any memories here for me.

I crept in anyway, just in case, kicking up dust, taking shallow breaths so I wouldn't sneeze. I went to the window and looked out over the tangled garden and woodland, the fields beyond, trying to feel some flicker of recognition.

In the garden, a broken swing hung from a gnarled old tree. Had I swung on it as a child? That patch of overgrown roses – had I thought they were pretty once? I could picture the little girl from the photos out there playing and exploring happily, but I couldn't feel her, I couldn't access her through memory.

After closing the door softly behind me, I went to the next room. Dad's room. I opened the door but didn't go inside. The furniture here was more modern, the dust hoovered away, but it didn't feel much more lived in than the other room. An open suitcase lay on the floor next to the unmade bed. The packing boxes in the corner were in the same arrangement as the day we'd arrived.

'Oh, Dad,' I sighed, and closed the door again.

The next door I opened though made hope flutter in my chest. I flicked through the photos. I had three of this room. In the oldest, my teenaged mother stood next to the double bed with its headboard of carved roses. She was wearing a puffy eighties cocktail dress, and she was beaming.

The next photo was some years later. Mum and Dad sat together on the bed, a newborn baby – me – in their arms. Mum's smile was even wider in this one.

The final photo showed the same room, but with the addition of a single bed in the corner. Young-Liz hugged a teddy on the bed, while my mother looked out of the window.

I stepped into the room, one hand gripped tight around my locket.

I eased myself onto the single bed in the corner, scrutinizing the squeak of the springs, as if they might tell me their secrets. I stretched out on the blanket, trying to lead my focus away from the immediate – from the ticklish catch of the dust and the tang of stale fabric – trying instead to open my mind and cast back . . . Just one memory, that's all I want.

'Liz?'

I half fell off the bed. 'Dad.' I coughed on the dust that poofed up from the mattress. 'Don't do that.'

'What are you doing in here?' He hovered in the doorway, frowning uncertainly. His eyes scanned the room like he was afraid something might leap out from a corner and bite him.

I held up the photos. 'Tracking down memories.'

Dad walked towards me, carefully, like he half expected to fall over a tripwire or for an alarm to go off. He took the photos I held out to him and looked at the top one. 'Ah.'

'This is the room we stayed in when we visited, isn't it?'

'Yes. It used to be your mother's room.' He gazed at the photo, one finger tracing its edge, a gesture of both affection and discomfort.

Not for the first time, I wished I could reach into his head and take some of his memories. This was the irony of Dad and I. He was tortured by having too many memories. I was tortured by having too few.

I stood and turned to the window, giving him a moment. Mum's old room overlooked the front of the inn, just like mine, but her view showed more of the driveway and less of the old tree.

I rested my elbows on the sill, taking care to avoid the dead flies. Did I remember this view? But all that came to me was a memory of that boy beneath my window last night.

'I wish I could remember,' I muttered to the glass.

'You can't force it, Liz.' Dad's voice was soft as the dust. 'You can't expect anything at all. You know what Dr Roberts said.'

I exhaled and nodded, still staring at the driveway.

Dad rested the pile of photos on the windowsill next to my hand. 'I'll put some food on. Come down in a few minutes, okay?'

He left, stirring the still air so it tickled my skin. I sank my chin to rest on my hands. In my mind's eye, horse-drawn carriages clopped down the driveway, dropping hotel guests and their suitcases at the front door. Ladies in long dresses walked on the lawn. Stable boys lounged under the shade of the big tree. My imagination did its best, but nothing came to me that could be a real memory.

The hairs stood up on my arms, and I rubbed them, the scratchy inside of my dress tickling my skin. No, not tickling – tingling. I froze, my breath catching in my lungs. Goosebumps prickled my scalp.

Oh, no. Where was it?

I saw it almost instantly. There – under the tree outside. Two brown-shoed feet faced directly towards me, as if their owner was watching me.

One of the feet tapped the gravel, slowly. Tap, tap, tap.

Another Glimpse.

I span and hurtled from the room, slamming Mum's door behind me.

Chapter Eleven

I couldn't sleep.

I stared up at my bedroom ceiling. It was pale with moonlight, striped with shadows that thrashed violently in time with the tree's creaks outside my window. Every few minutes, the tip of a branch scraped the glass like fingernails, making every nerve in my body spark.

I glanced at my bedside clock. 01.53. This was torture.

01.56

01.58. I clutched my duvet to my chin. Sleep, I willed myself. There'll be no more Glimpses tomorrow.

01.59

02.00

Crunch.

Oh no.

Crunch. Crunch.

I squeezed my eyes tight, as if that could block out the sound.

Images flurried across my mind. Whoever – whatever – was under that tree, they could just go away.

But the crunching didn't stop.

Clenching my fists, I leapt out of bed and pulled a dressing gown on top of my nightie. This was the last thing I needed tonight. If it was that boy again, I was going to tell him where he could go – that, or scream for Dad.

My heart raced hard against my chest as I stepped to the window, eased it open and leaned out just far enough so I could see down to the base of the tree. I found myself staring straight at the boy from the night before. I felt him staring straight back at me. I stifled a yelp.

'Don't be alarmed.' His voice was just loud enough to make out over the thrashing of the wind. His neck craned back to look at me. I had the horrible sense he'd been waiting for me.

The tree canopy shook above him, plunging him into shadow, illuminating him, plunging him into shadow again. In the flashes of moonlight he was vivid – bright green eyes, clear white face, red-gold hair. He wore clothes the colour of dead leaves.

He spread his arms. His smile was warm, as if to draw me in. 'Will you speak with me?'

My throat was too tight to speak. When I eventually forced my words out, they were small and hard as bullets. 'Who are you? Why are you here?'

'I want to talk with you. I want to know who you are.'

It made no sense that he'd come here for me. He was lying.

'Go away.' The wind whipped my words down to him. 'You shouldn't be here. Leave now or I'll call my dad.'

He took a step back. Lifting his arms higher, he turned his gloved palms to me. 'I apologize.'

'Stay away from my house. I'll call the police if you come here again.'

'I apologize,' he repeated, 'for upsetting you. I thought you would understand.'

He held my gaze for a long moment, then dipped his head in a funny little bow, and stepped back into the shadow of the tree. A moment later, his shadow raced across the grass in front of the outbuildings and disappeared at the edge of the woods.

I gripped the window shutter for support, my legs suddenly weak. My whole body shook with pent-up adrenaline. I strained my eyes towards the dark line of the woods. It made me uneasy that he hadn't gone back up the driveway towards the road.

I stood rigid in the darkness, staring out at the night, clutching the neck of my dressing gown in the absence of my locket. I couldn't move until I was sure he'd gone.

After a long while I gently lifted the latch on my window to ease it shut again, but as I was doing so a new noise from below made me jump. What the . . .?

My blood turned to ice as, looking down, I saw the driver's side door of Scott's new car ease open, and Scott sliding out, sneaky as a thief. He shut the door behind him, trying hard to be quiet. He didn't look up. With painstaking care, like an animal sneaking up on its prey, he tiptoed across the gravel and disappeared inside the outbuildings.

Chapter Twelve

Bang!

The door to 12G bounced open against the wall. I jerked my head up from my book as if it was attached to the door handle with string.

Scott swaggered into the room. A shaky cocktail of worry and exhaustion jittered through my veins. I didn't look at him as he thunked his weight down in the chair next to mine. But his very presence made my jaw clench.

Mr Scholars marched over to our table. 'Continue silent reading, 12G!' Then, lowering his voice: 'Scott, we're only a few days into the school year, and you're already late for registration. Did you at least sign the late register?'

Scott slouched back in his chair. I could hear the plastic bend. 'Nah, sir.'

Mr Scholars folded his arms, though he looked like he'd rather be folding his hands around Scott's neck. 'Get your book out. Sign in at reception on your way to class. You can explain to your next teacher why you're late.'

'I don't have a book, sir.'

Mr Scholars was starting to look like an overripe plum

– purple and fit to explode. I slid my open copy of *The Great Gatsby* in Scott's direction.

Scott pressed a gold-ringed finger down on the opposite corner of the book, and scooted his chair a little closer to mine. 'Sorted, sir.'

'Thank you, Elizabeth,' Mr Scholars said. 'It's nice to know someone in this class has manners.'

Scott snorted under his breath as Mr Scholars stalked away. I waited for our teacher to turn back and tell him off, but he didn't. He went back to his desk, muttering something about 'getting too old for this job'.

Scott had broken the studious mood, and whispered conversations sprang up one by one around the room. I'd planned to wait till break-time to confront him, but the sooner I got these poisonous questions out of my mind the better.

I glanced sideways. Scott met my gaze like he'd been waiting for me to look at him.

'I saw you last night, outside my window. What were you doing?' It was hard to keep my voice low so Katie and the others wouldn't hear.

'Don't know what you're talking about.'

'Don't play dumb. You were in your car. At two in the morning. And your friend, whoever he is, was creeping around too.'

Scott blanched. He obviously hadn't known I'd seen him. He covered up his momentary embarrassment with a one-shouldered shrug. 'Must be seeing things.'

I narrowed my eyes. That was a bad choice of words. 'You were there,' I repeated. 'Why?'

'I left something in my car. I came back to the inn to get it. Sorry if I woke you. I tried to be quiet.'

'And your friend?'

He leaned away from me, giving up the pretence of reading my book. 'That you are imagining. None of my mates have ever been over to the inn.'

I caught Katie frowning at us, and I buttoned my lip. But I burned to keep grilling him. Impatience gathered in my throat like wasps trapped in a bottle.

When the end-of-registration bell rang, Scott made an impressive transformation from slouched teen to marathon runner. But I was right on his heels as he swerved out of the classroom door.

'Seriously,' I said, catching up to him, 'you'd better tell me what you were doing. I don't want you hanging around my house at night.'

Scott swung his backpack like a barrier between us. 'I've got to go to reception. If you keep following me you'll be late to class.'

I ignored him and kept marching.

The corridors emptied as students disappeared into class-rooms. I followed Scott down a set of stairs. I could see the reception desk up ahead. I'd wait while he signed the late register and follow him to his next class if I had to, however late it made me with Miss Webb. This was much more important.

But before we could get there, Scott grabbed my satchel strap, jolting me to a halt.

He held up both hands before I could speak. 'I'm sorry, okay? How many times do I have to say it? I was just getting something out of my car last night. That's the truth.'

His eyes were so sincere, almost pleading. The anger in my blood dropped to a confused fizzle.

'Me and my dad are used to coming and going as we want,' he said. 'I didn't think. I'll be more careful next time so I don't disturb you.'

'Well.' I shifted my satchel on my shoulder, unsure whether to still be mad or not. 'Okay. But I'd rather you weren't sneaking around at all at night. And I will call the police if your friend keeps being creepy.'

'Yeah.' His mouth twisted. He tugged at one of his white-blond spikes. 'Seriously, none of my friends were there last night.'

Unease prickled across my skin. 'Well, someone was there. Right in front of your car, a minute before you got out. You can't pretend you didn't see him.'

'But I didn't.' He stopped twisting his hair and dropped his hand to his side with a sigh. 'There was no one there but me.'

I stared at him. Oh God.

Scott's face was open and seemed sort of sad, like he really meant what he'd said. Worse – like he felt sorry for me.

My hands began to tremble. I clenched them into fists to keep them still. Scott was messing with me. Okay, yes, I saw Glimpses, but he didn't know about those, and even so, that boy last night was nothing like a Glimpse. He was fully formed, fully corporeal, fully – well – fully there.

The corridors were completely empty now. I told myself to just walk away, but my feet wouldn't move.

'Look.' Scott took the smallest step closer, so I could smell his aftershave. His voice lowered even further. 'It's okay. I know. Your dad told my dad, my dad told me . . .'

My mouth went as dry as if he'd shoved it full of sand. 'Told you what?'

'That you had . . . issues after your mum died.' He tapped

his head. 'Nightmares, and the like. I know the other kids gave you a hard time at your last school about it.'

My jaw went slack with horror. 'That's not true,' I whispered.

He shrugged. 'Okay. Well, I just wanted to let you know that I know. But it's okay. Your secret's safe with me.' He smiled and stepped back. 'I'd better go. See you later, Liz.'

I was already late to History, but there was no way I could walk in there feeling like this. I could barely even walk, full stop.

I staggered to the nearest toilets, locked myself in a cubicle and sank onto the closed toilet seat. My mind churned. If a brain could vomit, mine would have done.

I couldn't believe Dad. What had he told Crowley? Scott hadn't mentioned my amnesia or my Glimpses outright, but if he knew I had 'issues' it was possible he knew everything. I covered my face with my hands. Scott had probably already told his gang. By the end of the day, it could be all over the school that the new girl was crazy.

I unlocked the toilet door and paced up and down between the sinks.

That boy, under the tree last night – there was no way he'd been a Glimpse. Glimpses gave me pins and needles. Glimpses were not entire people. But Scott had looked so sincere when he'd said he hadn't seen him.

I stopped still. I didn't know why I was even considering this. Obviously, Scott was lying. He'd heard about my problems, and he and his friends had decided to mess with my brain. The fact that he'd looked so sincere, that I'd almost believed him, only proved how dangerous he could be. At least with Derek, what you saw was what you got.

I looked at myself in the mirror, straightened my shirt dress, tried to wipe the look of angry panic from my face, and headed to History.

Chapter Thirteen

'So nice of you to join us, Elizabeth.' Miss Webb paused at the whiteboard as I entered the History room.

'Sorry I'm late.' I scuttled to my seat next to Susie at the front.

Miss Webb continued to glare at me until my textbook, pencil case and paper were on the desk. I could feel everyone in the class looking at me. It was a feeling I'd have to get used to if – when – Scott told people I saw things that weren't there.

Eventually, Miss Webb turned back to the board and continued speaking. I cringed over my paper, writing the date and underlining it.

Susie caught my eye and gave me a mock-alarmed look. *You okay?* she mouthed.

I nodded. But my smile felt tight as stretched rubber.

'As I was saying before our little interruption—' Miss Webb shot one more glance at me '—we're starting this term with a mini-project, in preparation for the assessed Historical Enquiries you'll be doing later in the year. You're going to research and present a historical topic of your choice. It'll be a great opportunity for some Speaking and Listening experience.'

Low groans emanated from the room.

Miss Webb smacked her pen down on her desk, her frizzy grey hair waggling on her head like a clown's. 'Come on now. You'll be interviewing for university or jobs soon, you should be grateful for the practice. You can choose any topic. The history of Hulbourn, witchcraft, the Spanish Inquisition.' She clapped her hands. 'Five minutes to find a partner and choose a topic.' The room erupted with voices and the scraping of chairs.

I looked at Susie. 'Need a partner?'

She'd already turned her chair towards me and uncapped a sparkly purple pen. She smiled. 'Obviously. What do you want to research?'

I let out a breath I didn't know I'd been holding. After my confrontation with Scott, I was more grateful than ever that Susie hadn't been put off me yet.

'I don't mind,' I said. My mind was too caught up with worry to care about some History project. 'Whatever you want.'

'Something with a little gore? Witchcraft, maybe, sounded good?'

'Already taken,' Miss Webb barked behind us, making us both jump. 'How about a project on our college's namesake, Mr Noyes? It would be the obvious choice, given that – working with Liz here – you'll have insider access to the inn, don't you think?' Miss Webb moved away to eavesdrop on someone else.

Susie rolled her eyes at her back. 'I'm sorry, Liz, but if I have to research that bloody Highwayman poem again, I'm going to die of boredom.'

'That's okay.' Miss Webb's suggestion had sparked my brain back to life. 'How about researching my inn though, if you don't have any other ideas? It's been in my family for generations and I hardly know a thing about it. There must be some stories we could dig up.'

'Hmm.' Susie considered.

She didn't look excited. But I was feeling more enthusiastic. My attempts at remembering my past hadn't gone so well yesterday, but I wasn't going to give up on them just because Scott had rattled me.

Susie's face brightened like a light bulb and she scootched to the edge of her chair. 'I'll research the inn with you. But on one condition.' She paused for dramatic effect. 'We research its ghosts.'

I pulled a face. My life was creepy enough. 'I don't know.'

'Oh, come on! It'll be fun. We can research the proper historical stuff too, but let's at least make part of our presentation entertaining. And you'd find out something about the people who used to live in your inn. What do you say?'

'I say . . .' I couldn't say no, so I shrugged. 'Sure.'

The rest of the lesson, Miss Webb had us planning our research and drawing up presentation outlines. Susie's enthusiasm for our project was contagious, and for most of the rest of the hour I almost forgot my concerns. But, as the hour went on, I found my thoughts slipping back to the vanishing boy last night, to Scott watching from his car, to Scott telling me he knew all about me.

'Susie, can I ask you something?'

'Yup.' She looked up from her scribbled notes, and suddenly looked crestfallen. 'You changed your mind about researching ghosts.'

'No, the project's fine. I wanted to ask you about those guys we saw in the corridor yesterday.'

She frowned. 'What about them?'

'What do you think of Scott Crowley? His dad works at my inn and Scott spends a lot of time around my house—'

'Scott goes round your house?' she interrupted. 'That's not good, Liz. You really want to stay out of his way.'

I raised my eyebrows. I hadn't expected such a strong reaction. 'Nobody likes him, do they? Is there something I should know?'

She chewed her lip. A long moment passed. 'Talk to me after class,' she said.

When the break bell rang, I followed after Susie in a bubble of silence. She looked through each of the classroom doors we passed, until she found an empty room. We both went inside.

I turned to her with wide eyes. I didn't know what reaction I'd expected to my questions about Scott, but it wasn't anything as serious as this.

'Hang on,' she said. 'I'm just going to text Matt not to wait for me.'

I nodded and perched on one of the desks at the front of the room, nervous, as if I was the one who'd done something wrong.

A moment later, Susie pulled herself onto the desk opposite mine. Her dark hair framed her face, her features set to serious.

'You're going to tell me something really bad, aren't you?'

''Fraid so.' She sighed. 'Just so you know, I'm only telling you this 'cause I have to. None of us talk about it any more. But if he's around your house . . . you need to know.'

I nodded and braced myself.

Susie hunched forwards and tucked her hands into the pockets of her black hoody. 'It started in year five. When we were in primary school, Scott was a bully. Not the worst kind, he didn't hit people or anything, but us girls and the nicer boys stayed out of his way.

'But then, right at the end of year five, he started being really weird. He stopped being so nasty, but he wasn't nice either. Most of us still stayed away from him, but this one girl, Lucy, didn't. She let him sit by her, and before we knew it he was giving her these little presents, walking home from school with her, that sort of thing. We were only ten, we all thought he was in love with her.'

I nodded again, unease creeping in my blood like an infection. I didn't know where this was going, but I didn't like the set-up.

'So, one day, right at the beginning of the summer holidays, Scott rang Lucy and invited her to the river to play with him and his mates. Next thing we all hear . . .' Susie dropped her voice to a whisper. 'Lucy's dead. Drowned.'

'Oh my God.' I clutched at my locket. 'You don't mean Scott . . .?'

'Officially, he's innocent.' She shrugged. 'But the police investigation went on all summer. Hulbourn was one big dramatic crime scene; it was all anyone talked about for months. They interviewed all the kids, all the parents . . . I mean, it's a small village, everyone knew Lucy and Scott.'

'But it was an accident?' I prompted.

Susie shrugged. 'Officially. But there was a lot of doubt around it. There was all this evidence against him. All the kids and teachers had noticed the attention he'd been paying Lucy, the weird presents. And, on the day it happened, he took her upriver from his mates – it was just the two of them; Scott was the only witness. Why would he do that? Even if he didn't kill her on purpose, a lot of people thought he pushed her in as a prank, that he was at least partly to blame. But he never admitted anything. When school started again in September, he just looked blank, like he'd put up a wall. He didn't smile any more, but he didn't look sad or remorseful either. It was creepy.'

I shuddered.

Susie kicked the table leg with her studded boot. 'Anyway. No one wanted to sit next to him in class after that, not even his old mates. A couple of parents even moved their kids out of the school. Then secondary school started and Scott began hanging out with these rough boys in the village, and it all went downhill from there. He's just got this really bad reputation. No one trusts him.'

I raised my eyebrows. 'I . . . think I'm getting that.'

My thoughts fluttered between panic and disbelief. I didn't know what I'd expected Susie to tell me, but certainly not this. This . . . this was just . . . more horrifying than I could have ever imagined.

Scott had been creeping around my house in the middle of the night.

He had been suspected of killing someone.

And now he knew too much about me.

The end-of-break bell rang, making every nerve in my body jump.

Susie slid off the desk and picked up her bag. She gave me a sympathetic look. 'I didn't mean to rattle you. I'm not saying Scott's a killer. But I thought you should know, especially if he's around your house. Just don't trust him, okay?'

'I don't,' I said. 'I didn't anyway, but now . . .' I shuddered. 'Thanks for telling me.'

She gave a small smile. 'No problem. And, please don't tell anyone it was me who told you? I don't want to get on Scott's bad side.'

Chapter Fourteen

After school, I speed-walked from the bus stop back to the Highwayman. The sooner I spoke to Dad, the better.

I'd barely reached the tree in the driveway before pins and needles jolted up my arms.

I scanned the outbuildings, the trees at the edge of the wood, the driveway I'd just come down. No Glimpse.

Then I looked towards the inn. In Granddad's bedroom window a hand pressed to the glass, thin and pale, five fingers stretching out. Only blackness behind it.

I wanted to be sick. I couldn't handle any more, not today. I doubled over, but nothing came out. When I stood up, my forehead damp with sweat, the hand in the window was gone.

Ignoring every instinct, I charged towards the inn, flung myself through the front door, dropped my satchel to the tiles, thundered up the stairs and threw open Granddad's bedroom door.

Relief and frustration flooded through my system simultaneously. The hand was gone. I marched into the room anyway. 'Go away!' I whispered (I would have screamed if

Dad hadn't been downstairs). 'Whatever you are, just leave me alone!'

I glared around me. Something on the window caught my eye. A five-fingered smudge, like a child had wiped their dirty palm on the glass. Goosebumps rose on my arms.

'Liz?' Dad's voice floated up the stairs, accompanied by an urgent creaking of floorboards. 'Liz, what's wrong?'

I turned from the window as Dad appeared in the doorway. He looked at me with something approaching panic.

I didn't have the patience to tiptoe around things any more. 'Did you know Scott might have killed a girl?' I demanded.

Dad's eyebrows went haywire. But the look of shock I was expecting didn't appear on his face. 'Who told you that?'

'Someone at school. You already know, don't you?'

'Yes. I know. It was a big drama, the last summer we were here. I didn't know Scott then, but your granddad gave Crowley time off to deal with it. I hope whoever told you also made it clear Scott was innocent.'

I folded my arms. 'They did. But there are a lot of people at school who aren't so sure that he is.'

Dad shook his head. 'Really, Liz? After everything you were put through at Jameson, you should be the last person to listen to gossip.'

'He's got a bad reputation, Dad. And—' I stepped forwards, my voice hardening '—somebody told him about me. You told Crowley about my problems, didn't you? And now Crowley's told Scott.'

'Ah.' Dad grimaced. 'Crowley and I were talking yesterday, about your mother and that you had a hard time afterwards. I'm sorry. I didn't think about him telling Scott.'

'And if Scott tells people at college?'

'Talk to him. I'm sure if you ask him, he won't tell anyone.'

Like I was going to believe a word Scott said, after his lies this morning.

'And anyway,' Dad said, 'you don't have those . . . problems . . . any more. So you don't have anything to worry about.' His words were casual, but I could feel him scrutinizing me.

'That's right,' I said, trying to be reassuring, matching my tone to his.

His face relaxed. 'Good. Well, I'll see you downstairs.'

He headed back down the corridor. As soon as he was gone, my whole body sagged.

It was obvious I was on my own with Scott. If I could have made Dad believe Scott's friends were sneaking round the inn at night, it would have been a different story. But if Dad confronted Scott, and Scott told him I was imagining things . . . well, I knew which of us Dad would believe.

I couldn't let him start worrying about my Glimpses again. As far as he was concerned, they were worse than the amnesia and not remembering Mum – they were the result of a brain damage the doctors hadn't been able to explain; a brain damage that Dad saw as his fault. I'd learnt quickly that the more I told Dad about my Glimpses, the more worried he became, the guiltier he felt, and the more he dragged both of us down.

I hadn't told him about any of my Glimpses for years and it had been months since I'd seen one in his presence. If he were to start thinking that I was seeing things here, now, Dad and I would be right back to square one.

I had to hand it to Scott. Whatever he and his mate were planning, they were planning it well. He'd backed me into a corner.

I gave the handprint on the window one last glare, and headed to my bedroom to change out of my school clothes.

Usually, Dad and I ate dinner on the sofa in front of the TV. But tonight I made an excuse about homework, and ate my microwaved lasagne at the kitchen table, in front of the laptop.

The inn's wireless broadband was mind-numbingly slow, but it existed, which was more than I'd hoped for when we moved in. Even with the slow internet, it only took a few minutes of typing and clicking to verify Susie's story about Scott.

Lucy Robertson. That was the full name of the girl who'd drowned. A black-and-white reproduction of her school photo showed a girl with a shy smile, a thin face and a blonde ponytail. 'A tragic drowning', the online article called it. There were details of a memorial service at Hulbourn church.

My lasagne turned sticky in my mouth. I put the fork down, my dinner unfinished. Susie's story felt so much more real now I'd seen Lucy's face. Even if Scott was innocent, I couldn't imagine how he could slope around school with that grin when there was something like this in his past. Dad crashing his car had been an accident too, but Dad and I had paid for that for years. Were still paying for it.

I closed the laptop and scraped what was left of my dinner into the bin. I needed to think about something else for a while. My heart was starting to feel like it could only pump poison.

'I'm going to check out the library,' I told Dad. I grabbed my notepad and a pen from my school bag and headed out of the kitchen. Doing some research for our History project would take my mind off things. I couldn't face any more worrying about Scott or drowned girls.

93

The library wasn't far from the kitchen. It wasn't even a real library, more of a cupboard under the stairs with the letters 'l-i-b-r-a-r-y' painted on the door, but it did have books, and when I'd told Susie about it she'd agreed it was worth investigating.

I propped the door open so I could still hear the TV – it was kind of comforting – and also to let out some of the stale, ancient, mildewed air. The room was only just big enough for a two-seater sofa and the bookcases. A brass-framed mirror opposite the door reflected grimy wallpaper, the sloped ceiling and the low door frame.

I approached the built-in shelves. The books were mostly old hardbacks, many without dust jackets: *Reader's Digest* encyclopaedias, a set of classic novels. It didn't take long to find what I was looking for. I had hoped Granddad would be the type to be interested in local history, or had at least thought some of the inn's guests would be, and I was right.

I pulled a few volumes from the shelves, dislodging a dead spider and a layer of dust. *Hulbourn Living Memories*. *Hulbourn: A History and Celebration*. *Hulbourn's Past in Photographs*.

A fourth book caught my eye, so thin I almost missed it. *Haunted Hulbourn*. A shiver tingled up my spine. Susie was going to love this one.

I retreated to the sofa and sank down, my right leg curled beneath me. I held my breath as dust poofed up around me and then settled. *Haunted Hulbourn* looked up at me from the top of the book pile. I knew I should save it for Susie rather than risk scaring myself, but just like I couldn't help peeking at the screen from between my fingers during scary movies, I couldn't stop myself opening its cover. I checked the index. 'The Highwayman Inn' was the first entry.

The Highwayman Inn stands at the edge of Hulbourn. With its long driveway, dark woods to one side and empty fields behind, it retains a sense of isolation from the village that has characterized it for five centuries.

The Inn itself is not as quiet as its location, however – the number of ghostly sightings reported there make it one of the most haunted buildings in Hulbourn. Records show that paranormal activity at the inn traces as far back as 1789, the year we first find reports of a ghostly highwayman. Numerous guests since then have reported seeing the highwayman, often in the company of a spectral black-haired young woman. These sightings no doubt inspired the poet Alfred Noyes to compose his well-known poem 'The Highwayman', for which the Highwayman Inn is now famous.

Other ghostly sightings at the inn range from phantom servant girls to black-cloaked old ladies. In the 1950s, a seance was conducted at the Highwayman by local psychic Meg Sanders. Unfortunately, there is no record of what transpired during the event.

I shuddered, and read the few paragraphs again. 'Most haunted building in Hulbourn'? Susie really was going to love this. I wasn't sure I did.

Over the years, I'd considered more than once whether my Glimpses might be ghosts. The medical experts – neurologists and psychiatrists, mainly – hadn't been able to explain the things I saw, filing my Glimpses under either 'unknown brain trauma' or 'mental illness'. For a while, part of me had hoped the Glimpses were ghosts – at least that would mean I wasn't the problem. Now, I wasn't so sure. Brain issues could be cured, seeing ghosts couldn't. And it was much less creepy to think of my Glimpses as imaginary. To believe I was seeing dead people would be a whole new level of scary.

I closed *Haunted Hulbourn* with a shudder.

As if on cue, the tingling started. I launched to my feet, wielding the pile of books like a weapon. To my embarrassment – and relief – my right leg gave way beneath me. I crumpled back onto the sofa in a heap. A roar of laughter floated down the corridor from Dad's TV as I rubbed at the pins and needles in my foot. No Glimpses this time, just bad circulation.

Rolling my eyes at my mistake, I picked up my notepad and the books and stood up again (gingerly) to go back to the kitchen. In the mirror opposite, there was a flash of white. Fast movement. Blue eyes.

I spun round, but the doorway was empty. I ran into the corridor, but the Glimpse had gone.

Four Glimpses in three days. Instead of getting better since coming to the inn, they were getting worse.

Chapter Fifteen

I stand on the lawn in silence. The rabbits peek at me between the long blades of grass. I'm waiting for something. I don't know what.

An explosion. A scream of metal.

Now I remember.

With awful certainty, I wait inside the car, bracing myself. Here she comes.

'Get out, get out, get out!' Over and over and over.

My mother's voice turns hoarse with repetition. I try to move, to get away from her. I'm thrashing now, back, forth.

'Wake up.'

I woke, wild-eyed and gasping for breath. It took me a second to realize where I was. For a moment, I just lay there, remembering. Then I snapped on my bedside lamp and reached for my locket.

'Are you all right?'

Adrenaline shot back through my veins. I *had* heard a voice. And I was sure I knew who it was: Scott's green-eyed accomplice.

Locket forgotten, I threw myself from bed and grabbed my dressing gown. Scott might have wheedled his way out of it, but I'd make sure this guy wasn't going to get away that easily. I was going to demand an explanation.

I pushed the window wide, letting in a gust of cold air, ready to lay into the creep. What I saw, though, made my voice freeze in my throat. I gripped the sill and gawped out at the night.

'What the hell are you doing?' I gasped.

The boy's pale face was level with mine, surrounded by dark leaves. He was perched on a branch no further than two metres away from my window, his body half lit by moonlight, half obscured by shadows.

A moth fluttered past, brushing my cheek, but I didn't even flinch.

'You sounded distressed.' His words were crisp as dry leaves in the cold air. 'I wanted to see if everything was well.'

I knew I should scream. I knew I should yell for Dad.

I did neither.

Instead, I leaned further out of the window and looked around for Scott. I didn't see him, only darkness. I looked back at the boy. He smiled kindly. I gave him my sternest look in return. I wanted answers.

'You were about to break in. That's why you've been sneaking around.' I had an even worse thought. 'Were you going to jump in my room?'

'I wouldn't be so disrespectful.'

'Where's Scott? I know he's here somewhere. I know you're in this together.' I scanned the ground again.

The boy's pale gold eyebrows drew together. 'The caretaker's son?'

'Don't pretend you don't know. I'm too tired for games. Tell me what you're doing here – a real answer this time – and then I want you gone. For good.'

'I told you last night.' His voice was calm, steady. 'I want to talk to you. We can help one another.'

I drew my dressing gown further around me and looked at the boy with suspicion. So far, trespassing aside, he wasn't talking or acting like one of Scott's gang. But I'd seen how well Scott could lie. And I certainly couldn't trust this boy.

'What could you possibly help me with?'

'You need answers. And I have questions.'

'What kind of answers?'

He narrowed his vivid eyes, considering. 'You were here as a child. But you're different now. You're troubled, and I believe I know why. There are things in your life you don't understand. I can explain them.'

He may as well have hit me with a taser. He knew me from before, he knew about my past!

While I knew it was probably a trick, I was too curious – too excited – to let it go. I wanted this to be true. If he'd known me as a child, he'd known Mum too. I had to find out more.

'Um, okay,' I blustered. 'Let's talk. But you have to get out of that tree.'

He grinned with relief. It completely transformed his face, the way moonlight transforms the night sky when it breaks through the clouds. 'Not a problem,' he said.

The branch that pointed from the tree to my window began to shake as the boy reached his full height, and I realized what he was doing.

'Oh, no,' I said. 'No, no, no, I didn't mean . . .'

I gaped up at him as he inched towards me. Closer and closer. He held his gloved hands out to each side, grasping smaller branches in his fists to keep from falling.

'You might want to move out of the way,' he said.

'You're insane!'

The boy crouched, perfect and controlled as a cat about to leap. I'd barely moved out of the way when there was a whoosh of air and a thud on the floorboards in front of me. The shock of his arrival trembled up through the soles of my feet.

'Are you crazy? You could have killed yourself!'

'No.' He smiled. 'I could not.'

I stared up at him. He seemed so much taller than he'd looked in the tree. Up close, his skin was less pale, his cheeks pink from the cold. There was a silvery scar, about an inch long, on his jaw. He smelled of night air and damp leaves, more tree than boy.

This, my brain whispered, is very bad. And incredibly surreal. A few minutes ago, I'd been sleeping, and now there was a tall, strong-looking boy in my room in the middle of the night; a boy who made jumping through windows look natural.

A boy who – if he'd lied, if his intentions were bad – could hurt me now more easily than he'd climbed that tree.

I took a slow step backwards. 'You didn't have to do that. We could have talked through the window.'

'This is more private.'

'Private' was the problem. But it was too late now. 'Let's make this quick,' I said. 'Tell me what you came to tell me.'

'We can make this quick.' He held a gloved hand out to me, like a gentleman meeting a lady in a classic novel. 'Zachary Wilson. It's a pleasure to meet you.'

I kept my hands behind my back. There was no way I was touching him. 'You promised me explanations. You said you knew me from before.'

'I didn't know you exactly.' His eyes scanned my face. 'But I have seen you at the inn before. Years ago. Your abilities were different then. That's what I want to discuss with you.'

Goosebumps rose on my arms. 'My abilities . . . ?'

'You see things that other people do not.'

I blinked at him. My whole body went ice cold, like I'd been plunged into a freezer. Scott must have told him. There was no other way this boy – Zachary – could know.

'What do you want from me?' I backed away from him, banging up against the wall. He had me trapped – wall to one side, my bed to the other. 'What are you and Scott getting out of this?' I glanced at the door. Before he could answer, I scrambled up onto the bed away from him.

'Wait. I have no intention of harming you.'

I jumped off the bed, onto the floorboards, spun round to face him. He stepped around the end of the bed towards me, his footsteps heavy.

'Stop where you are or I'll scream!'

He froze, one foot in the air. He lowered it slowly. 'For the final time,' he said, his eyes intense as though he could force me to believe him, 'I have no connection with the caretaker's boy. I'm here because of you. I know that you see things, because I've seen you see things. It's evident that you don't know what they are. And I can explain them.'

There was no way. He was crazy. I looked around the room for a weapon. My bedside lamp would have to do. I inched towards it and clasped my hand round the heavy brass stem. I felt safer.

I fixed my eyes on him, unblinking. Perhaps it was the lamplight making the room look smaller, but he seemed to take up too much space; Zachary filled the room with his presence, tall and solid as a standing stone.

While I scanned him, he scanned the room, the white walls and dark-shadowed corners. His attention caught on the pile of Granddad's books on the dresser. He leaned towards them, reading their titles.

'Don't touch anything,' I said.

He turned to look at me, his eyes glittering. 'This.' He lifted a gloved finger and pointed at the cover of *Haunted Hulbourn*. 'This is what I came to talk to you about.'

My skin prickled. 'An old book?'

He straightened, his smile back. 'No. I want to talk about the spirits you see.'

I opened my mouth to laugh, to protest. Nothing came out, my throat was thick with panic. My mind raced. He wasn't meant to say what he just had. No one, ever, was meant to say what he just had.

'You *are* one of Scott's friends,' I whispered. 'And you're messing with me.'

His face grew solemn, like it was carved out of stone. 'I wish, for both our sakes, that was the case.'

My skin crawled, goosebumps dancing across my scalp. Then the tingling scurried up my arms like a mouse, and I gasped.

Zachary jolted to attention. He stared at my bedroom door, alert as a panther stalking a gazelle. I looked behind me, panic making my breathing loud. But there was nothing at my door.

'Hear that?' he asked, his voice barely louder than the breeze outside my window.

102

I listened. Nothing. Then, *tap, tap, tap.* Soft, heeled footsteps in the corridor outside my room.

Pins and needles consumed my skin. There was a Glimpse outside my room. Zachary and I locked eyes for an instant. He crept silently towards me, shifting his gaze to the door. Oh my God. He could sense it too.

He was close enough for me to make out every tangle in his hair, every jagged edge around his scar. A moment ago, I'd have run. Now, I didn't want to.

He stopped, his head turned towards the door. 'You hear her, don't you?' he breathed next to my ear. 'You sense her.'

I gave the tiniest of nods.

'Spirit.'

Fresh fear prickled over my skin, as if he was saying the word for the first time.

'I regret she's here,' he whispered, 'because now I have to depart. But we need to speak about this again.' He drew back, his green eyes questioning.

I nodded my answer.

'When?' His thin lips barely moved.

'Saturday,' I whispered.

He nodded. 'The other side of the woods. Early evening.'

I nodded again, more firmly than before. God, I was terrified. But I'd also never been more excited in my life. He saw the same things I did. He was like me.

He smiled at me, not his wide grin from before, but something more solemn, more heartfelt. Then he looked again at the door. 'I have to go.' He took a step back. 'Don't be alarmed. She cannot harm you.' He paused. 'What's your name?'

'Elizabeth,' I whispered.

'Then I look forward to seeing you again, Elizabeth.'

In one fleet movement, he was at the other side of the room, crouching on my windowsill. He lifted a gloved hand in farewell then leapt off gracefully, silently, into the darkness. I didn't worry about him. I didn't have time. The tree outside rustled and creaked, then fell quiet.

I turned back to the door. My hand on the lamp sent shadows spidering out around the room.

Tap, tap, tap, from outside my door. Then *tap, tap, tap*, again, from further away down the corridor. As the footsteps faded away, the pins and needles faded too. I was left alone with a racing heart and the all-consuming stillness of night.

Chapter Sixteen

I opened my eyes with a gasp. My room was unmenacing in the morning light.

I sank back against the pillows, my hands over my face. The events of the night raced through my mind, more surreal and intense than any nightmare.

That boy, Zachary, jumping from the tree into my room. The Glimpse outside my door. A Glimpse he had sensed too.

If Zachary was right, that thing outside my room last night – all the countless fragments I'd glimpsed in the last seven years – had been spirits; had been dead things.

Black dread filled me, cloying as ash. But, underneath it, glowed an ember of hope. I got out of bed and looked at the list stuck to my wardrobe door. 'No more Glimpses'. I was no closer to getting rid of them, but for the first time, someone had provided an explanation that corroborated their existence. For the first time, I wasn't in this alone. My Glimpses were outside of me, not all in my head.

I was closer to understanding this than ever before.

Zachary said my Glimpses were spirits, but he hadn't told me how he knew that. In the cold light of day, I realized I had far more questions than he had answered. For a start, who the hell was this guy? Why did he have to leave so urgently when he heard the steps outside the door? And – the biggest question of all – if he wasn't Scott's friend, how did he know all about me?

I pulled open my wardrobe door. Operating on autopilot, I took out a new pair of jeans, and scanned the hangers of boring new tops. I didn't have the mental energy to remember which T-shirt was meant to go with which cardigan, which cardigan with which jewellery, and this morning I didn't care. I reached for one of my vintage items instead – a purple velvet tunic with a white lace collar. It wasn't standard teenage issue, but after the revelations of last night, it seemed ridiculous to spend time matching clothes.

The scent of coffee mingled with the inn's usual mustiness as I plodded downstairs with my school bag. Dad was up already. Yawning, I headed into the kitchen.

I jolted to a halt in the doorway. 'Scott.'

'Delighted to see you too.' Scott looked me up and down from his perch at the kitchen table. One leg was curled casually under him as if it was perfectly normal for him to be there. His white teeth sparkled into a smirk as he took a sip of coffee.

I narrowed my eyes at him. 'Why are you here?'

'I left something in the office last night.' He nodded at a Maths textbook on the table next to his mug. 'Thought I'd give you a lift to school, since I'm here. Show you my new wheels.' He smiled again.

I looked from Scott to Dad. Dad stood at the kitchen counter, buttering toast. He gave me a look that warned me to be polite.

I really didn't know what to make of Scott. After last night, I was fairly sure that he had been telling me the truth about not knowing Zachary, but that still didn't explain why he had been spying on us, or why he'd lied about it. And the news that he had been linked to the death of a girl was not going to shake off that easily.

I took a seat at the opposite end of the table to him. 'Thanks, but I'm okay getting the bus.'

'Liz,' said Dad, thrusting a plate of toast at me. 'Scott has very kindly waited for you.'

I groaned, and reached for the plate. 'Okay.' I managed a smile. 'A lift would be nice. But just this one time.'

Scott nodded, but a flicker of something crossed his face – uncertainty? Disappointment? He looked down at his mug and tugged at the fake-diamond stud in his ear lobe.

I bit into the toast, my crunching loud in the suddenly awkward silence.

'Want a slice?' I nudged the plate towards Scott as a peace offering. I had no reason to apologize to him, but it wouldn't do to aggravate him. And I didn't want Dad upset either.

'I already ate breakfast,' Scott said.

I chewed slowly, watching him watching me out of the corner of his eye. In between sips of coffee, his fingers constantly moved, pulling at his hair or his eyebrow ring, teasing a splinter in the table. He was nervous about something, I realized.

After a few minutes, he leapt up from the table. 'Mind if I use your bathroom?'

'Go ahead,' Dad said.

'Liz, I'll see you in the car in five.' Scott brushed past me, in a cloud of aftershave. I pulled a face – the tang did not go well with toast.

107

The moment he left the kitchen, I sat back in my chair and rubbed my fingers across my forehead.

Dad sat in the seat Scott had vacated. 'You look pale.'

'I didn't sleep well.'

Dad grabbed one of my uneaten pieces of toast. 'I thought I heard noises in the night. Bad dreams?'

I glanced at him. Made my voice breezy. 'Yeah. Not too bad though.'

Scott's footsteps creaked and banged through the ceiling. It sounded more like he was shifting furniture around than using the bathroom. A minute or so later, he pounded back down the stairs.

I picked up my satchel with a sigh. 'See you later, Dad.'

'Have a good day.' Dad dropped his voice to a whisper and added, 'Give Scott a chance, eh?'

Outside, Scott was leaning against his car, waiting for me, kicking at the gravel. He stopped as soon as he saw me, folded his arms and squinted at the sky. 'Does that tree bother you?' he asked.

It was the last thing I expected him to say. Immediately, I thought of Zachary's face framed by leaves last night, Zachary jumping through my window in the darkness. I tried to keep my face neutral. 'Why would it bother me?'

'My dad thinks it's getting too close to your window. Blocking the light. Scratching the glass. He's been talking about cutting off that big branch.'

'Oh.' I paused. 'Well . . . I kind of like the tree the way it is.'

Scott shrugged. 'I'll tell him you said that. Let's get to school.'

I frowned as he turned his back to get into the car. Surely those questions had to be coincidental. I tugged on the passenger door handle and clambered inside. Scott started the engine and we crunched out of the driveway.

'You seem nervous,' he said. 'You don't mind cars, do you? After what happened with your mum and dad and all?'

'I'm fine,' I said, my voice one degree warmer than frosty.

'Good.' Scott paused the car as we pulled out of the driveway. 'I've only had my licence a few months, but I'm a decent driver. You can trust me.'

I sank down in my seat as we passed the bus stop – I didn't want Katie or Susie to see me. I just wanted to get to school in one piece, without having to talk too much.

But Scott had other ideas. 'Look, sorry again, about you seeing me the other night in my car,' he said, pulling up at a traffic light. 'And about you thinking I had one of my mates over.'

'Really. It's fine.'

He looked at me, an expression on his face that I couldn't decipher. 'Did you really think you saw someone?'

I looked away from him, out of the window. 'I'm not sure any more. It could have been shadows, I guess. New house and everything.'

He grunted. 'I hope that it was just shadows. If anyone was hanging around the inn at night, I don't think they'd be a good person, do you know what I mean?'

I didn't respond straightaway. I leaned my head back against the headrest so Scott couldn't easily see my face. 'Yeah?' I prompted.

'Yeah. Well, it's obvious.' His voice was almost painfully casual. 'Any guy who hangs around girls' bedroom windows at that time of night, would have to be dodgy. Certainly nobody you should be talking to. I mean, you start talking to a guy like that, he might think he was welcome inside. Who knows what it could lead to.' He paused to change gear. 'So, you know, I'm just glad to hear it was probably nothing.'

I hugged my bag to my chest. Scott had seen Zachary: he had seen him the night before, and he had seen him again last night jumping into my room.

Scott had been spying on me.

The car slowed as we entered the school car park. I hadn't even noticed driving in through the gates. Scott pulled to a halt in a parking space then turned to face me. We looked at each other for a long moment. His face was bright and curious, as if nothing he'd said was strange.

'You can tell me, you know,' he said, 'if you imagine any more people around the inn.'

'Thanks,' I said. 'But I won't. See anything, I mean. Like I said, I just saw some shadows.'

'Suit yourself. Only trying to help.' He shrugged and got out of the car. He paused to brush a streak of dust off his shirt, then walked away.

I yanked the passenger door open and jumped out after him. Without turning around, Scott pointed the keys over his shoulder and the car beeped locked. He disappeared into the crowd outside school.

I stayed in the car park a minute, to gather myself together before anyone saw me. For the second morning in a row, Scott had rattled me as if he'd put my bones in a bag and shaken me up.

He had seen Zachary, I was sure of that now. Whatever Scott's motivations for denying it, it was obvious he was trying to mess with me. And being messed with by a boy who some people thought capable of murder . . . It could never be good.

I needed to sort out my life before it got any more complicated. On Saturday, I'd get as much information as I could out of Zachary and, in the meantime, I needed to stay far away from Scott.

Chapter Seventeen

I could have hugged Miss Webb when I got to History and she told us we had the whole hour to go to the school library and do project research. I didn't think I could have handled a 'real' lesson.

Susie nabbed us one of the more private tables between the stacks of shelves. I could have hugged her, too, for that.

'Love your top,' she whispered, as we sat down. 'It's so unique.'

'Thanks.' I tugged self-consciously on my lace collar, then pulled Granddad's books out of my bag. 'So I found these at the inn last night.'

'Good one.' Susie sorted through the books, and she soon spotted *Haunted Hulbourn*. 'Seriously? This is perfect! Liz, your granddad had great taste in books.'

She cracked it open and started to read, her brown eyes darting wildly. I fiddled with my pen and waited for her to finish. I hadn't plucked up the courage to read the entry on the Highwayman Inn again, not after last night. I remembered it vividly enough.

'Hey, I know this woman.' Susie jabbed a lacquer-black fingernail onto the page.

'What woman?'

'Meg Sanders.' Susie twisted the book so I could see, and pointed again at the text. 'The woman who did the seance at your inn in the fifties. She lives down my road.'

I blinked at Susie. 'Are you sure? Wouldn't she be really old by now?'

'Mrs Sanders is ancient; I'm sure it's her. She read my mum's tarot cards once for a tenner.'

In a flash, and for the first time that morning, she had my full attention. 'We have to talk to her!'

'Exactly what I was thinking.' Susie's white cheeks had gone pink. 'This is perfect. Think of all the things she can tell us! And Miss Webb'll love us if we include an interview in our presentation.'

I nodded. 'Can you arrange it?'

'I'll speak to my mum at break. She can ring Mrs Sanders for us. Maybe we can even see her tonight.'

I squeezed my locket. If the inn really was haunted, if I really was seeing ghosts, if Zachary was right, perhaps the psychic would know. And maybe when I met Zachary tomorrow, I'd have some information to tell him.

I texted Dad on the bus ride home to let him know I'd be late. It took me a few tries – my phone was on its way out, I was badly in need of a new one. Then I walked with Susie and Matt into the village centre. They spent most of the walk murmuring together, hands intertwined, as if it was the first time they'd seen each other all month, not since break-time. At school, their all-consuming infatuation with each other sometimes made me blush – they were sweet together, but so unguarded, so open about their feelings. I couldn't help imagining myself in Susie's place and feeling both shy and a little bit envious. Maybe one day I'd feel confident enough about myself to let someone as close to me as Susie let Matt, but I couldn't even imagine it now.

This afternoon, however, I didn't need to feign an interest in the pavement or the sky during their more lovey-dovey moments. I had bigger things to think about, like how to ask a little old lady about the dead people that haunted my house.

Matt left us at the street before Susie's. 'Have fun with the ghost lady,' he said. 'Don't get possessed.'

Susie rolled her eyes at him, then led me down her terraced street. 'That's Meg's house—' she pointed ahead '—the one with the broken gate. Are you excited?' She clapped her hands. 'I'm excited.'

Meg's garden gate wasn't the only thing broken about her house. (What did I expect from an old lady psychic – window boxes? Wind chimes?) The garden itself was overgrown with bindweed and nettles, and her front door was a disgrace of scabby, peeling brown paint. It rattled on its hinges as Susie banged the brass knocker. Long moments dragged by.

'Are you sure she's in?'

Susie nodded. 'Mum said she might take a while to get to the door. Meg must be, I don't know, eighty-something.'

There was a scrabbling from the other side of the door then the sound of bolts being shot back and a key being turned. The door creaked open to reveal a woman with papery skin and thinning hair hunched over a walking frame. She blinked at us from behind wide-rimmed glasses.

'Susan?' she said, in a voice that sounded like a scratched gramophone record. 'What happened to your hair?'

Susie smoothed her black and lollipop-red fringe. 'Hi, Mrs Sanders.'

'And who's that?' Meg peered around Susie to look at me. She wobbled on her frame, and Susie had to grab her arm to steady her and stop her falling against the door.

I smiled. 'I'm Elizabeth, Susie's friend.'

Meg gave me a displeased look. 'I thought only Susan was coming. Well, you're here now. Don't just stand around out there. You're letting the cold in.'

I caught Susie's eye and raised my eyebrows. Considering the things I wanted to ask her about, I'd hoped Meg would be more approachable.

'Come on, girls!'

Susie and I followed her into her narrow hallway. A musty smell hit me, reminding me of the inn, but more claustrophobic somehow – as if Meg's old furniture was trying to stuff itself up my nostrils. The decor was dark and museum-like. All that was missing were a couple of sinister waxwork figures in fifties period costume.

Meg led us through to the living room and gestured at a sunken sofa. Susie and I perched on the edge of it and, waved on by Meg, we each took a dubious biscuit from a greasy plate on a coffee table cram-packed with a teapot and too many tea-stained mugs.

I looked around me at the cabinets full of ornaments and dusty knick-knacks. Random objects cluttered the surfaces, far more than at the Highwayman. Some matched what I imagined an old lady should own; some, like a fruit bowl full of what looked like small bones, did not.

I realized Meg was staring at me with suspicion. I snapped my attention back to her with a too-bright smile.

'Thanks for seeing us, Mrs Sanders,' I said. 'We're here because we're researching the Highwayman Inn's ghost stories for a school project. We're hoping you can help. I—um, I actually live there now.'

Meg leaned forwards and squinted at me. 'The Highwayman Inn. It's a long time since anyone's asked me about those spirits. You live there, do you, you say?'

I glanced at Susie. 'Um, yeah.'

'Well, you've come to the right place.' Meg leaned back in her chair. 'I know all about the spirits at the inn.'

It was exactly what I'd hoped to hear, but her words, combined with her unfriendly demeanour, made me feel apprehensive. I nibbled my stale digestive, trying to hide my anxiety.

'That's amazing,' Susie said, her bright tone soothing my nerves. 'We hoped you'd have some good stories.' She pulled *Haunted Hulbourn* from her bag – she'd insisted on keeping it today to show Matt. 'This book mentions your name. It says you did a seance at the inn in the fifties.'

'Show me the book.'

Susie open *Haunted Hulbourn* to the right page and handed it over. Meg brought it close to her eyes. '"Most haunted building in Hulbourn",' she read out loud. 'Most haunted building in the county, more like. I've encountered any number of spirits, girls, but none so frequently as at the inn.'

Susie clapped the tips of her fingers together excitedly.

I thought of the snarling face I'd seen on Monday, the footsteps outside my door last night, and coughed on a biscuit crumb.

'What do the spirits look like, when you see them?' I asked, trying to sound casual.

'Not like they do in the films, I can tell you that,' Meg said. 'The way I see spirits has changed over the years. When I first saw them, they looked like . . . fragments. Small pieces of spirit. A hand here, a leg there.' She narrowed her eyes at me. 'You know what I mean.

'But as my psychic powers developed, I found I could see more and more. And as I opened myself up to the spirits, the spirits were better able to communicate with me. Some were even able to touch me. These days, if I see a spirit, they look and feel so real, I could almost think they're a living person.'

'Ugh.' Susie shuddered, making the sofa rock. 'That must be so weird.'

Meg's gaze locked with mine. I tried to keep my face blank. I didn't want her to see that she'd rattled me. I didn't want to be like Meg. I didn't want my Glimpses to get worse.

'So what ghosts have you seen at the inn?' Susie asked.

'Oh, too many to say. Tea?' Meg smiled, reached precariously for the pot on the coffee table, poured stewed tea into three of the least tannin-browned mugs and shoved a milk jug towards Susie.

'Can you describe some?' I asked. 'For our school project?'

I was grateful to be able to take a mug and sink back into the sofa. I lifted the mug to hide my mouth and I listened. I tried to match what Meg described with my own Glimpses – did Meg and I really see the same things? – but it was impossible. I had no way of knowing if the face I'd seen had belonged to a servant girl or an inn guest; if the footsteps outside my door last night had belonged to a barmaid or a dead relative.

Susie took furious notes. 'It's all so creepy,' she said with delight.

It was creepy. But I was not the least bit delighted.

Meg shook herself exaggeratedly, as though shaking off an unwelcome topic.

'Enough of this dark talk.' She glanced at me. 'You two girls should be heading off. I'm sure your mothers will want you home.' Pain bristled through me at the word 'mothers', but Meg smiled at me, oblivious; sweet innocence embodied. 'Have you finished your tea, Elizabeth? Let me take your cup.'

She pulled the mug out from my hand, and dropped it straight onto the floor next to the coffee table. I gasped as warm liquid splashed up my jeans and into my ballet pumps.

'How clumsy of me!' Meg's hand flew to her pale cheek.

I stared at her. She'd done it on purpose!

Susie leapt to her feet. 'Where are your towels, Mrs Sanders?'

'There are some rags in the airing cupboard upstairs. Get a couple, would you, there's a love.'

Susie nodded and ran from the room, her heavy boots pounding up unseen stairs.

Before I could ask what she was playing at, Meg stooped forwards towards me in her chair. 'Elizabeth.' She spoke fast. 'You need to stop what you're starting at the inn, do you hear? There's a powerful spirit, and you've caught its eye. Stop—' she raised her white eyebrows '—for your own good.'

I felt the blood drain from my face. 'What do you mean?'

'I'll put it bluntly. Stop talking to boys, Elizabeth,' Meg hissed.

'Are these all right?' Susie reappeared in the doorway, a ratty tea towel in each hand.

I dropped my gaze to my wet shoes, not trusting my face to look calm. Susie crouched at my feet. She pressed one rag to the stained carpet and handed the other to me.

I dabbed at my jeans with a shaking hand, and stole glances

at Meg over the top of Susie's head. The old lady looked coldly back at me.

There were an awkward few moments as Susie and I finished cleaning up the mess Meg had made. Then we gathered our bags.

'Thanks, Mrs Sanders,' I said, as we stood up. 'You've been so . . . helpful.' I narrowed my eyes at her. 'Maybe I could talk to you again?'

'Oh, no.' Meg said. 'I don't think so. I've told you all I can.'

Susie's gaze flicked between me and Meg. Then she said, with unnatural brightness, 'Shall we go, Liz?'

But I wasn't finished here.

'You can see yourselves out,' said Meg.

We headed out of the living room and back into the dark hallway. I exhaled for what felt like the first time in minutes. Susie stepped outside and I went to follow her, but stopped and rolled my eyes in fake exasperation. 'Sorry,' I said, 'forgot my granddad's book. Back in a sec.'

I darted back to the living room. I'd already had one cryptic warning today from Scott, I refused to go home with another. I had to make Meg explain what she meant about powerful spirits and not talking to boys.

I hurried round the doorway to the living room. 'What did you mean—'

I didn't reach the end of my question. Tingling. My skin felt like I'd plunged into a bucket of needles.

Meg still sat in her chair. But hovering in the air next to her was a disembodied head.

I gasped and staggered backwards.

The head whipped round to look at me. The malevolent blue eyes, the pink lips opening in a snarl – it was the same

Glimpse I'd seen at the inn! But this time, brown ringlets framed the face, fine-boned shoulders sloped beneath the neck.

Meg glared. The Glimpse glared. I froze to the spot. Then Meg threw *Haunted Hulbourn* at me. The book bounced off my leg, jolting me to life.

'Shoo, girl!'

I barrelled back down the hallway like I'd been shot from a cannon.

Susie squealed as I nearly flattened her into the weeds in the front garden. 'Oh my God, what happened to you?'

'Sorry, sorry!' I pulled back, struggling to keep myself from hysteria.

Susie tugged on my sleeve and pulled me out of Meg's front garden. We both ran and didn't stop until we got halfway down the street, then we collapsed on the kerb. Susie laughed. I just tried not to be sick.

'I heard her yelling at you,' Susie giggled. 'Oh my God, she's crazy! Did you do something bad to her in a past life or something? She spilled tea on you!'

I looked at Susie, then groaned and hid my face in the cover of *Haunted Hulbourn*. 'You saw that?'

'It was so obvious.' Susie bit her lip, her laughter subsiding. 'Sorry, Liz, I didn't know I was taking you to a crazy lady. Did you see she had bones on her bookshelves? I can't wait to tell my mum.' She shook her head.

I took a deep, gulping breath, and stood up off the kerb.

Susie stood up too, dusting off her long black skirt. 'You know the way back, right? What now – shall I get my Ouija board, then back to yours for some ghost hunting?'

I couldn't hide the look of horror on my face this time. Susie burst back into giggles. 'Joking!'

I rolled my eyes, but managed a smile. 'I'd better go. Thanks though, for organizing this. See you at school on Monday.'

'No problem. You fancy another crazy evening sometime, you know where I live.'

I turned and started walking away before my grin became a grimace. I barely made it to the end of Susie's street before I started to shake.

That Glimpse in Meg's house – that ghost in Meg's house – had been the exact same one I'd seen at the inn. And it – she – had been talking to Meg.

I didn't trust that old lady any more than I'd trusted Derek. And even if I could trust her, Meg's warnings made no sense. She'd said I should 'stop what I was starting', she'd said I had attracted the attention of a powerful spirit, she'd told me to stop talking to boys. By 'boys' she could only mean Zachary or Scott, but I didn't see why she should care who I spoke to.

It didn't matter. Meg was crazy. Meg hung out with ghosts – seemingly by choice. I might see spirits, but I'd never reach a point where I'd sit calmly while there was one in my house.

As for what Meg said about not talking to boys, I'd already decided I wasn't going to talk to Scott if I could help it. Zachary, though . . . he, at least, had promised me straight answers. He was one boy I was definitely going to be speaking to again.

Chapter Eighteen

To my relief, Scott's car wasn't in the driveway when I got back to the inn. I ran to the front door anyway, just in case, my satchel banging against my side. I avoided looking at any of the upstairs windows – I couldn't handle any more today.

'How was your project research?' Dad asked, wandering out of the kitchen as soon as I got through the door. 'How was your friend?' He smiled.

I paused in taking off my tea-sticky shoes. My face was probably sheet white, but I managed a real smile for him. 'Susie? She's okay.'

Dad waved his coffee mug at me. 'One week into school, and you've got yourself a pal. I'm proud of you, Liz. I knew you could do it.'

I finished taking off my shoes and jacket as he went back into the kitchen. Dad's words had penetrated the fraction of my brain that wasn't absorbed with what had just happened at Meg's house. Susie really was becoming a friend, I realized. Even after today, even after hearing all those ghost stories, Susie hadn't freaked out. She actually seemed to like hanging out with me.

I wondered what she'd think if she knew I was like Meg. It was one thing hearing weird stories from an old lady, it would be another thing entirely if the girl you sat next to in lessons started talking that way.

I pulled myself up the stairs, desperate for my duvet. I wanted to do nothing more this evening but lie in bed and think – about my Glimpses, about ghosts, about Scott's threat, about Meg's, about the Glimpse from the inn appearing at Meg's house, about meeting Zachary tomorrow.

Most of all, I needed to work out how I could – if I could – stop the Glimpses happening. I refused to end up like Meg, apparently crazy and alone, with no one but scary ghost-girls for company.

I got to the top of the stairs and padded down the corridor towards my room. Granddad's bedroom door was ajar. I reached out to close it as I passed but paused as, through the gap, I saw yet another open door.

Instead of shutting the door, I pushed it open. At the foot of the bed was a built-in closet, its door wide open, revealing darkness inside; and leading into it – or out of it – were dusty trails, running across the carpet. I frowned. No ghost could have done this, and I couldn't imagine Dad coming in here – there were photos of Mum everywhere. Even if he had been in, he wouldn't have left it in such a mess. No. Crowley had been here. Or . . .

I remembered Scott's bathroom trip this morning, the dusty marks on his clothes.

In two strides I was at the closet, groping in the darkness for the light-pull.

A bare bulb fizzed to life, illuminating the small space. A rail of black morning suits filled one wall. The only other objects in the closet were an empty shoe rack and, leaning against the wall, a stack of gold-framed paintings.

Checking behind me – no Glimpses, no Scott – I edged into the small room. The closet was uncarpeted, the floorboards grimy. Scuffles in the dust led me in as clearly as if Scott had chalked an arrow on the floor. The trail stopped at the stack of paintings.

Feeling more confused now than frightened, I crouched down by the paintings and started to look through them. Unless one of the ornate gold frames held a mirror, I couldn't imagine Scott having any interest in them. I couldn't really imagine anyone having an interest in them. Scene after boring rural scene – sheep, clouds, quaint Victorian milkmaids – languished under a blanket of dust.

I leaned the stack back against the wall. Maybe Scott hadn't done this after all. It made no sense that he'd break into my granddad's closet to rummage through old oil paintings.

Holding my grimy hands away from my clothes, I closed the door and followed the dust tracks back into the corridor. The scuffs in the carpet continued down the corridor, and, alarmingly, stopped right outside my room.

I ran to my bedroom and flung the door open. Unease twisted in my belly. In the middle of my bed lay a huge picture frame, face down.

I held my breath, listening hard. When I was sure I was still alone, I tiptoed towards the bed.

The gold frame was huge, bigger than any of the ones in Granddad's closet. It sank into the duvet with its weight, smearing my white covers with grime. It took some effort to flip it.

I expected another farm view, more sheep, but this was no

landscape. This painting was a scene of darkness. Luminous in the moonlight, a young woman stood at an open window, with full, half-parted lips and long dark hair twisted into a red-ribboned plait. A moonbeam struck a white bed behind her. A white bed in the middle of a white room.

Paranoia seized me and I ran to my wardrobe and yanked it open – no one there. I stuck my head under the bed – no one there. No one behind the door, which I slammed shut. I lifted the painting, my breathing quickening under its weight, and placed it shakily on the chest of drawers. For a long moment, I just stared at it. The white room, the girl at the window, her dark hair.

It couldn't be coincidence that the room in the painting looked exactly like my bedroom, right down to the white beams and the white, low-framed door.

And the girl . . .

I stepped closer to the painting, scrutinizing every brushstroke. I tugged my own plait over my shoulder and fiddled with it as I looked at the painted girl's braided hair. I examined her dress, long, simple and elegant; the dreamy look in her eyes as she looked out of the window; the thin layer of dust over everything.

Something tugged at the corner of my mind. I felt as if I'd seen this painting before. Maybe I had – it could have hung in the inn when I was a child, and I wouldn't remember.

Or maybe . . . Out of nowhere, I remembered Alfred Noyes' poem.

He whistled a tune to the window, and who should be
   waiting there
But the landlord's black-eyed daughter,

Bess, the landlord's daughter,
Plaiting a dark red love-knot into her long black hair.

Bess. The dark hair, the red ribbon, the romantic eyes, the ghost, waiting at a window. I knew who the girl was. But that didn't explain why Scott, or whoever, had left it in my room.

I turned back to the bed and my heart lurched. Framed by the rectangle of dust left by the painting, was a folded piece of paper.

Hardly breathing, I picked it up and unfolded it. It was a piece of A4 ruled paper – the same paper we used at school. Printed on it, dead centre, was a single word:

FAMILIAR?

What? It just had to be Scott, and I wasn't sure whether to be annoyed or scared. Either he was purposefully trying to confuse me, or he was wrong in the head, or both. He'd been suspected of killing someone when he was just a child – surely you didn't come away from an experience like that without it affecting your mind somehow. Whether he was innocent or not, he had to be a little bit screwed up.

Gravel crunched outside, jolting me back to reality. I went to the window. Scott's little red car pulled up next to the outbuildings. I narrowed my eyes as Scott and Crowley climbed out. Their laughter drifted faintly up to me as they went into their office.

Gripping Scott's note, I marched from my room and downstairs. I paused in the hallway. 'Dad?' I called. 'Have you been in Granddad's room today?'

'No,' he called back. 'Why?'

'No reason.'

I pulled open the front door and stepped outside. I'd had enough of this. I was going to confront Scott about the painting, and if Crowley was there too, so much the better. He needed to know how strangely his son was acting.

The outbuildings were a part of my new house that I hadn't yet explored. They were single storey, reaching to only halfway up the inn, their rough stone contrasting with the adjoining whitewashed walls. The low building, once a stable block, had three doors and a couple of small, net-curtained windows. A pile of gardening tools was propped up against the wall.

I knocked on the door in the middle – the one Scott and Crowley always used – and waited.

Crowley answered. 'Liz.' He smiled, a beat too late. 'Everything all right?'

I tried to see around his bulk to the room beyond. A TV flickered in a recess in the wall, a football game playing at low volume. 'I need to talk to Scott.'

For a moment, I wondered if Crowley had heard me. Then he stepped back, gesturing for me to come in. 'Sure. Scott, what have you done?' Crowley's tone was joking, but his eyes weren't.

Good. This was serious, and I wanted Crowley on my side.

I stepped into the office, trying not to wrinkle my nose at the combined odour of damp, aftershave and sweat. I glanced quickly around. It wasn't what I'd expected. The room was almost bare, the only furniture being a coffee table laden with a kettle and mugs, and a two-seater sofa on which Scott spread out. The walls were bare, the concrete floor covered with a simple red rug. Was this really where Scott and Crowley spent all their time?

Scott stood up when he saw me. He looked from me to his dad and back again. He didn't smile. 'What's up?'

I held up the piece of paper, dirty now with my fingerprints. 'This is what's up. Have you been in my room?'

Crowley slid the paper from my unresisting fingers and opened it.

I kept my eyes on Scott. He blanched, his mouth opening and closing like a fish. 'No,' he said, 'why would I?'

'What is this?' Crowley held the paper up, so the word 'FAMILIAR?' was visible. 'Scott?'

Scott said nothing. He refused to look at the note.

'Why on earth do you think my son was in your room?' Crowley asked me.

'Someone took a painting from my granddad's closet,' I said. 'They left the door open and dust all over the carpet. Then they left the painting on my bed, with that note. It definitely wasn't my dad. Scott was upstairs this morning, so it must have been him.'

'Really—' Scott's voice was low and desperate, as if he wished I'd shut up '—it wasn't.'

Crowley stayed silent. 'What was the painting of?' he asked, not taking his laser-beam gaze off Scott.

'A girl at a window,' I said.

'Well, that sounds very odd.' Crowley pulled his thumbnail hard over the fold in the paper, zip, zip, zip, as though he was about to rip it apart. 'Very odd.' He looked back at me. 'But I don't see why Scott would do that.'

Crowley's gaze was solid and cold. He didn't blink. Zip, zip, zip.

The certainty I'd felt a moment ago that Crowley would be on my side fell away.

'You don't think it was Scott?' My voice was flat.

'He says it wasn't him. It certainly doesn't sound like anything he'd do,' Crowley said. 'Scott can be a joker, but this doesn't seem very funny. I was out this afternoon, probably your dad had friends over in the day and one of them went sniffing around.'

I looked from Crowley to Scott, letting my disbelief and outrage do whatever they liked with my face. Crowley's expression was hard and very still in response. Scott was pale, his eyes trained on his father.

'This is stupid,' I muttered under my breath. I looked at Scott. 'Don't go in my room again.'

There was nothing else I could say. I stomped past Crowley's fat stomach and outside, not bothering to close the door behind me.

Propped up in bed in my pyjamas, I studied the painting by the light of my bedside lamp. I was still sure it was Scott's doing, but it unsettled me that I didn't know why he had left it in my room. That aside, it was hard to keep my eyes off it. Something about the painted girl kept dragging my gaze to her.

I got out of bed and padded to the mirror hanging over the painting. I swept my plait over my shoulder, then, feeling slightly silly, turned my profile from one side to the other in the age-spotted mirror until I found a pose that looked something like the girl's.

She looked so calm. So sure of herself. Maybe that was why I couldn't stop looking at her. I'd made a friend since coming to Hulbourn, and I'd managed to avoid the weird things about me becoming general knowledge, but I still didn't feel the self-confidence the painted girl clearly had.

I was more determined than ever now to tick off the points on my Normality List. I refused to turn out like crazy Meg. All I wanted was to recover the real Liz, the Liz I'd been before the car accident, and get on with my life.

I climbed back into bed. I was meeting Zachary tomorrow, I reminded myself. If anyone knew how to stop seeing Glimpses, if anyone could give me answers about my past, it was him.

In my dreams, I'm the painted girl.

I open my eyes and sit up in bed. Excitement leaps in my chest. Anticipation. I'm not sure what for.

Familiar shadows toss and turn against the far wall of my bedroom and with a jolt I remember – Zachary! I jump from bed and run to the window.

Joy saturates me as he steps from the shadows at the base of the tree trunk. He smiles, his face lighting up the night.

There's a posy of wild flowers in his hand. His golden hair and green eyes and the blues and reds of the flower petals have taken all the colour from the world for themselves. He takes a rose from the bunch, throws it up to my window for me to catch and press to my chest.

A thorn snags my skin, and I flinch. Something warm and wet runs down my finger. But when I look down, there's no mere trickle of blood, my hands are slick with it.

Chapter Nineteen

After dinner on Saturday evening, I excused myself as soon as seemed reasonable, telling Dad I was going to read in bed then get an early night. He'd never have let me leave the house alone if he knew what I was really doing.

Up in my room, I shrugged an old blazer on over my navy tea dress and slipped my phone into my pocket. Then I crept back down the stairs, hoping Dad wouldn't hear the floorboards creaking over his TV show, slipped on my pumps, and darted outside into the waning light.

I couldn't believe this moment was here. I'd been nervous all day – worrying about lying to Dad; worrying that Scott or Crowley would see me; worrying that Zachary wouldn't be there, or that he would; worrying that I wouldn't get back before Dad found I was gone.

I crunched as fast as I could across the gravel by the out-buildings, head down, and darted into the woods that bordered the inn.

It was only 6.30, but there was less than an hour of daylight left, and it was already close to dark under the trees. The air was damp and cool and smelled of rotting leaves. I wound between the trunks, stumbling over roots and through clumps of ivy and mulch, trying not to panic. Tonight was about getting answers, about reclaiming my life – about facing my fears and laying them to rest.

But I couldn't deny that I was very alone, about to meet a boy who was practically a stranger to me. To talk about Glimpses and ghosts. My blood raced in my veins, and I had no way of slowing it.

I'd taken a good look at the woods from my bedroom window, and guessed that if I walked through them in a straight line it would take just a few minutes to reach the field on the other side. To my relief, a dull light broke through the tree canopy and dappled my blazer. Up ahead, the flat plain of a field was visible between the trunks. I was there.

I stopped at the final line of trees and looked around. I wrapped my arms around me, against the chill of the evening. 'Hello?' I called into the field.

No one answered. Disappointment drowned out my flicker of relief. Perhaps I'd got the wrong time, the wrong place. Or maybe the boy had decided not to come.

'Elizabeth.'

He was here! I turned in the direction of Zachary's voice. For a moment, I didn't see him; then, as if he was an optical illusion, he materialized before me. His clothes, his red-gold hair, blended so well with the hues of the trees that he appeared almost more woodland animal than boy. Then he lifted a black-gloved hand in greeting, and beamed his huge smile, and some of the tension released from my muscles.

'You came,' he said, as he walked closer. 'I wasn't certain if you would. I was concerned I might have frightened you to excess the other night.'

'It wasn't the most relaxing night of my life,' I said. 'You left me with a lot of questions.'

Zachary stopped under one of the trees next to me. He was just as tall as I'd remembered – I had to crick my neck back to look at his face – and built solid as the tree trunk. I could see the muscles in his arms as he leaned back against the bark, supporting his weight.

I did my best to look calm. If he wanted to hurt me, he'd had plenty of chances already.

'Good.' He smiled. 'We both have questions for each other then. I'll abide by tradition and let the lady go first.' He pushed his weight off the tree trunk and held a gloved hand towards the field. 'Shall we walk?'

I stepped out of the shadow of the trees after him and into the field. In the dimming light, Zachary's skin was as luminous as it had been in moonlight, his eyes as vibrantly moss green.

I hesitated, and glanced behind me into the dark woods. 'Actually, I'd rather stay near the inn. I don't want to be long.'

He turned his whole body to face me. 'I realize I'm asking a lot of your trust. But you have my word – you can trust me.' His eyes darted over my shoulder, towards the woods. His voice turned grim. 'We were disturbed last time we spoke, and we have a strong chance of being disturbed again if we remain near the inn. If we are to speak properly, we should move further away.'

I remembered the tap-tap-tap of the Glimpse-feet outside my door, and everything inside me tightened. But I still hesitated. I wanted answers, but being here at all – with a stranger who looked, I now realized, strong enough to lift me under one arm and run off with me if he wanted to – was already so risky.

'Answer one question first,' I said, 'so I know you're for real.'

He hesitated, then dipped his head. 'Ask away.'

'You said you saw me when I was little.' I bridged the space between us, my hand at my locket. I opened it and held it towards him. 'Did you know her?'

My whole body burned as he leaned down to look at the tiny picture between my fingers.

He drew back and looked at me. 'The older lady? Your mother?'

I nodded. He knew!

'I have seen her before. But a long time ago, just like I saw you.'

'So you haven't . . . seen her spirit?'

'No.'

I nodded again. I closed my locket with a click. 'If I come with you, will you tell me what you remember of her?'

'I will.'

I felt for the reassuring shape of my phone in my pocket. 'Come on then. I want to be home before it's properly dark.'

Zachary set off down the side of the field, keeping in the shadow of the trees. I had no idea where we were going; presumably – hopefully – just away from the inn so we wouldn't be overheard by anyone, or any . . . thing.

I walked by his side, my hands in my pockets. Even though it was chilly, my palms were sweating.

'I have so many questions,' I said. 'I don't know where to start.'

'Begin with the basics.'

'How long have you seen Glim—ghosts?'

'For almost as long as I can recall.'

'Have you always seen them?'

'No.'

'What made you start?'

He paused, considering. 'An encounter with death.'

That made sense. The Glimpses had only started for me after the car crash that almost claimed my life. 'Same for me,' I said. 'But if you're not Scott's friend, how did you know to find me at the inn? That's the part I don't get.' I looked down at the furrowed soil, watching my feet move back, forth, as I waited for his answer.

'I've been visiting the inn for a long time,' he said, as if choosing his words carefully. 'I witnessed you seeing a spirit.'

I frowned. 'But the other night was the first time there was a ghost around at the same time as you.'

I looked sideways at him. He looked back at me. His face was set, but his eyes scrutinized me like I was the part of this that didn't make sense.

'It astounds me that you don't know,' he said.

'Know what?'

He gestured ahead. We'd almost reached the end of the field. A blackberry hedge blocked our way. 'Follow me to the road, and I'll show you.'

Before I could ask what he meant, he darted forward and disappeared through a gap in the hedge with the ease of a person half his size.

I looked back the way we'd come. The inn's roof poked through the trees in the gathering dusk, and it looked a long way away. An owl hooted, making me jump and reminding me how close we were to nightfall.

'I don't want to go any further,' I called.

'Trust me.' Zachary's voice floated through the hedge. 'I

promise you. One minute longer and you'll be in full possession of the truth.'

I bent to look at him through the brambles. He gazed steadily back at me.

I sighed. Too late to turn back now. I shoved myself into the hedge. Thorns ripped at my tights and tangled in my hair, tugging some of the curls loose from my plait.

On the other side of the hedge was the road Zachary had promised. It crumbled at the edges into an overgrown verge. The white lines painted down the middle were faded out to barely there, and a little further along the way this road met another, forming a crossroads.

Zachary walked to the crossroads. He stopped on the grass verge there, his arms poised at his side like a boxer's, his back to me.

I followed him, uncertain. When I got close, he turned around, and my whole stomach tightened. His jaw was clenched, making his face appear angular; the effect was to highlight his scar. His chest rose and fell under his brown sweater, like he was full of adrenaline.

'I'll tell you the truth now,' he said. 'You should prepare yourself. I don't want you to be alarmed.'

I had no idea what he could tell me that could be so much worse than 'I know you see ghosts', but there was something, and I was afraid to hear it. I hugged myself tight. His gaze on me was intense, hopeful and fearful at the same time.

'Okay.' I sounded stronger than I felt. 'Tell me.'

'Elizabeth, there is a reason I knew you could see spirits from the first time I saw you.'

I raised my eyebrows.

'It was because you could see me.'

My brain ground to a halt, then started up again twice as fast. 'What?' I snapped.

'The inn has been my second home for centuries. That's the reason I'd seen you before, that's how I saw your mother, and that's why neither of you saw me. My physical body was buried here.' He gestured at the grass beneath his feet. 'I'm spirit.' He said it without flinching.

Tears pricked at my eyes. I hardened my jaw, not letting them out. He'd lied to me, made me look such a fool.

'I should have known I couldn't trust you.' My voice trembled. 'Scott put you up to this, didn't he?'

'No. I speak the truth.'

'Yeah, right. I'm not an idiot!' I looked at the hedge. I should just run. I couldn't believe I'd let this happen. I'd known it was dodgy, him just turning up at the inn. I'd seen Scott watching us. I was beyond stupid to have thought he could help me.

The pain and humiliation and disappointment were so strong, they burned in me like acid. I had to get out of here before I corroded. I refused to let him see me cry.

'I'm going,' I said, turning from him. 'I hope you've had fun.'

'Wait,' he said. 'Please.'

His voice was so defeated, I couldn't help but look back. His face had softened. He looked infinitely sad. I scowled in response.

'I've told you nothing but the truth, Elizabeth, and I'll prove it to you. Don't walk away.'

I should have kept going, but I didn't. I marched back towards him, folding my arms. 'You want to prove you're a ghost? I'd like to see you try.'

He pulled off his glove and held his hand out to me. 'Touch me.'

I looked at his hand and rolled my eyes, as much at myself as at him. For a moment, he'd almost taken me in again. I'd actually been interested to see what he'd do. But this was blatantly just another trick.

'I'm not going to touch you,' I snapped. 'Like I said, I'm not an idiot.'

He let his hand fall. His disappointment was so convincing, he must have been the star of his school drama class.

I stormed back to the road, ready to race back to the inn – I couldn't stand even looking at him any more – but was stopped when car headlights cut through the dusk, heading towards us too fast for me to cross the road to the hedge.

I stepped further back onto the verge with a groan of frustration.

Zachary did the opposite. He stepped into the road.

'It seems I'll have to prove myself another way,' he muttered, as he passed.

'What the hell are you doing?'

He stood right in the middle of the road, and looked back at me. 'Making you believe me.' He spread his arms, and faced the oncoming car.

'Oh, no.' Panic flooded my system. I looked frantically from Zachary to the headlights and back again. 'Don't be stupid. Get out of the road. Now!'

Zachary just shrugged. The headlights raced towards him, lighting him up like a beacon, bleaching his face. It was happening too fast, I was powerless.

'Move!' I shrieked. 'Move! MOVE!'

But he didn't move. And the car didn't stop.

I screamed as it ploughed into him.

Chapter Twenty

The car squealed to a halt, its front bumper grinding into the hedge. I ran forwards. Zachary!

I stopped, gaped, trying to piece together the impossible scene before me. The top half of Zachary's body seemed to perch awkwardly on the bonnet of the car, like a torso sculpture set on a plinth. Arms spread, jaw clenched. Looking right at me. Then he moved – or it moved – and from the side of the car, Zachary emerged, walking towards me, entire and solid and alive-looking as before.

I gasped, inhaling burnt-tyre fumes. I was going to be sick. Right there and then, I was going to vomit. I clapped a hand across my mouth and whimpered into it.

The car door burst open. A man with a shaved head and tattooed arms leapt out. He looked at me, then back at his car. 'What the hell just happened?'

'You . . . you ran over someone,' I whispered into my fingers.

'What?'

I dropped my hand. Panic bubbled in my lungs. 'You ran over a boy!'

The man's face twisted, draining of colour. Then he turned and dived towards the front of his car. He sprawled on the concrete. 'Where?' he yelled. 'Shit, I don't see him! It's too dark.'

Zachary looked at me from the side of the road, his expression solemn and resigned and more than a little sympathetic.

'No,' I said. 'He's . . . he's not under there.'

The man levered himself up from the concrete. His face wasn't white any more. Even in the dim light, I could see it was blotched over with red. His expression was shifting rapidly from panic to something I liked even less.

'Then what the hell do you mean I ran over a boy?'

'He's . . . he's there.' I pointed at Zachary, my whole arm shaking.

The man stared at me. 'Are you crazy?'

'No!' I staggered into the road and held a trembling finger an inch from Zachary's chest. I could see his ribcage rising and falling, muscle and bone moving. 'Here! He's here! I don't know . . .'

There was a long silence. The man stared at me, not blinking.

Finally, the man's face loosened and he let out a long breath. 'Shit,' he muttered. 'Shit.' Still muttering under his breath, he turned back to his car and examined the paintwork on the bonnet. 'Any damage, you're paying.'

I stared after him, my finger still an inch from Zachary's jumper. I couldn't look at Zachary. I let my arm hang.

This couldn't be happening.

'Elizabeth.'

I gave my head the tiniest of shakes. No. No, no, no.

'Elizabeth, look at me.'

I had no choice. Very slowly, I turned, my lungs growing tighter with each degree as though they were in a vice. I met his gaze, and gave my head another tiny shake. I didn't want him to say anything.

'He cannot see me.'

No, please don't say any more.

'Hey, crazy girl!' the man called. 'You escape from some mental ward or something?'

I looked back at the man. I shook my head.

'Then get out of the road. If you're still here when I drive back this way, I'm calling the police, got it?'

The car reversed out of the hedge and skidded away. Zachary and I were left alone.

'Come on. Let's move out of the road.' He gestured at the grass verge, and, not knowing what else to do, I stumbled to where he pointed. He followed me, keeping his distance.

I collapsed to the ground and dropped my head into my hands. The cold seeped through me. My lungs rasped. There was no way that what I had just seen could have happened, for real.

But I had seen it. Maybe I was crazy after all. Maybe I still had brain damage from the crash.

Zachary crouched to the ground near me, still a respectable distance away. I stared at him between my fingers.

'I apologize for putting you through that,' he said. 'It was the only way I could think to prove myself to you.'

I gulped. 'Am I imagining you?'

He gave a wry smile. 'I'm real, Elizabeth. As real as you are. I'm simply not alive.'

'You're really . . . you really think you're . . . dead?'

He nodded.

My breath hiccuped into my hands, half hysteria, half sob. 'Oh my God,' I whispered.

My brain felt like a match that wouldn't ignite. My thoughts struck against each other – *He's dead, he's a ghost* – but failed to flare into anything that made sense.

'You seemed ready to accept that you saw spirits before,' he said, softly, 'why do you find it so hard to believe now?'

I shook my head, still holding my hands to my face. 'But you're nothing like . . . like them. You don't make my skin burn. You're so fully formed. You're too real.'

Funny, then, that having this conversation was so thoroughly unreal.

I bit my lip hard enough for it to hurt. Part of me wanted him to tell me this was all a trick. But there was a dense, frightened mass deep inside me that knew he wouldn't, knew it wasn't.

Zachary's face was unreadable in the almost-darkness. 'I don't know why you ever thought me alive,' he said. 'There have been others at the inn who were able to see me, but no one has ever mistaken me for a living man.'

He sat down on the grass next to me, stretching out his long legs, sending a gust of earth scent my way, which had made me think of trees before, but now made me think of freshly dug graves.

The sun had dipped below the horizon and the sky was almost entirely pencil-lead grey. It felt like the normal world had followed the sun over the horizon too, leaving me in this cold, dark universe that made no sense.

Bats swooped and darted in the twilight above us. The moon was full, and its rays shone down on Zachary, lighting up his tangled hair.

I let my hands fall from my face. I wrapped them instead around my locket, as if for protection. The metal felt cold but reassuring.

'How long have you been . . . like this?' I whispered.

'A long time. Longer than you've been alive.'

I nodded, and shivered. Once I started shivering, I couldn't stop. The night had turned so cold, so suddenly.

He was dead. I saw ghosts. But none of the other spirits I had ever seen were anything like him.

Then I remembered Meg telling me she'd learned how to see spirits so they looked almost like living people. That was happening now, with Zachary.

I sat up straighter, just as scared, but more focused.

'I've considered our connection many times since I realized you thought I was alive,' Zachary said, as if joining in with the conversation in my head. 'Elizabeth, I believe we were intended to find each other.' He looked at me. 'It's many years since I believed in God or fate, yet our meeting cannot be an accident. You're clearly a powerful spirit-seer. You can help me. And I can help you.'

I shook my head, clasped my locket tighter. 'I can't help you.'

'Yes, you can,' he said gently. 'I'm searching for someone. A fellow spirit. There's nothing in this world more important to me than finding her. If you help me, I'll owe you an eternal gratitude.'

He sat very still, waiting for my reaction, almost as tense as the moment before he'd told me he was dead. His shadowed eyes glittered like cut glass in the darkness.

'You want me to look for a ghost for you?' My voice was a squeak.

'I do.'

My throat constricted. The whole point of this meeting had been to find out how to get rid of the Glimpses, not to sign up for going out and finding more! I hugged my knees to my chest. I knew I should run. I should jump to my feet right now, and run like the wind. Instead I stayed stock still, and began to consider what it would mean to offer to help him.

I looked at him. I could make an excuse for why I couldn't help him. But I had been stripped bare by everything I had seen, heard, felt out here tonight. It was too late for lies.

'Here's the problem,' I said, my voice almost a whisper. 'I might be able to see you, but I don't want to. I don't want to see anyone, anything, like you.'

He nodded. I could practically see the hope drain out of him, the way the last of the light had drained from the sky.

'I understand,' he said. 'I realize the weight of what I'm asking you. I also know I cannot do much to help you in return. Yet I would do anything, within my power, to repay you.'

But you can't help me not see you.

A long moment passed.

'Are you frightened of me?'

'No.' I said it automatically, but then I considered it, and was surprised to find I'd spoken the truth. 'I'm not scared of you. You seem a good person. I'd help you for sure if you were . . . like me. What I'm scared of is being able to see you at all. I'm scared of what it means about me.'

'It simply means your abilities are powerful,' he said. 'If you understood them better, perhaps your fears would lessen. And that is something I can help with.'

I chewed my lip. 'How?'

He hunched his shoulders around his tall frame. 'If you help me, I would help you in every way I can. I cannot tell you how to stop seeing me, but I can tell you all I know about how the spirit world works. About who can see me, and who cannot. I can help you understand yourself.'

An ember of hope flickered to life in my chest. 'And you could tell me everything you know about my mum,' I said, my voice stronger. 'I don't remember her, and I want to.'

The shadows shifted as he smiled. 'I could. And I would.'

Maybe I was stupid, but the low hum of excitement had overtaken my jittering nerves. Maybe Zachary was right, and this was meant to be. Other than Meg, I was the only one who could help him. He was the only one who could help me.

For the first time, my Glimpse-seeing abilities would be useful. And maybe if I helped him, if I understood my Glimpses better, I could find a way to make them stop. Or, at least, take away some of their power of frightening me.

I considered a moment more, but I already knew what I was going to say. I'd spent seven years trying to escape my Glimpses, and it hadn't got me anywhere. This was the only way.

'Okay.' I shrugged. 'Let's do it.'

Zachary beamed, and he was bright as the moon. Despite myself, I smiled too, though my smile felt weak as cake mix.

Then he took off his glove, and stretched a tentative hand across the space between us. 'Shake on it?' he asked.

I looked at his hand, and my nerves clawed their way back out from under my excitement. It was one thing agreeing to look for ghosts, quite another to touch one. But somehow, I steeled myself. I'd survived the last hour, and felt far stronger than I would ever have expected to. If I could handle everything else, I could handle this. Literally!

As I reached for his hand, I could feel my heartbeat in my fingertips. I braced myself for the sensation I'd felt on the rare occasions Glimpses had touched me – a thickening in the air, something physical but soft as moth's wings or spider's feet.

I inhaled sharply as my fingers touched his. It was like touching something in a dream – real, but at the same time not. Otherworld. His hand enclosed mine, warm, his skin rough, more solid than a normal Glimpse but still not solid enough. Touching. Not touching.

We pulled our hands away at the same time. Zachary touched his palm with his other hand, as though reliving the feel of me. He looked as dazed as I felt.

'Have you touched someone like that before?' I asked, my voice barely more than a breath.

He shook his head. 'Not so strongly.'

'Me neither.'

The bats dived in the grey-black sky above us. Night frost bit hard, but I could still feel the rough warmth of his hand.

I hugged my knees again, and made a concerted effort to pull my mind back to reality before it floated off too far, too fast.

'So tell me who you want me to look for,' I asked.

Zachary pulled his glove back on before answering. 'Her name,' he said, 'is Bess.'

Chapter Twenty-One

I looked at him sharply. 'Bess?'

He nodded.

'But you don't mean . . . Bess, as in the landlord's daughter?' I prompted.

Zachary's face blanched, turning him even paler – something I hadn't thought possible. 'You know her?'

I shifted into a crouch, in an effort to stay still. 'Bess, as in the landlord's daughter, plaiting a dark red love-knot into her long black hair?' I was incredulous.

'Good God, Elizabeth, tell me, have you seen her?'

'No!'

He sank back onto the grass as if all his muscles had given way.

My mind whirred. Could 'The Highwayman' poem be real?

'Zachary, was Bess your girlfriend?'

He gave me a pained look and nodded.

'How did you die?'

'I was shot.'

'You were a highwayman?'

'Yes!' His voice rose. 'Elizabeth, what do you know?'

I leapt to my feet, fuelled by adrenaline. My mouth half grimace, half grin. 'Oh my God.' I paced a small circle, my dress damp and cold through my tights.

I wished Susie was here. I wished anyone was here. I couldn't handle this on my own, but I couldn't tell anyone, either. It was just me and Zachary.

'Elizabeth!' Zachary's voice was tortured. He twisted and turned around me, trying to see my face.

I forced myself to stop still and face him. 'You're the highwayman, aren't you? From the poem.'

'Please. I am begging you. Tell me what you know.' His voice was shaky, but firm. 'Have you seen her?'

The pain in his voice focused me. I pursed my lips and shook my head. 'No. I don't think so. I'm sorry.'

He pressed his hands to his face, and breathed out through his fingers, part exhale, part groan.

I ran my locket back and forth repeatedly on its chain, watching him. When he dropped his hands, his face in the moonlight was both pale and dark, both ghost-like and corporeal: it was like I was seeing him – really seeing him – for the first time. I tried to fit his image with the highwayman of the poem I'd read in school.

'When did you die, Zachary?' Zip, zip, zip, went my locket on its chain.

'Seventeen hundred and eighty-nine.'

1789. The year *Haunted Hulbourn* claimed the ghost-highwayman had first been seen at my inn. I nodded. 'Yet you seem so young,' I said.

He scrubbed a hand through his hair and sighed, apparently still recovering from the shock I'd inflicted. 'I'm nineteen, or over two hundred years, depending on how you count it. I exist in the same world as you, Elizabeth. I'm not trapped in a time bubble. Now explain to me how you know so much about Bess.'

'There is a poem about you and her,' I said. 'About Bess and her highwayman. It was written over a hundred years ago, right here at the inn. The inn's famous for it. When you told me you're looking for a girl called Bess . . . I am sorry, I didn't mean to get your hopes up. I just can't believe . . . It's just a lot to take in.'

'I have heard a poem talked about at the inn,' he said. 'So many people saw Bess and me over the years, and I understood a text had been written about us. But I wasn't aware that it's well known.'

'You're famous.'

He raised an eyebrow, but I couldn't tell in the darkness whether it was with excitement or disbelief.

I thought of the poem, of the tragic love of Bess and the highwayman that lasted beyond the grave. The whole point of the poem was that the lovers were together forever.

It hit me for the first time what he was saying.

'But why isn't Bess with you?'

He exhaled and rolled his eyes up to the stars. 'I wish I knew. She disappeared years ago. I've been searching for her since. Every night, I visit the inn, looking for her. I no longer expect her to be there, yet I still hope. That's how I saw you. Your room used to be hers. The night I first saw you there—' he smiled, but not happily '—for a moment, I thought you were her.' He looked at me again, his face sad and solemn and shadowed as stone.

The poem's story was true.

Bess was gone.

And the last of my hysteria died.

'This is terrible,' I said. 'Of course I'll help you search for her. Just tell me where to look.'

'Thank you.' His voice was rich with gratitude. 'I mean that, Elizabeth, from the depths of my soul.'

Some warm feeling blossomed inside me. I gave him a small smile. 'So what's her full name?'

He exhaled, his shoulders relaxing. 'Bess Richards.'

'I have glimpsed one girl at the inn,' I said. 'She's petite, and has brown hair in ringlets. But she seems too . . . angry to be Bess.'

Zachary grimaced. 'Ann Barton. Keep your distance from her.'

Car headlights appeared down the road, jolting my thoughts away from snarling Glimpse-faces and tapping feet in the night.

'Oh, shit,' I whispered, suddenly remembering Dad. How long had I been gone? I pulled my phone from my pocket to check the time, but when I pressed the button, the screen stayed blank. 'Oh, this is so bad.'

'What's the matter?'

'My phone's dead, er, I mean, the battery . . . I have to go back to the inn, right now. But you have to come with me. I've got so much to ask you.'

The car's headlights grew brighter, its engine whirring closer. I squinted and stepped back from the verge, waiting for it to pass so I could dash across the road and back through the hedge.

But instead of passing, the car began to slow. It pulled up to the verge next to me. I tensed. I was in the countryside, in darkest night, with a broken phone and an invisible companion. This was bad.

The driver's door opened. I had the too-late urge to run and I scrambled for footing, but a voice I recognized shouted my name. I froze, and turned to see Crowley step out of the car, stretch his bulky arms, crick his neck and saunter over to me.

'Do you have any idea,' he said, 'how long your father has had me driving around looking for you?'

Dad. I was in serious trouble.

Zachary sidestepped as Crowley nearly walked into him.

'I was just on my way back. My phone broke, I was going to ring him.'

'Save your explanations for your dad.' In the darkness, Crowley's eyes were shadowed pits. He jerked his thumb at the car. 'Get in.'

I cast a glance at Zachary. I hoped he could see how sorry I was.

Crowley spun round to see what I was looking at and I held my breath as he looked directly at Zachary. But he turned back, frowned at me, and reached for the driver's door.

As we pulled away, I imagined Zachary behind us, still standing in the road, watching as we disappeared into the distance.

Chapter Twenty-Two

I'd been gone for almost two hours. It was past eight.

I knew I was going to be in trouble – a lot of trouble – when I got home, but I felt numb to the panic. The evening had left me feeling strangely detached from reality.

I chewed my lip and glanced at Crowley. His stomach pressed grotesquely against the bottom of the steering wheel. His face was rigid with annoyance that was a mere preview of the anger I knew was coming my way.

Too soon, the car's headlights cut across the tree in the inn's driveway, illuminating the open front door.

Crowley pulled up next to the outbuildings. 'You're in for it now, sweetheart,' he muttered.

Dad met me halfway across the gravel. 'Where the hell have you been?' His words shot like bullets, jolting me suddenly alert.

Behind me, I heard Scott ask Crowley: 'Where was she?'

I hung my head and walked towards the inn. 'I'm sorry, Dad. Let's talk inside.'

He stormed alongside me. The moment the front door shut, he let rip. 'Where were you? Tell me!'

I wanted to sink into the floor. 'I'm sorry. I really am. I just went for a walk—'

'A two-hour walk? In the dark? Without telling me?'

I walked towards the kitchen. I couldn't handle this now.

Dad raced after me. 'I looked for you everywhere. We searched the whole inn. I had Scott looking for you in the woods, Crowley combing the streets. You left no note. You didn't even answer your phone. I was worried sick!'

I sat down at the kitchen table and pulled my phone from my pocket. 'I did take my phone, but it must have broken. I only just realized when Crowley found me. I'm sorry.'

Dad paced around the table. He puffed like a volcano about to erupt. 'You went for a walk.' He stopped pacing and scrutinized me. 'Look at you. You're freezing. You're almost blue.'

It was true. But compared to everything else that had been happening, it was so insignificant. I'd barely noticed how cold I was till now.

Dad pulled out a chair, scraping its legs violently on the tiles, and sat down at the table opposite me. His eyes were red, and his hair stood up in a hundred different directions.

Guilt twisted inside me. I leaned across the table towards him. 'Dad, I am so sorry,' I said, as solemnly as I could. 'I really am. I should have told you I was going, but I didn't think I'd take so long, and I did take my phone. I lost track of time. It won't happen again.'

'It had better not.' Dad swept a hand across his mouth. He rolled his eyes to the ceiling. 'God, Liz,' he muttered. 'You've got to understand that you are all I've got left. You can't scare me like that. If I lost you, it would destroy me.'

'I know,' I whispered. 'But I'm almost eighteen. I'm not some little kid any more. You're not going to just lose me.'

'I didn't think I was going to lose your mum, either. But I did. We did. And living here—' his gaze took in the kitchen '—in her old house, just metres down the road from where . . . it's impossible to forget.'

I stared at my hands and sighed.

'It's not been easy for me, you know. Moving here. But I've done it – for you. Because you wanted this, because you wanted to have your new start.'

'I know.' I was trying to be sympathetic, but I just felt impatient. I didn't want to listen to it any more, not with everything else I was trying to deal with.

'Do you, Liz?'

'Yes.' My voice was flinty. There was a new tightness in my throat. 'But things haven't been easy for me either, Dad. You have no idea some of the things I go through, and I have no one to talk about them with, because I don't want to upset you.'

He frowned. 'What's that meant to mean?'

'You!' I gestured at him. 'You're so caught up in feeling guilty and being depressed. Sometimes I think you only want me to get better so you can feel better. You're my dad, you're meant to set an example. I came much worse out of that car accident than you, but I have tried so much harder. There are all these old photos of you playing piano, of being happy, but you might as well be a different person now. All you do is watch TV. You've never even tried to get your career back.' I glared at him, my eyes wet with sudden tears.

Dad looked taken aback. 'You've never said any of this before.'

I rolled my eyes at the floor. 'I have, Dad,' I said. 'Maybe not so directly as that, but if you'd been paying attention – I have.'

He said nothing.

'I am sorry, though, for tonight. I really am. I shouldn't have done it. I was inconsiderate and dumb and I am sorry for worrying you.'

Dad nodded. He didn't look at me. Then he exhaled, long and low. 'I hear what you're saying, Liz.' His eyes glittered wetly. 'And maybe you have a point. I will try harder. For you. I'll start job hunting properly on Monday.'

I nodded. I didn't know what to say. I'd half expected him to yell back at me.

'I don't want you to feel like you can't talk to me. If there's anything you want to tell me about, I hope you'll feel you can.'

I thought of Zachary, of everything I'd learnt tonight. I pressed my lips together, and nodded.

'And if you feel like going for a "walk" again . . .' He made quotation marks in the air around the word 'walk'.

'I'll tell you,' I said. 'I promise.'

'Good.'

We looked at each other for a long, solemn moment. Then Dad sighed and stood up. 'I think we both need a cup of tea.'

I stood up too. I caught him round the middle as he passed, and gave him a sideways hug – for reacting so well to my outburst when he had every right to still be mad with me; for just existing when Zachary was so alone.

'Love you, Dad.'

After a stunned moment, Dad said, 'Love you too.' Then he hugged me back, and went to put on the kettle.

Chapter Twenty-Three

I gazed blearily at the computer screen as Susie clicked on yet another illustrated image of a ghostly Bess.

'None of these are real,' I said. 'Just imagined, after the poem. Go back to the search screen?'

Miss Webb had booked us research time in the computer suite today. I was exhausted, overwhelmed, but determined to put our session to good use. I had so much I wanted to find out.

'What did you say her name was again?' Susie asked.

I told her. Susie carefully Googled 'Bess Richards', along with 'The Highwayman Inn' and '1789'. She squinted at the search results. 'Well, it looks like she definitely lived at your inn. Good job on tracking down her name. It seems pretty clear she'd be the same Bess as in the poem.'

I blushed. I had told Susie I'd found another book on the inn in Granddad's library. It was the only excuse I could think up to explain why I suddenly knew the names of three of its former residents. Susie had been disappointed when I told her I'd 'forgotten' to bring in the actual book.

'What were the other names you got?' she asked.

I consulted my notepad. 'Ann Barton and Zachary Wilson.' Susie typed slowly.

It took almost all of the lesson and a lot of clicking to dig up any information, and even then it wasn't much. Ann Barton was named in a long list of people associated with Hulbourn, and there was a note that her grave was in the local churchyard.

There was nothing on Zachary.

'Save your work and log off,' Miss Webb called, as the end-of-lesson bell rang.

I sighed, and shoved my notepad into my satchel. I'd hoped to find out more, especially about Bess. As far as Zachary's girlfriend was concerned, the internet was a dead end.

But the mention of Ann's grave had given me an idea. If Zachary was buried at the crossroads and he didn't stray far from his grave, maybe Bess's ghost did the same.

'Fancy going to the graveyard after school?' I asked Susie. 'We could get a photo of Ann Barton's grave for the project, and Bess's too if we can find it.'

She gave me an amused, sideways glance. 'You're getting well into this ghost thing. Let's do it.'

The hours until the end of school were just as nerve-wracking as the hours before we'd gone to Meg's house.

The graveyard – seriously? I had one single, solitary memory of having been to a graveyard before – for the funeral of Dad's aunt when I was eleven. I had refused to get out of the car, because a pair of Glimpse-hands had been knocking on the windscreen. Since then, I'd done my level best to avoid even walking past a graveyard. If by mistake or misfortune I did, my skin would creep and crawl for sickening hours afterwards.

Looking back, it was obvious my Glimpses had always been

ghosts. But I'd convinced myself it was the closeness to death that set them off; that it was some abstract reminder of the car crash that killed Mum, a trigger in some messed-up part of my brain. Now I knew better.

Dad had given me his phone since mine was broken, so I called the inn on my walk to the graveyard to let him know I'd be late.

Susie and I turned a corner, and the village church loomed up ahead, dark grey stone against a grey sky.

'Are you all right?' Susie asked, her pencilled eyebrows pulled together in concern. 'You seem kind of agitated.'

'Do I?' I pushed a curl behind my ear. 'It's nothing, I'm just . . .' I sought for a good answer. I couldn't think of anything. 'I'm fine.'

Susie nodded, and kept silent as we walked through the cemetery's huge iron gates.

Immediately, the tingling spread across my skin like static, growing stronger with each step we took towards the graves. Headstones stretched ahead of us, regular as shark's teeth. The sky was dull and moody, doing nothing to alleviate my fear.

'I think the oldest ones are in that corner.' Susie pointed to the back of the graveyard, where the headstones disappeared into a line of trees.

I nodded. I didn't trust myself to speak. My skin felt hot and cold, rippling like something alive. I knew exactly why.

Even with my eyes narrowed, I could see at least three different Glimpses. To my right, a pair of legs strolled between the headstones. To my left, a woman's disembodied face sang a breathy, high-pitched song. Ahead of us, a pair of hands tried, and failed, to rearrange a bouquet of grave flowers.

It took all my effort to keep calm. It was like being covered in ants and being powerless to swipe them away; it was a nightmare.

I had to concede that Project Normal was not going at all well. Twenty-four hours ago, I'd have been as likely to ask Scott on a date as to come to a graveyard voluntarily. But I kept Zachary's moonlit face in my mind, his heartbreak and his hope, his longing for peace – mine too – and forced myself to keep moving forwards.

The ghosts can't hurt you, I told myself. It didn't help.

We'd almost reached the trees that marked the end of the graveyard. The graves were oldest here, their mossy stones crumbling into the grass.

'Ann Barton and Bess Richards, right?' Susie asked. I nodded. She set off between the rows of headstones, obviously expecting me to follow.

I eyed the limbless torso hovering on the path ahead of her. 'I . . . think I'll go this way,' I said, pointing in the other direction.

'Okay.' She shrugged.

I scuttled off between the headstones, cursing under my breath. I could tell Susie thought I was acting weird. She didn't know the half of it: even I was impressed with my own heroic restraint in the face of abject horror.

I clasped my locket in my fist, my amulet, breathed in slow and scanned the crumbling headstones as fast as possible, working methodically so I didn't miss one. No Ann. No Bess. I already knew there wouldn't be a Zachary.

'Over here!' Susie called, excitement in her voice.

I weaved between the graves towards her. Susie stood in front of a headstone set flat in the grass. 'Look.'

I read the words written on the grey, mossy stone.

Here was interr'd the Body of Ann Barton of Hulbourn, who departed this Life August 13th 1789 in the 18 Year of her Age.

'It's her,' I said.

'Do you think she really haunts your inn?' Susie pulled her phone and a notepad from her bag. 'So weird. You're standing over her bones, and yet she could be spying on you in the shower every morning and you wouldn't know.'

I shuddered.

I pictured Ann's snarling face, in my bedroom and at Meg's house. Keep your distance from her, Zachary had warned. As if I needed telling.

'Any sign of Bess's grave?'

Susie shook her head. 'I haven't looked over there yet—' she gestured further down the rows '—if you want to.'

I nodded, and left her taking photos of Ann's headstone.

It only took a few minutes to confirm that as far as Bess was concerned, I was putting myself through this for nothing. She wasn't here.

I wandered back the way we came. I glanced over at Susie. She was still at Ann's grave, but had switched from taking photos with her phone to talking on it, presumably to Matt. Her black skirt with its rag-like strips floated around the headstones; if anyone looked like they should be seeing ghosts here, it was her. But she was completely oblivious to the stiff-backed torso that floated just inches away from her gesticulating hands.

I clutched my locket and took a deep breath. A new determination gripped me. I hadn't told Susie, but there was one more grave I wanted to find, since I was here.

I walked up through the rows, scanning the death dates. Ten years ago, nine years ago, eight years ago . . . seven.

I had only seen her headstone once, in a photo Dad kept separate from all the others.

I caught sight of it between the rows. Pure white marble, slightly sparkling, the heart carved at the top as clean as if crafted only yesterday.

Mum's grave.

I walked towards it. I glanced at Susie to make sure she was still on the phone, then lowered myself to my knees in front of the stone.

'Juliette Rathamore', I read, 'died, aged 30, leaving a husband, Paul, and a daughter, Elizabeth. Forever in our hearts.'

I put my locket to my lips, and waited to feel something. I emptied my mind, and gazed at Mum's name; pictured the smiling woman in Dad's photos, imagined her buried far beneath me.

Feel something, I urged myself. Remember.

I bowed my head – that's what they do at gravesides on TV – and strained for a memory. I couldn't get any physically closer to Mum than I was now. If I was going to feel something, it should be here.

But all I felt was a familiar frustration, and the same detached melancholy I felt when I looked at any of these graves.

Frowning, I rearranged the fresh roses in the graveside urn. Dad had been here recently, maybe even today. That made me feel sad. The blank lower half of the headstone, clearly intended for him, that made my throat tighten.

But everything else about Mum's grave . . . nothing.

I became aware of something floaty and black in my peripheral vision a moment before Susie spoke.

'Is that your mother?'

I shot to my feet, the blood rushing to my face as if I'd been caught doing something bad. I nodded.

'I didn't know.' Her voice was quiet. 'You should have told me. I could tell you were weird about being here. I could have come on my own, if you'd said.'

'No.' I shook my head, managed a flash of a smile. 'It's okay.'

Susie looked at the headstone, her face solemn. 'God, you must have only been ten. You must really miss her.'

Tears sprang to my eyes. 'Actually, I didn't know her.' The words came out before I knew I was going to say them.

Susie looked confused. 'You didn't know your mum?'

Good one, Liz. But the fear I'd felt when faking my past in English last week didn't come. After everything that had happened in the last twenty-four hours, it seemed pointless to keep such secrets when I had so many others chewing away at my heart.

I felt I could trust Susie.

'We had a car accident in the village when I was ten,' I told her. 'My mum died, and I . . .' I waved a hand at my head. 'I lost some memories. I don't remember her.'

I waited for the secret, now unleashed, to do something. I had always feared ridicule, feared that by speaking the truth out loud I would invoke some disaster.

But nothing happened. I spoke, and the words just . . . floated away, light as mist.

Susie was silent for a long moment.

'Liz, I don't know what to say, but I think that is the saddest thing I've ever heard. And I'm sorry.'

And that was it. It was over. And it hadn't hurt at all.

'Thanks.' I smiled.

Susie mirrored my smile. Then she bent to the grass, picked a daisy, and pushed it in amongst the roses.

'Come on.' She tugged gently on my arm and turned towards the exit. 'There's this place in the village called the Cocoa Pod that does the best hot chocolate, and you deserve one with whipped cream and sprinkles.'

Chapter Twenty-Four

Scott was tinkering under his car bonnet by the outbuildings when I got back from the village. He stopped what he was doing to watch me approach, holding a spanner in his fist.

'Hey,' he called.

I kept walking, ignoring him. My stomach was warm with hot chocolate and a blissful hour spent chatting to Susie about 'normal' girl stuff like homework and TV. I didn't want Scott to bring me down. My policy on staying out of his way had become law since his weird antics with the painting on Friday.

'Hey,' he called again. He marched across the gravel, blocking my path. 'Didn't you hear me?'

'I heard you,' I said, 'but I have nothing to say. So let me through.'

He brandished his spanner at me. His T-shirt was flecked with oil and sweat. 'You owe me an hour's worth of petrol for last night's shenanigans.'

I pulled an exasperated face. 'Fine. Tell me how much. But you're not going to intimidate me, Scott, so just leave me alone.' I sidestepped, and shoved my way past him.

He caught my arm. 'You should be intimidated by me,' he said, his voice low.

I shook my arm free. 'What?'

'I didn't mean that.' Scott wiped the back of his hand across his face, leaving a smudge of grease on his cheek. 'But, God, Liz, you're making this really hard for me.'

'I haven't done anything to you.'

'Oh, yeah? Do you have any idea the bollocking I got on Friday night because of you?'

I raised my eyebrows. I was so sure that Crowley had taken Scott's side. 'Well, good,' I said.

He glared at me, his blue eyes hard and cold as ice cubes. 'You're so dumb sometimes. No wonder you had to be in all the special classes in your last school. You really are clueless, aren't you?'

My face hardened. 'Just leave me alone,' I said, marching off before my anger could turn to pain.

My alarm went off at 1.45 a.m. Within seconds, I was awake, my eyelids heavy with sleep, but my limbs fuelled by adrenaline. I switched on my bedside lamp, climbed out of bed then pulled on one of my warmest long dresses, twisted my hair into a plait and went to the window.

I barely had to wait for Zachary. The moment I stuck my head out into the cold air, he stepped from the shadows of the tree. Even through the darkness, I could see his smile. I waved hello, pointed at the tree and stepped back from my window.

The tree rustled and creaked outside as he climbed. My hands started to tremble in anticipation. Though I'd thought of little else but Zachary and what he'd told me the night before, it still felt incredible that he existed, that he was here again, this secret boy who nobody but me could see.

He landed inside my room with a soft thump and a rush of cool, tree-scented air.

'You were waiting for me?' I asked.

'Ever since the sun set.'

'You should have woken me up.'

'I was tempted.' His eyes smiled, then grew serious again. 'What happened last night, after the caretaker stole you away from me?'

I pulled a face. 'Nothing worth repeating. But I have something else to tell you . . .'

I trailed off. Zachary had gone as still as a standing stone. I followed his gaze to the painting of Bess on my dresser.

'That was one of the things I wanted to tell you,' I said.

He took a slow step forwards. Then a faster one. He made it to the painting in four strides. 'Where did you find this?' He stared at the painting, like he couldn't believe it was real. He lifted a hand to the canvas; his fingertips went straight through the layers of paint and dust. 'I haven't laid eyes on this for years.'

'It's Bess, isn't it? I found it in my granddad's closet.' It was easier than explaining the truth.

His cheeks were flushed with emotion, but with pain or elation I couldn't tell.

'She's beautiful,' I said, my voice soft. 'Is that what she really looks like? Is she who I'm looking for?'

'It's a close enough representation.' He considered, stared at the painting. 'Though Bess never approved of it. Her opinion was that it made her look vulnerable, comely but fragile. She was not fragile. She jumped out of that window as many times as I jumped up to her.'

166

'Really?' I was impressed.

'Admittedly, many of those occasions were after . . . 1789. I wouldn't recommend you try it.' His gaze drifted back to the painting.

I gave him a few minutes to just look at it, to be with Bess, even if it was only her image and his memories. But I had so much more to say. I twisted my dress sleeves around in my hands until I couldn't contain my words any longer.

'So, I went to the village graveyard today.'

That got Zachary's attention. He turned fully to me, his eyebrows shooting upwards. 'What for?'

'To look for Bess's grave. I figured since you stay near your . . . um, body . . . she might do too. I found Ann's grave—' Zachary flinched at her name '—but not Bess's. What's the deal with Ann, Zachary?' I glanced at the door, half expecting the tap-tap-tap of her footsteps on the other side. 'I've seen her a few times, and she seems . . . scary. Is she bad?'

His face darkened. 'Yes.'

'Why?'

'She believes she's in love with me.'

Surprise twisted my face. 'I thought you were going to say something awful.'

'She is awful. She plagued Bess for being with me, both before and after our deaths.'

I raised my eyebrows, more sympathetically this time. 'You've known her since you were alive?'

'Ann was a barmaid at the inn, alongside Bess. They died on the same night. The redcoats managed to kill a number of the inn staff while they were waiting for me.' Guilt and resentment flashed in his eyes.

'But is she dangerous?' I asked.

167

'Is she able to touch you?'

'I'm not sure. She hasn't tried. But no spirit has ever touched me as strongly as you.' A thrill of embarrassment went through me at the memory of Zachary's skin on mine, absurd though it was. He might be a ghost, but he was still handsome. I looked at the painting, rather than meeting his eye. 'Why do you think we could do that?'

He considered. 'Perhaps because you can see me so fully. It must be part of our connection.'

I nodded. That made sense. Meg had said she could touch spirits better as she got used to seeing them. And I saw no Glimpse as clearly as Zachary.

'So where should I look for Bess?' I asked. 'Unless you know where her body is, I don't know where else to check.'

He looked at me for a long moment, his gaze piercingly intense. 'Put on your overcoat and follow me.'

I hesitated for a microsecond, then got my jacket and pumps. I slipped Dad's phone into my pocket. 'We're not going back to the crossroads, are we?'

He pulled a humourless smile. 'No. We're staying nearby tonight.'

He walked to the door, and gestured for me to open it. I did; the light from my bedside lamp spilled into the corridor. I stepped into it on tiptoes, praying for the floorboards not to creak, and cast a glance towards Dad's door. If he caught me now, dressed to go outside, I'd be in big trouble.

Zachary followed me into the corridor, ducking to fit under the low door frame. I pulled the door closed, plunging us into darkness.

'Where are we going?' I whispered.

'Downstairs. Outside.'

I inched forwards, arms outstretched like a zombie, until I felt the wall. Trailing my hand along the wallpaper, I began to shuffle in the direction of the stairs.

Zachary's gloved hand brushed the back of mine, soft as a whisper, making me jump. 'Do you mind?' His words were barely audible. 'It'll be swifter. I'm used to the dark.'

I nodded, and held my breath as he wrapped his hand around mine. His touch was light, both solid and not, but it felt even firmer than I'd remembered from Saturday. His leather glove was warm and soft, and I could feel the press of his fingertips against my palm. He led me forwards in the darkness, with confident strides.

'Stairs,' he whispered.

We went downwards more slowly, Zachary walking a few steps ahead of me. When we reached the bottom, he guided my hand to the front door handle and let go of me. I opened the door onto the night, letting in a rush of cold air. The night smelled damp; it must have rained while I was asleep. The tree blacked out the sky above us, but there were stars visible between its branches, and it wasn't as dark as it had been indoors. When I turned, all I could see was Zachary's tall, dark outline.

'This way.' He strode across the front of the inn, away from the outbuildings.

I followed, my feet crunching on the gravel, so loud compared to him. I tugged my coat around me, but my ankles were already freezing where they poked out of my long dress. We headed down the side of the inn and across the lawn. A chill dampness soaked through my pumps and reached between my toes.

All I could see ahead of us was blackness. I trusted there

was a point to this venture, but what it was, I didn't know. I remembered Dad's phone, pulled it out of my pocket and pressed a button, illuminating a small patch of the path before us with a greenish light. A rabbit froze next to an overgrown rose bush, its eyes wide in the eerie glow before it darted away.

I knew from looking out of the window that the inn's back garden was huge. But Zachary didn't go far. He headed towards one of the near corners, and stopped beneath a gnarled tree.

'Here,' he whispered.

I shone the phone questioningly in his face. He squinted in the weak light and pointed beneath the tree.

I angled the phone down at the ground, my stomach fluttering sickly as though I'd swallowed a moth. At first all I saw was a tangle of bindweed and ivy. But then I spotted it – the top edge of a stone.

'Oh,' I breathed. I bent and tugged the worst of the weeds away. Rain coated my legs and the weeds tugged at the bottom of my dress, but I barely noticed.

Because there was Bess's grave.

Her headstone was small, smaller than the ones in the churchyard, and the stone was dark and crumbling round the edges. The top right corner had fallen away completely. Its face was barely legible, the carved letters eroded by the years and covered with moss and lichen, but I could read enough to know what I was looking at.

'Bess Richards,' I read, mentally filling in the letters that were obscured. 1771. 1789.

And that was all. No 'Forever in our hearts', not even a 'RIP'. The stone was hardly big enough to fit more on it than was already there.

Water dripped down my cheek. I wiped it away, expecting

it to be rain, but it was warm against my fingertips. I licked my lips and tasted salt. Tears.

The phone's light blinked out. I didn't turn it back on. I crouched in the weeds in the darkness, waiting for the lump in my throat to ease. Black emotions clawed through my body, welling up from some deep place I hadn't known existed, had no experience of.

She shouldn't be here, I wanted to tell Zachary. Nobody would ever know Bess's grave was here. This wasn't right. There was no one left alive to remember Ann, but at least people would read her name in the churchyard; maybe someone would wonder, now and then, who she was. But here, Bess – the real Bess, who was more than a girl in a poem – would be completely forgotten.

I stood and faced Zachary. I didn't turn the phone on again, but my eyes had adjusted to the darkness enough to be able to tell he looked solemn, his jaw more chiselled than a gravestone.

'What's she doing here?'

'She isn't here. Only her bones and her name on a stone. Bess died by her own hand; she wasn't eligible for a churchyard burial. It could have been worse. She could have been buried at the crossroads like me, and have received no headstone at all.'

'That's ridiculous.'

'Perhaps. But I'm glad of it. If she had been buried in the churchyard, we couldn't have been together.'

'Why?'

He pursed his thin lips together. 'I have to remain near my body. I can only be at the inn because of its proximity to the crossroads. If Bess had been interred in the churchyard, she might never have been able to come back here.'

I frowned at him. 'Are you sure?'

'Bess and I tried countless times to leave. I can only travel as far as the entrance to the inn's land. Bess could move further into the village, yet certainly not as far as the church.'

'What happens if you try?'

'There is a barrier, like a wall of glass. I can see beyond it, but I cannot pass through it. It was the same for Bess. That's why I can't comprehend how she departed. And it's why I haven't been able to leave to look for her myself.'

A new emotion choked my throat. 'You haven't been further than the inn in over two hundred years?'

'No.'

I wiped the wetness off my cheeks. I'd been so excited to think the romance of the poem was real, but the reality of it was worse than anything I could imagine. Even while Bess had been with him, they'd been trapped like prisoners, for hundreds of years. And now Zachary was trapped here alone.

No, not all alone.

I frowned. 'There must be a way for you to leave. Ann's grave is at the churchyard, but she can be here. And I've seen her somewhere else in the village too.'

'Elsewhere?' His voice was sharp.

'Yes, at an old lady's house. How is that possible, if spirits have to stay near their bodies?'

'I don't know.' He sounded baffled. 'Ann boasted that she had a headstone in the churchyard, but I assumed her body must have been buried at the inn. There is no other way she could be here. Are you quite certain it was her you saw?'

'Positive.' My mind whirred. 'Which means there must be a way for spirits to move around. Perhaps Bess knows something you don't – some secret, or a trick of some sort – and that's how she left.'

172

'She would have surely told me.'

I said nothing. An owl hooted above us, mournful and low. I shivered, and looked back down at the shadows that shrouded Bess's grave. I'll find you, I promised her. And when I did, I would clear away these weeds and place fresh roses here instead.

I pictured the roses on my mother's grave; guilt stabbed like a thorn. There must be something broken in my heart that I could feel this bad over a girl I had never met, yet feel nothing at my own mother's graveside.

I looked at the ground and clenched my teeth before I could start crying again. 'Let's go,' I said.

We walked back in darkness and silence, alone with our thoughts. Zachary must have sensed my change in mood, because without me asking, he guided me through the grounds with the barest touch on my arm.

We stopped at the inn's front door.

Zachary stood in front of me, close enough for me to smell his leafy, earthy scent. His outline was a huge black negative in the night. 'I apologize if I made you melancholy.' His voice was low. 'It wasn't my intention.'

I shook my head. 'It's nothing you did. It's nothing to do with you at all. I was thinking about something else.'

'Do you want to speak with me about it?'

For a moment, I was tempted. If anyone could understand how very alone I felt sometimes, it would be him. But how could he understand a girl who looked at her mother's grave and felt nothing? No one would be able to sympathize with that. And I was too ashamed to confess it to him. 'You don't want to hear my problems,' I said.

His voice was low. 'I wouldn't be so certain.'

I smiled, but with more pain than happiness. 'I should go inside. Will you be here tomorrow night?'

'I will. Goodnight, Elizabeth.'

'Goodnight.'

He turned, and the darkness swallowed him whole.

I stood for a long moment, my hand on the door, letting my heart rate return to normal. Then I went inside, guiding my way up the stairs and along the upstairs hallway by the green light of Dad's phone. The warm glow of my lamp spilled under my bedroom door, a beacon welcoming me back.

I opened my door, pulling off my coat as I did so. I didn't register the tingling until the door had closed behind me.

I gasped and moved back up against the wall.

Ann.

'Oh, Elizabeth,' she sing-songed. Her voice was sweet, her brown ringlets bobbed around her shoulders as she smiled, yet I was horror-stricken. She knew my name.

Ann tapped across the floor towards me. Delicate brown shoes stuck out beneath the trim of a brown dress. Small hands folded in front of her. But the rest of her body up to her shoulders was empty air.

I pressed harder into the wall. But I stood my ground. 'Stay away,' I said.

Ann drifted to my side. 'How amusing. Just what I was about to say to you.' Her mouth stretched, showing small, childlike teeth. Her gaze swept over me from head to foot, her pretty face twisting in distaste. 'I assume you're enjoying being alive. So stop talking to him, Elizabeth.'

Then she tossed her curls, and vanished out of my bedroom through the wall.

★

I wait on the lawn. Everything's quiet. The breeze ripples the grass, the rabbits chew. The day is bright with summer sun.

The screech of metal shatters the silence. I start to run. The air fills with black smoke from the car's mangled body, which I see the moment I turn the corner. From somewhere inside it, I can already hear myself screaming.

Zip.

The door rips open.

'Get out, get out, get out!' my mother snarls. She rips at me with her fingernails.

But – and this is new now – I am not looking at my mother. For the first time, I see Ann's face, peeking over my mother's shoulder. Her glossy curls frame her expression, equal parts savage and sweet. She stares straight into the wreckage of the car, smiles at me. Then,

'Get out.' The voice that joins my mother's is crystalline, childlike. And then they're chanting together, a dreadful harmony of hatred. 'Get out, get out, get out!'

Chapter Twenty-Five

I took a deep breath, adjusted my satchel on my shoulder, and pushed open Meg's sagging garden gate.

I'd barely slept last night. Zachary had told me Ann couldn't hurt me, and logic told me it was true, but he'd also said to stay away from her; and I couldn't get her threat out of my head. *I assume you're enjoying being alive.* The memory of her words made me tremble. Which was one reason I had walked home with Susie after school. Meg knew about Ann. And, psychic as she was, I hoped she knew far more – about Zachary, about my mother, about how I could master my power. Maybe she even knew where Bess was.

I didn't want to talk to Meg again, but now, more than ever, I couldn't afford to wait to find the answers to my questions.

I knocked on Meg's door, and composed my face into calm determination.

After a long minute, Meg opened the door a crack. For a moment, she looked like just an old, harmless lady, but then she registered me and her expression blackened.

'You again,' she said. 'I told you last time, I don't have any more to say to you.'

She began to push the door closed; I caught it before she could. 'Please, Mrs Sanders. I just have a few questions. It's important.'

Meg frowned at me through the gap in the door.

'You're the only person alive who can help me,' I said, truthfully. 'And I need help.'

She gave a sigh of exasperation and stepped back. 'I charge twenty quid a reading. And hurry up. I'm on a schedule.'

I exhaled – I hadn't been sure she'd even let me in the door – and stepped into the house before she could change her mind. Meg shuffled back down the dim hallway ahead of me, one hand on the wall to steady herself, muttering irritably under her breath.

I followed her into the living room and perched on the edge of the sofa nearest the door. Meg eased herself into her armchair with a groan.

'I hope you're not expecting biscuits again. Well, girl? What do you want? Quick, now.'

I placed my hands on my knees, and started with the most conventional question I had. 'I want to ask you about my mother.'

'What about her?'

'She died years ago. Which you obviously already know,' I added, seeing Meg roll her eyes. 'I know you do mediumship readings, pass on messages from beyond the grave, that sort of thing. I wondered if you could . . . do the same for me with my mum.'

Meg flapped a hand, as though shooing away a fly. 'Next question. I can already tell you, she won't have any messages for you.'

I tried not to let my frustration show, but it was impossible.

'How do you know? I'm going to pay you, can't you at least try?'

'I don't need to try, girl. I know.'

'Can you at least tell me if she's still around as a ghost?'

'That one, you can answer on your own.'

I narrowed my eyes at her. Meg matched my unimpressed look with one of her own. Maybe it had been pointless coming here. She might have let me in the door, but apparently that didn't mean she was actually going to help me.

'Next question,' Meg repeated. 'I assume you've got more?'

I nodded. I wasn't sure there was much point asking. If she wouldn't even answer a 'normal' psychic question, then I doubted she'd answer my others, but I had to try.

'I want to know why some people see spirits and others don't,' I said. 'And if a person can see them . . . I want to know how they can make them stop.'

Meg gave a small smile. 'Now, that's a better question.' She settled back in her chair and smoothed her skirt. 'Seeing spirits is a gift. Some, like myself, are born with it. Others develop it after an event brings them in close contact with the dead. You are one of the latter.' She smiled, showing off her false teeth. 'I've never seen a girl so touched by death as you, I must say.'

Shivers bristled down my spine. 'So is there a way to stop it?'

'Can you stop your eyes seeing? Stop your ears hearing? It's a sense, girl; you can't turn it off. Not even in death.'

Disappointment poured through me like cement. 'Are you sure?'

'Never been more sure. Especially in your case. Are we done? Time's ticking.'

178

I sighed and looked back up at her. 'I heard that spirits have to stay near their bodies. Is that true?'

She nodded.

'So how come I saw a spirit from the inn here in your house, someone who was buried in the old churchyard across the village?'

For the first time, Meg looked flustered. 'All sorts of spirits communicate with me. I'm the strongest psychic in the area.'

'So spirits can move from their bodies then,' I said. 'How? Do your psychic abilities override the pull of their bodies, or something?'

'No. I didn't say any of that.' Meg adjusted her glasses. She looked uncomfortable. 'There are physical rules to the spirit world just like there are to the living one. Spirits can no more escape their bodies than you and I can escape gravity. If I want to communicate with a spirit, I must go to them, or find a way to bring them to me.'

I frowned at her, confused.

Meg looked around, as though checking we weren't being overheard, then leaned forwards in her chair. 'No spirit can move to where their body is not, girl.' She held my gaze, then flicked her eyes towards the bookcase.

I followed her gaze. A shiver rippled through me as I saw what she was looking at.

The fruit bowl, with its small pieces of bone. I looked with slow horror from the bowl, to Meg, and back again. Meg raised her thin white eyebrows.

'Are those . . . human?' I whispered.

'I'm not answering any more, so don't ask me.' She sounded as much nervous as annoyed. 'I've said quite enough. Work it out for yourself.'

I snapped my mouth shut.

Meg's gaze darted around the room once more. 'It's time for you to leave. But I will tell you one more thing before you go.' She leaned towards me again, and the confidence returned to her voice. 'I know you ignored my advice. You've been carrying on with that boy, haven't you?'

I sat very still.

'Zachary.' Meg looked at my face and nodded. 'You should look alarmed, girl. I'll tell you a thing for free, about dealing with the dead. They do not change. How can you trust him, this boy who once attacked the vulnerable in the night, stole from them, left them for dead? Do you think a person with that level of selfishness could ever be good, even in death? Has he told you he murdered his own brother?' Meg chuckled at my aghast expression. 'I thought not. Oh, yes. His poor brother, Philip. Zachary was ruthless. Notorious. The dead do not change, they simply learn to manipulate. And you're valuable to him. If there's anyone he'd want to manipulate, it would be you, powerful as you are.'

My heart pounded. 'Why should I believe you?'

'Because I've been there. I know.' Her smile turned wry. 'You'll learn, my girl, how the dead try to twist those of us with power to their own purposes.'

I stayed very still. I didn't know how to respond. A thousand objections filled my mouth, but I didn't let one of them out, because of the single voice that whispered, *What if she's right?* It was true that I didn't know anything about Zachary, not really; only what my instincts and the poem told me. It was true that he had more to gain from our connection than I did.

Meg patted the arm of her chair. 'I think that's enough for one afternoon.'

I stood up. My legs were jelly. I fished for my wallet in my satchel.

'No charge,' Meg said. 'Not for what I've told you.'

'Um. Thanks.'

She narrowed her eyes, but for once she looked more contemplative than mean. 'You're welcome. Now, don't come back.'

I headed back down the hallway and out into the front yard. The sky was heavyset and overcast, but even so, stepping outdoors felt like a release. I stood on the weed-cloyed path to compose myself then continued on my way, picking up my pace.

I had to talk to Zachary.

Chapter Twenty-Six

'Liz, I swear you'll give me a heart attack.' Dad leaned over the back of the sofa and looked at me over the top of his glasses. 'Calm down.'

I pushed the cupboard door to. I'd already reorganized the cutlery drawer, gone through all the food checking best before dates, and loaded the dishwasher. Before that I'd tried flicking through magazines, zoning out on the internet . . . but every time I sat down, all I did was think about Zachary. Whatever I did to pass the time, the clock refused to get any nearer bedtime.

It wasn't that I believed Meg as such – I'd only spoken to Zachary a handful of times, but I trusted him like I'd known him much longer – it was just that I couldn't deny what Meg had said about him being a highwayman. When I put the romance of the poem aside, I had to admit he had been a criminal. He had stolen from and maybe even hurt people. Meg said he'd been feared and notorious, once upon a time.

But murdering his own brother . . .? Surely that was something that could never be left in the past. If it was true, Zachary was – or at least, had been – capable of something I'd never have thought possible of him.

And why would Meg lie to me? She had to know I'd ask him. If it was a lie, it was a silly one.

I didn't know what to think.

'Liz, do I need to stage an intervention?' Dad said. 'Step away from the washing up and sit down. Tell me what's wrong.'

I sighed, and walked over to the sofa. I'd put on my longest, swishiest skirt after school, and I wrapped its folds around me like a blanket as I sat down next to Dad. 'Nothing's wrong.'

He assumed his best, attentive-father pose, which I noticed he'd been working on since our argument at the weekend. 'I thought we made a bargain. I try harder, and you keep me in the loop with what's happening with you.'

'It's not a big deal.' I paused. Normally, I would have left it at that, but Dad had been trying so hard lately, that I let myself continue. 'I just heard something today about one of my new friends that I didn't expect.'

Dad nodded, and frowned with exaggerated thoughtfulness.

'How do you know if you can trust someone, Dad?'

'Aha.' He rubbed his bristly chin. 'I didn't realize we were wading into such philosophical waters. Can you give me any details?'

I shook my head.

'Okay. That's fine. Trust; it's a tricky one.' He considered. 'Although I did see a great daytime talk show about it the other day.'

I smiled and rolled my eyes. 'Shame I missed it. I'm sure the advice was stellar.'

'It wasn't bad actually. I think the conclusions were to talk to the individual about your worries, and that their actions speak louder than words.'

Zachary's actions were the problem. Because his words had, so far, been pretty much perfect.

Manipulative, Meg's voice whispered through my mind. I squashed it away. I refused to think badly of Zachary until I spoke to him. But the poison of doubt had begun to infect my mind at its roots.

'Does that help?' Dad asked.

'Maybe.'

'Good.' He glanced at the TV, which had been chattering to itself this whole time, and turned it off.

I was surprised; the TV never went off while Dad was awake.

'Now, come with me,' he said, 'because I've got something to show you.'

Dad heaved himself off the sofa and headed out of the kitchen. I followed, expected him to go upstairs – the only other part of the inn we used – but instead he turned left and opened the door to the inn's old dining room.

The air was stale of course, but I could tell Dad had been in here before he turned on the lights. The spider-webbed chandeliers illuminated a freshly hoovered carpet. And right in the middle of the room stood the inn's piano – shiny and clean and with a piano stool ready at the keyboard.

Dad looked at me with an almost shy smile, then walked right up to the piano, sat down at the stool, and flipped up the lid.

For a long moment, I was dumbstruck. Dad's hands skated across the keys, filling the room with a perfect, bittersweet melody. In seven long years, I had never once heard Dad play. It was like watching one of the old photos come alive.

I drifted over to his side. With the old, dusty tables and empty chairs around us, it felt like the evening had morphed into a dream.

'I had the piano brought out of the drawing room today and tuned.' Dad smiled up at me. 'I didn't think I'd remember how to play, but it's all stored up here somewhere.' He paused to tap his head.

'Your playing—' I sought for the right words '—it's amazing.'

'This is nothing.' He hit a wrong note, weaved it into the melody, and kept going. 'If only you could remember the way I played before.'

Dad bent over the keys, and I closed my eyes, feeling the music vibrate through me, unfamiliar yet familiar at the same time. I didn't know if I was remembering, exactly; all I knew was that this felt right. Music filling this empty dining room, Dad happy and more at ease than I had seen him in forever.

'And the best part,' he said, 'is that I rang a few of the local music studios this afternoon, and it turns out the one in the next town has a vacancy for a sound engineer. So I have an interview on Saturday.'

He brought the music to a dramatic, over-the-top crescendo, and I laughed and clapped enough for a whole inn-full of hotel guests.

I didn't bother trying to sleep. I didn't even get changed out of my clothes. I just sat up against my pillows, examining the painting of Bess by the light of my bedside lamp, looking at the picture of my mother in my locket, thinking about Dad and Meg and Zachary.

And all the while, Dad's playing echoed round my head,

bittersweet, like the promise of a new start tinged with regret at something lost.

After the piano had fallen silent downstairs and Dad had creaked his way to bed, I waited another hour, all my thoughts now on Zachary. There would be no running around in the dark tonight. I needed to know that I could trust him before I got in any deeper.

As before, Zachary stepped out of the shadows under the tree the moment I moved to my window.

'Come up,' I whispered. I didn't stay to watch him climb. I retreated to my bed and sat back against the pillows, running my locket over my lips as I waited for him.

He thudded softly into my bedroom, with his usual panther-like grace. 'What's the matter?' he asked immediately.

I looked up at him. Was I that easy to read? I'd been trying to look neutral. I didn't want him to think I'd already judged him when I asked what I had to.

'I need to talk to you,' I said. 'Sit down.' I flicked my gaze towards the end of the bed.

Zachary looked at the bed and hesitated. Then he folded to the floor instead, leaning against the wall. He tipped his head back to look at me, his red-gold hair spilling across his brow, which was creased with concern. 'Has something happened?'

I didn't say anything for a minute, just looked at him. I tried to imagine him as a highwayman. It was all too easy. With his slim, muscled body, his clothes the perfect colour for hiding in the dark, his practical boots and gloves, he was built for the outdoors, made for the night. He'd look good on a horse.

He'd look good in a fight.

He was tough enough to be a highway robber – that was for sure. But could he hurt people? Would he kill?

'Elizabeth. Speak to me.'

I sighed. Then I got off the bed and joined him on the floor, pressing my back against the wall beside him, bunching my skirt around me. He smelled like a boy-sized piece of night; he made me think of darkness, of trees and earth and stars.

'Zachary, I have a question.' I held his gaze and paused – there was no easy way to ask this. 'I've been thinking about you being a highwayman. Were you good at it?'

He looked at me, not blinking. 'I was.'

'Were you notorious?'

'I . . . had a reputation.'

'Did you kill people?'

He started, the sole of one of his boots scraping sharply on the floor. But he didn't break eye contact. 'Why do you ask?'

'Because that's what highwaymen did, wasn't it?' I licked my lips, suddenly nervous. 'And because I spoke to a psychic who came to the inn a long time ago, and she told me you'd murdered your brother.'

'It was not murder.'

'But . . . you did kill him?'

He squeezed his eyes shut as though in pain. 'Who was this person? What did she tell you?'

I drew my knees up to my chest and hugged them. 'Her name's Meg Sanders. She's old; she came to the inn decades ago. She didn't tell me much.'

'How does she know about Philip? Is he spirit, like me?'

'She didn't say.'

He nodded. Then he wiped his hand over his face and exhaled. 'It's so long since I've heard his name.'

'I'm sorry,' I said. 'I didn't mean to upset you. But I know so little about you.' I didn't know how to explain. 'I have no context for you, Zachary. I don't see you with other people. I don't get to hear what other people think of you. I only see you in the dark, at the inn. You need to tell me more about yourself.'

'What do you want to know?'

'Everything.'

Chapter Twenty-Seven

'So many years have passed since I last told my story.' Zachary bent his knees and draped his arms over them. 'But I will tell you what I can remember.

'My life ended at an inn, and it began in one too,' he said. 'My parents owned an inn near London, on Hounslow Heath. It was smaller than the Highwayman, the number of rooms was only enough for our small family and a few travellers, but the bar was constantly busy.

'My childhood memories are not fond. It was both hard work and dull; harsh by today's standards, but common enough for the time. When my brother Philip was ten years old and I was seven – which was when my parents judged us old enough – they had us working in the inn: sweeping; waiting tables; serving drinks; taking guineas, which they were always careful to check at the end of the night.

'Our parents' lives revolved around money. Everything they did, everything they made Philip and I do, centred around it. I could not fault them for that, they made sure we had clothes and enough in our stomachs, but love and affection—' he pulled a face '—was lacking. I had my brother to look up to, but he had no one.

'I could see the strain it put on him. As the years passed, he changed. He developed a hard shell and, in the absence of other ambitions, he became as obsessed with cash and appearance as our parents. When he grew into adolescence, he lost interest in me altogether, and instead spent his free time in the bar making merry with the drinkers.

'His favourites were the highwaymen. "Heroes on horse-back". "Gentlemen of the road". To Philip, they represented everything we lacked in our own lives – freedom, glamour, danger, vigour, romance. Hounslow Heath was infested with highwaymen, he had no shortage of examples to envy, and he became obsessed. If someone who had been robbed came into the bar, he would be at their table in moments, absorbing the grisly details. If an actual highwayman came in, I would be running the bar by myself for the night. And that happened frequently.'

'Didn't your parents report them?' I asked.

'No. Highwaymen were good business. They spent a lot of cash and told amusing stories. They had a kind of following. My parents made extra guineas selling information to them: which of our customers were most worth robbing, who would put up a fight. I have no doubt they got a few people killed they'd fawned over in the bar the day before.

'One of my parents' regulars was a highwayman called Sawney. He was a particular favourite of Philip's. Sawney would sit in the corner, drinking his port and swishing his ridiculous curled locks, and the women – and Philip – had eyes for no one else.

'I should have seen it coming. One cold night in the spring,

Sawney was prancing around the place even flashier than usual, doling out his stolen money and poor advice. He told my brother he was wasted on inn-keeping, that he would make more money in one night as a highwayman than he could in years slaving for my parents. No doubt he was trying to flatter his way to a free tankard-full; but it was all the encouragement Philip needed. He came to me that night and told me he was leaving.'

'To be a highwayman? So it was your brother's idea?'

Zachary nodded. 'He was going to be "a gentleman of the road". Those were his words. But he didn't have the guts Sawney gave him credit for. Highwaymen always worked alone, but Philip persuaded me we would do better as a pair; that there would be no risk of disloyalty between brothers; that he'd miss me if I stayed. I knew he was frightened. And I certainly had no love for my life with my parents. So we left together.

'Our first night as highwaymen was a shambles. Philip was clueless, despite all his time spent listening to their stories. I was barely sixteen and had done nothing more than wait tables. We were a mess. We stole two horses from our parents' stables and had one rifle between us, which neither of us knew how to handle properly. The only person we dared detain that night was a postboy travelling on his own. He wept the entire time the robbery was underway. Our first major problem arose when we had to conclude it. I'd barely considered the realities of what our new lives would mean until that moment; I'd thought only of following Philip.

'But Philip knew the reality. We had to shoot the boy, he said, so he couldn't identify us to the thief takers. He didn't have the nerve to pull the trigger, and I wanted no part of it whatsoever. So we tied the poor boy up and left him on the roadside, and started our careers with intimidatingly large rewards on our heads from the Postmaster General – one of the worst blunders a highwayman could make.

'I realized then that Philip and I had doomed ourselves. We were wanted men, we couldn't return home, but unless we could shoot to kill, we would not survive.

'The knowledge made me nauseous. It made Philip angry. He took our money to the nearest town and procured two flintlock pistols. I determined I wouldn't kill, whatever the necessity of it, but Philip, fuelled by anger, felt differently.

'I tried to delay the "next time". But the coins from the hold-up bled from our pockets. Philip wanted to emulate Sawney, and within a week of plentiful beer, excessively good food, the fashionable clothes Philip insisted on and stabling for the horses, our pockets were empty.

'We chose a moonlit night to stage our next hold-up. We needed enough light to see what we were doing, despite the risk we would be more easily remembered. Philip insisted we hold up a coach – the more people we stole from, the more guineas we'd get, and the more time we would have before we had to do it again.

'We concealed ourselves in the bushes by the side of a road. When a coach drove past, Philip burst out on horseback, his flintlock raised. After he got the travellers out of the carriage – three men and a lady – it was my cue to run out from the undergrowth and relieve them of their goods, while Philip held them at pistol-point. All was going well, until I approached the final man. He whipped a blunderbuss from his cloak. Philip shot him before the man could shoot me.

'Philip yelled at me to get back. He dispatched the second

man. Then the third. The lady cowered on the road, wailing. I demanded Philip stop – three men were dead and the lady was clearly defenceless – but he kept his pistol raised.

'The woman entreated Philip to spare her. She told him she had two children waiting for her at the end of the road. She offered him everything she had. But I could tell he was going to kill her. He was crazed with adrenaline and power and fear; he didn't look like my brother any more. I railed at him. It did nothing. I ran at him, but he refused to lower his arm. So I took out my own pistol and pointed it at him. I told him to drop his gun, or I would shoot him in the leg.

'Philip ran forwards and shoved me. We fought, just like we had a hundred times before, but we'd never fought with guns between us. Somehow, my pistol went off. The bullet exploded in my brother's stomach.'

Zachary paused. His voice was lower when he continued. 'It took an unendurable time for him to die. The lady ran, and it was just Philip and myself, on the road in the dark, in the quiet, with three corpses around us. I'm unsure whether he could not speak, or simply refused to, but in any case he remained mute, only stared at me until he fell still. When I try to remember him now, that's the clearest image I have of him – pale and sweating, pain and accusation in his eyes, staring up at me.'

I felt bruised, somehow. Tender and pained.

'That's horrific,' I said. 'I can't . . . I can't even imagine it.' I leaned towards him, making him look me in the eyes. 'It was awful of me to ask you to tell me all of this. I wish I could take it back.'

'No.' His eyes were flat as stones. 'I didn't intend to kill my brother, but, yes, I did kill him.'

'But it was a terrible accident, and you were only trying to stop him shooting that poor woman.'

'I attacked him when he was holding a gun. It was reckless. I've considered this countless times. If I'd only found the right words, or spooked his horse and made it run, or put myself in front of the lady, or prevented us from leaving our family home in the first instance, then—'

'It was an accident,' I interrupted. I thought of Dad, how he'd tortured himself for seven long years over Mum. It was tragic to think that Zachary had suffered guilt like that for over two hundred.

'You were doing the right thing,' I said. 'You didn't want to kill. He did.'

'That's as may be. But it's not that simple. Philip was attempting to save our lives, harsh though his methods were. Yet I did not even inter his body. Another coach came by and I hid. The next day, his tarred corpse swung at the crossroads a few towns from here, a macabre warning to other highwaymen. It tortures me that he might yet be there now, in spirit, like me; I have no way of knowing. I abandoned him.'

I wanted to tell him I was sure Philip was fine, long gone to wherever spirits went to, but I couldn't begin to fathom how the spirit world worked. For all I knew, Zachary might be right.

'Didn't his death make you want to stop being a highwayman?' I asked, my voice soft.

'It should have. Yet it was the event that made me a highwayman. I'd had my brother to consider before, now I had no one. Witnessing him die scoured every good feeling from my heart, leaving only desperation and self-loathing. I no longer cared if I died. It made me the perfect criminal.' His smile was rueful. 'I made a promise to myself that I would never kill – I'd be a 'gentleman highwayman' or die – but I robbed, I tied men up and gagged them, I slit bridles and let countless horses escape, I got in fights and broke bones. I was ruthless in every other way.

'I was pursued and almost caught countless times. I passed numerous corpses swinging at crossroads, just like Philip had, and knew it was only a matter of time before I met the same fate. Yet I did not stop. I couldn't. I had no home, no other means of making a living. I would always be hunted even if I did. I believed I'd sealed my fate.'

'How did you get your scar?' I looked at the jagged silver line on his jawline, resisting the urge to try to touch it.

Zachary put his fingers to his skin, as if he'd forgotten the scar was there. 'That? A short knife. I was in the habit of checking for weapons before I took my victims' goods, but on one occasion I was careless. The man tried to cut my throat. Luck was with me that I suffered no worse than this scar.'

I shuddered, but I couldn't take my eyes off the scar's blunt line.

'Two years after Philip's death,' he continued, 'my travels took me back to London, and who should I meet in an inn but Sawney. I always imagined the beating I'd give him if I saw him again, but I'd lost so much of myself by then, that I bought the man a drink. He hardly recognized me, but he remembered Philip. He laughed to hear how we'd followed his flawed advice, and that I'd become a highwayman with a reputation matching his own. He gave me a final piece of advice as a farewell gesture – how to make more money than ever. The Newmarket races.'

'Newmarket? That's near here, isn't it?'

'It is. It's also close to where Philip died, but even that horror couldn't stop me. I set off for Newmarket, planned a few hold-ups along the way to finance my journey, and when I drew near I stopped off at—' He held out his hands, as though to encompass the whole room.

'My inn.'

'Your inn. It wasn't named the Highwayman yet. It was the Honest Lawyer, and advertised itself with a painted sign of a headless attorney. I considered the sign amusing, so I stopped. I only intended to rest a night or two. The races were drawing nearer and I wanted my pick of the takings. But my room was comfortable, and I was growing tired of running. And then there was Bess.' He smiled.

'She was everything that the other girls I'd met since becoming a highwayman were not. She was beautiful, that goes without saying.' Zachary glanced towards the painting on my dresser. 'But more than that, she was . . . simply herself. She worked behind the bar, yet she wasn't a slave for her parents, like Philip and I had been. She worked alongside them, as an equal and out of desire not duty. She was kindly and good, yet strong-willed – she would throw out bad guests, no matter how much money they had.

'I would order extra plates of food, simply so I could be served by her. We'd talk and laugh. I had not laughed while sober for years and it truly brought my soul back to me. When we began spending our free time together, I extended my stay at the inn; I didn't want to leave. During the races, I rode to Newmarket at night and would be back at the Lawyer, with my Bess, by sunrise.

'She realized, soon enough, what I was of course. I had managed to keep it from her for a while, but she was a smart girl and knew me by instinct. When, eventually, she found me out, she did not become afraid of me, or act enamoured by my dashing career. She disapproved, but didn't judge; she only felt fearful for me. For the first time in three long years, I'd found someone to care about, and someone who cared about me.

'That was when I decided to end my days as a highwayman. But my purse was almost empty; I could not stop immediately. I allowed myself until the end of the Newmarket races to replenish it. I planned to stage hold-ups every night of the races until I had enough money to purchase an inn of my own, and then I would ask Bess to marry me.

'She knew my intentions. She desired a life with me just as much as I did with her. She told me that she would wait for me, here—' he looked up at my window '— watching for me to come back each night. And she did.'

He glanced at me. 'Yet, as you know, there was no happy ending. There was a reason highwaymen needed to keep moving. Up until then, I hadn't attracted too much attention, but working the same roads, staying in the same inn for too long, was dangerous. Someone at the Lawyer took a dislike to me, or perhaps they wanted the reward money – I was worth two hundred guineas to swing – and the redcoats came.

'You know how it ends. I'd rather not elaborate on that part.'

I did know how it ended: Bess shooting herself to warn him, Zachary dying the next day.

'But it didn't end,' I said. 'Because you and Bess were still around.'

He nodded. 'It took a day and more for us to be reunited. After the redcoats shot me, I followed them to the crossroads, where they strung up my body. I was in shock at first. It took me a while to think of coming back to the inn. But when I did, I found her, in this room. Her room – now yours.

'We had planned a lifetime together. And we got multiple. But we never had a life. We could not leave, we couldn't grow old, we could not change.'

'Wasn't there another option?' I asked. 'If I understand it right, not everyone who dies remains here, a ghost. Couldn't you have gone . . . wherever they go?'

He shrugged. 'If it was an option, it was not open to me. There were no angels urging Bess to heaven, no devils to drag me to hell. No ethereal lights to walk into or doors to open. Only this—' he spread his hands to indicate the room '—the same world we had always known.

'I have considered it, of course. That this is a purgatory, and that Bess might have found her way to wherever it is that spirits are meant to go. But she would not have left without telling me. That I cannot believe. We'd been together for so long. It felt like half of me was ripped away when I discovered she was gone. It still does.'

Zachary rubbed his hands through his hair, with a humourless laugh. 'That was intense. I never thought I'd tell anyone those stories again.'

My heart felt like it had grown too big for my chest. I wanted to wrap my arms around him and tell him everything would be okay; I wanted to run outside and not come home until I had found Bess for him; I wanted to go to Meg and tell her she was wrong about his brother, and that there was nothing she could say because I was never going to stop talking to Zachary.

I looked up and caught him watching me. He bumped me with his shoulder – the touch weaker than my brain told me it should be, but very real – and smiled. 'It's your turn to tell me something about you.'

I looked down at my hands. 'Believe me, you don't want to hear it.'

'Believe me, I do.'

'Another night,' I said.

'I'll hold you to that.'

After Zachary left, I spent a contemplative hour on the end of my bed, looking out of the window at the moon.

It was hard to get his face out of my head. The way he'd looked when telling his story, so sad and elated by turns – his eyes sombre then sparkling, his thin lips downturned then stretched wide – tugged at my heart even now he was long gone in the night.

I had to help him find Bess. I couldn't bear to think of the suffering he'd gone through and still was going through. He should be happy, always. The 'always' part was the whole point of the poem he was famous for. Something was wrong with the universe for allowing it be any other way.

Zachary was meant to be with his love. If that couldn't be made right, if his suffering was pointless, what hope could there be for me – Liz, just some unimportant, messed-up girl – to have the life I was meant to? The life, I realized now, in a way that I hadn't realized before, that I truly wanted.

I would find Bess. Because it was the way things had to be. Even if it meant Zachary never needed to speak to me again, even if his smiles and glances all went back to her. I would find her. For him.

It was ridiculous to feel sad over the prospect of no longer seeing Zachary, something I had wanted and wished for just days ago. I forced my thoughts back to the practical. I'd been to Bess's grave, now I considered my other options.

There weren't that many. I could trek the length of the country looking for Bess, but that could take a lifetime, especially since Zachary couldn't come with me. The only obvious next step was Meg. I was sure she could find Bess if she wanted to. But she'd made it clear she didn't want to help me.

For the first time, I wished I shared more of Meg's abilities. She had ways of bringing ghosts to her, something to do with that bowl of bones. If I could only learn to do the same—

All of a sudden I remembered Susie the other day, on Meg's street, joking about doing an Ouija board. She had said she'd wanted to be a paranormal investigator. Well, perhaps it was time to give it a try.

Chapter Twenty-Eight

Scott glared at me all through registration the next morning. He was so obvious about it that the whole table stared at us, but I succeeded in ignoring him. I had bigger things to think about than him.

When the bell rang for first lesson, I took my time putting my book away and picking up my satchel, waiting for Scott to leave. But he didn't. He sat right by my side until the classroom was almost empty. Only then did my calm shift to worry.

I stood up. Scott stood too, like my shadow.

I headed for the door. Scott followed close on my heels. I speed-walked through the corridors towards the Geography block, trying to shake him off. He couldn't do anything to me here, I told myself, not in a school full of people.

My satchel strap tugged tight across my chest, yanked from behind. I gasped, stumbling. Before I could right myself, Scott opened a door and shoved me into an empty classroom.

He let go of me, and I stumbled towards the nearest table. I quickly recovered my balance and spun back towards the door. Scott was already blocking it, hands lifted.

I opened my mouth to shout for help.

'Don't!' he said. 'I'm not going to hurt you. I just need to talk. Two minutes.'

'What are you doing?' We were in an empty Maths classroom.

'I'm giving you a final chance. That's why we're here.'

I looked back at him, my eyes wide. He was crazy. 'A final chance for what?'

'To stop what you're doing at the inn.'

'Stop what?'

'You know what.' He dropped his head and looked up at me through his blond lashes. 'I've warned you before. You're not the only one who can be awake at night, you know.'

I froze. Was Scott warning me about Zachary? That was all kinds of bad. I needed to know exactly what Scott knew. 'I don't know what you're talking about.'

He took a step towards me, but not far enough to unblock the door. 'Yes. I think you do. I'm not letting you get me in trouble again. So this is my final warning. Stop what you're doing, or something bad will happen, and you'll be to blame.'

That was it. I squared my jaw, walked forwards, stopped in front of him. I could see the door handle. I could grab it easily, if Scott didn't stop me.

'You think you can bully me, Scott,' I said, my voice low to keep it from shaking, 'but the more you threaten me, the easier it'll be for me to persuade my dad to sack your dad. Especially now I know about Lucy. So leave – me – alone. I really mean it now.'

Scott started at Lucy's name, as if I'd shocked him with a live wire. He looked angry, and hurt.

I reached past him for the door handle. He blocked my way.

He grabbed my satchel strap and tried to wrestle it over my head.

'Hey!' I shrieked.

The strap broke with a snap. Scott stumbled back with the force of it, but he had my bag. He spun, holding it away from me.

I shouted then for real. 'Get off my bag!'

I heard the door of the adjacent classroom burst open. Scott heard it too and threw my bag back at me.

A teacher's face appeared in the glass of the door. She flung the door open. 'What's going on here? Scott Crowley, what is this?'

I turned round to the teacher, panting, hugging my bag to my chest, the broken strap dangling.

Scott looked between me and the teacher. 'I wasn't doing anything, miss.'

The teacher gave Scott an unimpressed look. 'Are you all right?' she asked me.

I hesitated, then nodded. I was only glad Scott had decided to take his aggression out on my bag instead of me. I shouldn't have said those things to him, and especially not about Lucy. I didn't know what I'd been thinking. I'd wanted to get him off my case, but instead I'd just tripped his switch.

He'd become aggressive so easily. I thought of the inn. Its many rooms, its isolation. He could do much worse there than just break my bag, and nobody would be there to stop him.

The teacher was clearly annoyed. She looked at me. 'What's your name? Who's your form teacher?'

'Elizabeth Rathamore. My form tutor is Mr Scholars.'

'I'll make sure he knows about this. Neither of you should be in here. Get to lessons.'

Scott was out of the door first. By the time I got into the corridor, he was already at the other end, as if he was the one who needed to get away from me.

I'd calmed down by the time I arrived at History, though the telling-off I'd endured from Miss Kirwin for being late to Geography hadn't helped.

Susie took one look at my face as I sat down, and whispered, 'Are you okay?'

I nodded, then changed my mind and shook my head. But before I could think how to explain, Miss Webb launched into a lecture about presentation structure.

Susie threw me wide-eyed glances for the next ten minutes. When Miss Webb stopped talking and allowed us to start pair work, Susie demanded, 'What is it? You're all pale.'

I didn't know what to tell her. I couldn't mention Scott's warnings, without having to tell her about Zachary. But I had to say something or I'd explode.

'It's just Scott,' I said. 'He's being weird.'

Her face grew properly concerned. 'There's no such thing as "just" Scott. What's he done?'

I struggled for words. 'He followed me after registration and, well, we got into a tussle. He broke my bag.' I held up my satchel, with the knot I'd made in the strap to hold it together.

'What did he do that for?'

'I don't know.'

'Was he trying to steal it?'

I shook my head.

Susie lowered her voice. 'You remember what I told you about Lucy? I don't like it if he's getting violent.'

I lowered my voice to match hers. 'Of course. But it's okay.

I'm going to be really careful around him.' That much was true.

Susie nodded, but the worry stayed in her eyes.

'Girls,' Miss Webb barked behind us, 'this doesn't look like presentation work to me. Look, you haven't even written anything down yet.' She reached between us and flicked my blank notepad. 'Chop chop.'

Susie and I bent studiously over our work. As soon as Miss Webb moved away, Susie slumped back in her seat. 'Be careful, Liz, okay?'

'I am. I will.' I smiled, and clicked the top of my pen, wishing I could snap Scott out of my mind just as easily. I had bigger goals today than avoiding him. 'So, about this presentation,' I said. 'I was wondering if you're up for a teensy bit more research?'

Chapter Twenty-Nine

Susie needed no persuasion to agree to doing an Ouija board. It was all she talked about, all break-time.

'I don't get why we can't do it at yours though,' she said. 'It's so much bigger. Your dad wouldn't have a clue what we we're doing if we did it at yours. My mum'll ask all kinds of questions.'

That was my only condition for doing an Ouija board – that we do it at Susie's house. She was quite right, it made more sense to do it at the inn, but I couldn't risk it. Not with Ann around. And Zachary of course. I wasn't sure how Ouija boards worked – I'd only read about them, and seen the odd movie sequence – but the possibility of summoning Zachary through one made me shudder, in a completely different way to the idea of summoning Ann. I wanted to keep him separate, somehow, from my other Glimpses.

'Do you think the inn's ghosts will even hear us at my house?' Susie pushed.

'Isn't that the point of Ouija boards, that they can summon ghosts from anywhere?' I said. 'And anyway, my dad's kind of religious,' I lied. 'He'd kill me if we did it at mine and he found out.'

Susie just shrugged and said, 'All right then. We'll just have to say the names of the inn's ghosts when we're doing it, I suppose.' Then the certainty left her face and she whispered, 'Do you think we should ask for Lucy's ghost too?'

Shivers spidered up my spine. Susie was right: if anyone could tell me how worried I had to be about Scott, it was her.

Bess, my mum, Philip and Lucy. Was it stupid to hope that, out of all the spirits in the world, they would be the only ones that came through?

After the bus journey home, Susie, Matt and I took the long route back to Susie's street. Matt fished a bag of chocolates out of his backpack and passed them around as we walked.

I took a small handful, grateful for the distraction – my nerves were jittering like Mexican jumping beans – before I saw what was in my hand. 'Chocolate ghosts?'

'Bought them at lunch,' Matt said. 'All the shops are getting stuff in for Halloween. Thought they were appropriate, considering you two are turning into the Noyes College ghostbusters.' He smiled, and bit the head off a spook. 'Suze, you've totally corrupted our new girl.'

'I haven't corrupted her.' Susie slapped his chunky arm. 'She asked me.'

'You're two freaks together, then.' Matt leaned down – a long way; he was so much taller than Susie – to kiss her temple. 'Rather you than me, Liz.'

'Wuss,' Susie muttered.

They play-fought, snatching kisses in-between fake punches. I looked away, as I always did when they got smoochy, before my face could start burning. No boy had ever looked at me the way Matt looked at Susie. Which had never seemed a big deal before; I'd never met a boy I wanted to look at me the way Matt looked at Susie.

But now, I couldn't help imagining Zachary in Matt's place, me in Susie's. I imagined Zachary smiling at me, his attention all on me. It was almost too painful. Even if it wasn't for Bess, even if Zachary liked me, we could never be like this. He was dead.

I swallowed my chocolate ghost and made a show of eyeing Matt's all-black outfit, his studded dog collar, his wrists full of rubber bracelets and his dyed-black hair. 'You're scared of ghosts? I thought you'd do Ouija boards over breakfast.'

'I'm not scared,' he said. 'I'm sensible. You know it's only evil spirits that come through those things. My brother's friend got possessed when he did one. It made him kill his hamster.' Matt grinned, and pulled another ghost from his bag of sweets. He waved it in Susie's face with a 'Woo-ooo!'

Susie shrieked and grabbed my hand, and we ran, giggling to the end of the road. Matt laughed and chased us, trying to flick sweets into our hair.

Running was easy. Giggling was too, though it felt more like hysteria than laughter. There was enough jittery energy running through my system to power the whole of Hulbourn.

I had a full minute to contemplate Susie's house before we went inside, thanks to the prolonged kiss goodbye that Matt-and-Susie were enjoying. Susie's house was the same size and layout as Meg's, but I could already tell it would be very different inside. And about as different again as the Highwayman.

Cheerful, red cotton curtains hung in the windows, framing a windowsill full of money plants and a huge, dozing ginger cat. Glass wind chimes hung from the curtain pole, reflecting colourful shards of light back into the front garden. When Susie finally unlatched her lips from Matt's and opened the front door for me, the whole house smelled deliciously of baking.

'Mum brings her work home with her,' Susie said, leading me into the small front hallway. 'She's always trying out new recipes to make at school.'

The family cat emerged from the living room with a heart-melting meow. Susie scooped him up and carried him into the kitchen ahead of me.

'Hi, Mum,' she called.

'Hi. Hey, Liz.' Susie's mum smiled at me from the counter, where she was doing something with Rice Krispies, chocolate and a bag of dried fruit. She'd swapped her dinner lady tabard for a long, floaty black dress, like a grown-up version of something Susie would wear.

'Hi, Ms Boyd,' I said. I felt suddenly shy. I'd seen Susie's mum plenty of times in the school dining hall, but this was different. I'd never been invited to a friend's house in my memory, and I wasn't entirely sure what I was meant to do.

'Whatever you're baking,' I said, 'it smells amazing.'

'Thank you. It's banana loaf.' Susie's mum smiled.

'Mum's obsessed with making cakes that contribute to your "five a day",' Susie told me. 'She made chocolate and beetroot cake last week. It was so gross.'

'It wasn't that bad,' her mum said. 'It's all part of the job. School dinners are more complicated than they sound, you know. I'm just doing my bit. You liked the green tea cupcakes I made earlier in the week, didn't you?'

Susie rolled her eyes, and turned to me, the cat in her arms. 'Here, hold Marmalade for me. I'll get us something to drink. I can make an ace replica of the Cocoa Pod's hot chocolate.'

'Sounds yum,' I said.

Susie rolled the cat into my arms. I didn't have much experience with animals, I'd never had pets, but Marmalade didn't seem to care. He lay in my arms, well fed and purring, squinting up at me.

I rocked him – just like a baby – glad to have something to do as Susie and her mum weaved around each other in the small space.

'Don't use all my sprinkles.'

'Mum, we've got two packets. Where are the cinnamon sticks?'

'Cupboard on the left. Make me one too, would you?'

'I'll swap you for a couple of those crispy cakes. Unless there's something weird in them.'

'Only raisins.' Susie's mum looked back at me. 'Are you all right with Marmalade, Liz? He's a bit of a porker. Put him down if he gets heavy.'

'He's fine. Thanks.'

I lifted the cat up, and rubbed my nose in his fur as Susie and her mum continued bustling, their banter and laughter flying back and forth. I knew from school how well Susie and her mum got on, but seeing them like this, now, made it impossible to ignore. I felt like I was intruding on something private. But what was more painful was the thought that they were like this every day.

I loved Dad, but we didn't have what Susie and her mum had. Maybe that would change now he was getting better, but he'd never be my mum.

I'd heard the way adults talked about me behind my back,

especially when I was younger. *Poor girl, growing up without her mother.* It hadn't meant much to me – my only experience of what mothers were meant to be like came from TV – but seeing Susie and her mum now really rammed it home.

Was this what Mum and I would have been like, if she'd lived? I'd never know. Either way, my life would have been completely different.

Marmalade was interested in my heart locket, which dangled around his whiskers. He lifted a paw to bat at it, squirming in my arms. It was like trying to hold treacle. I let him ooze down towards the lino, feet first. When he found the ground, he meowed and went to sit by his food bowl.

'You're fat enough,' Susie told him. She turned and handed me a steaming mug of chocolate. She picked up a second mug and a plate of crispy cakes, which her mum had decorated with fresh fruit.

'We've got History project stuff to do,' Susie told her mum. Behind her mum's back, she grinned at me, her eyes round and sparkling. 'Ready, Liz?'

I nodded, though I was pretty sure my smile was part-grimace. I'd almost forgotten about the Ouija board.

'Thanks for the cakes, Ms Boyd,' I remembered to say, as we left the kitchen.

Susie danced up the stairs to her room. I followed. I was half tempted to go back and get the cat – he wouldn't protect me against Glimpses, but his presence would be a comfort.

'Wow,' I said, as Susie opened the door to her room. 'It's like a monster and a fairy mashed their bedrooms together.'

'Exactly the look I was going for.' Susie smiled, and pointed at her bed, which was covered on three sides by a black mesh princess canopy. 'Sit.'

I sat, balancing my hot chocolate on my knee, and gazed around me. Her walls were covered with heavy-metal band posters. Girly, black lace cushions littered the floor. A vase of fake, black roses sat on the windowsill – I didn't need to ask to guess they were from Matt. Every other surface was covered with objects – black candles, stuffed bears with vampire teeth, dirty plates, open pots of make-up.

I couldn't help thinking of my own bare, white room, its only decoration the painting of Bess, and my Normality List. I wondered what Susie would think of me if she knew.

Susie knelt on the floor, fishing for something under the bed. She pulled a box out and wiped off the lid. 'Here it is,' she said, sitting cross-legged on the carpet.

I exhaled the tightness from my lungs, and crouched down on the floor next to her.

'Perhaps we should be drinking bat's blood, instead of hot chocolate,' I joked. 'Can spirits come through when there are marshmallows in the room?'

Susie laughed. 'Haven't you ever seen *Ghostbusters*? Marshmallow man? Just let me read the instructions.' She pulled a slip of paper from the box and squinted at it.

'You've done this before, though . . .?'

'No. Never.' She shrugged. 'Mum only let me buy a board when I turned sixteen, but I never found a willing partner-in-paranormal-crime to do it with me. Until now.' She looked up at me through her red fringe, and grinned.

I gripped the handle of my mug so hard, my knuckles burned against the ceramic. 'Some ghost-hunting expert you are.'

'Wannabe ghost-hunting expert. Okay—' she flapped the instruction sheet '—it sounds pretty straightforward. Can you light those candles on the bookcase? There's a box of matches next to the big candle.'

I did as she asked.

'Oh . . . no, actually,' she said. 'Blow them out again. The candles are meant to be white – black candles call bad spirits.'

I blew them out with such force that I spat at her tea lights. 'Here. Let me read those,' I said, almost snatching the instructions off her.

Susie lay the board on the carpet between us as I skimmed the printed sheet. She was right, the instructions were straight-forward, but the list of printed warnings made me sweat.

'Let's get this over with,' I said. I opened her curtains wide to let in as much daylight as possible, turned on the main light, and sat down at the board. I rested my fingertips on the wooden indicator.

Susie placed her hands on the board next to mine with a squeak of nervous excitement. 'Do you want to ask the questions, or shall I?'

'I will,' I said. It took me a minute to calm my mind, but eventually I was ready. 'Is there anybody there?' I asked.

This could either be the most enlightening experience of my life, or one of the most foolish things I'd ever done.

Chapter Thirty

Susie and I stared at each other. Her smile wobbled nervously, her eyes slightly vacant, as, like me, she put all her focus into her fingertips.

Nothing happened. I asked again. 'Are there any spirits in the room?'

This time, there was a jolt beneath my fingers. Susie gasped, 'Oh my God, oh my God,' as the indicator slid towards 'Yes'. 'Are you pushing it?' she asked.

I shook my head. I didn't need to ask Susie the same thing. My whole body vibrated. There was a Glimpse here, and it was close.

I hadn't expected this to happen so fast.

Unable to stop myself, I twisted round, looking for it. I didn't find a thing out of the ordinary.

Susie was focused intently on the board. I heard her breath quicken. 'How many spirits are in the room?' she asked.

The indicator slid to the number one. Heat prickled across my skin.

'What's your name?' I asked.

The indicator slid across the board, skating the alphabet

slowly, as though teasing me. But it passed B for Bess; J for Juliette, my mother; L for Lucy and P for Philip, and came to rest simply on 'No'.

No? What kind of an answer was that?

Goosebumps joined the prickling on my skin. Too late, I realized with a gasp that I'd forgotten to start the Ouija by refusing the bad spirits – the instructions had been explicit on this.

'No bad spirits here,' I said, my voice too loud. 'If you're a bad spirit, you can leave.'

'Ask about the inn,' Susie hissed.

My throat was tight. 'We're looking for some spirits,' I said to the room. 'We're looking for Bess Richards. Do you know her?'

The indicator jolted under our fingers and slid back to the alphabet. Fast, jerky movements spelled out 'G-o-o-d' then 'r-i-d-d-a-n-c-e'.

'Good riddance?' Susie frowned.

My fingertips began to tremble on the indicator. Whoever this spirit was, they knew that Bess had disappeared. 'Where is she? Do you know where she's gone?'

Susie's frown deepened. I knew that I was risking a lot, straying from the History project in this way, but right now I didn't care. I held my breath as the indicator hurried back across the alphabet.

'S-t-o-p l-o-o-k-i-n-g'.

I swallowed, hard. 'Why should I stop?'

The indicator slid to Z. And dread balled in my stomach.

'Z-m-i-n-e', spelled out in slow letters.

'Z mine?' Susie repeated.

I met her gaze, eyes wide, my lungs pumping, skin burning raw. 'Ann?' I whispered.

The indicator rushed to the Z and starting making its way back towards A.

'Shit—' Susie's voice was small '—this means the spirit's trying to get out of the board, right? Take it to Goodbye—'

But I'd already let go of the indicator. I crawled on my hands and knees, searching the room for Ann, as her tinkling laugh filled the room.

'Oh, Elizabeth, you are hilarious!' Ann's voice.

In the corner of the room, Ann's laughing head and shoulders appeared against the wallpaper, followed by the rest of her – all of her. She didn't look solid like Zachary, but she was the closest thing to human I'd ever seen another Glimpse become.

Terrified, I leapt to my feet. 'Go away!' I wished my words were solid so I could throw them at her. 'You're not meant to be here.'

'Oh, but I thought you wanted to talk.' Ann's gaze darted to the Ouija board. 'It would have been rude to ignore you.' She smiled, rosebud lips stretching over her creepily small teeth.

I spun and grabbed the nearest thing that came to hand – one of the black candles – and ran forwards. Susie dived out of the way as I charged right over the Ouija board. I barely registered it crack in two beneath my feet.

'Liz! What . . . ? Liz!' Susie gasped.

I threw the candle at Ann; it sailed right through her small-boned chest and thunked against the wall behind her. 'Go away!'

I heard Susie shriek.

'Leave me alone,' I said, 'I'm nothing to do with you!'

Ann's fake-sweet smile vanished. 'Now, that wasn't very nice.' She took a step towards me. 'This is your final chance,

216

Elizabeth.' She took another step, her brown dress moving stiffly around her ankles. 'Keep speaking with Zachary, keep searching for that girlfriend of his, and this—' she gestured up and down my body '—will be over.'

It took all my self-control to remain still. 'You can't hurt me,' I hissed. 'I'm not scared of you.'

Ann flashed me a brutal smile. Then she jerked her arm up to hit me, her hand flying towards my face. I flinched away, my eyes closed against the anticipated slap. It didn't hurt – it felt like a feathery tickle – but the violence of it made it seem like it should. When I opened my eyes, Ann was gone.

I gasped, as if I'd just been rescued from drowning, and staggered back.

'Oh my God, Liz.' Susie's voice shook from somewhere below me.

I looked down at her. Susie was jammed against the side of the bed, her face paler than I'd ever seen, her eyes huge. Splinters of the Ouija board, doused in spilled hot chocolate, covered the carpet at her feet.

'I'm so sorry,' I said, as I stooped to pick up the mess.

Susie caught my wrist. 'Liz.' Her voice was firmer. 'What just happened?'

I stared at her. Suddenly, I imagined what she'd just seen: me, shouting at thin air, hurling candles at the wall. I sat back and put my hands to my face. I was damp with sweat. I must have appeared insane.

'Liz!'

'I'm sorry.' It was all I could think to say. My voice shuddered. 'I am so, so sorry.'

My only friend; the only person, other than Dad and Zachary, I'd become close to in seven years. And I'd ruined it.

I scrabbled to my feet, grabbed at my bag. I had to get out before I made things even worse. 'I'm sorry,' I said again, then flew out of her room and down the stairs.

Chapter Thirty-One

I stumbled, half running, back to the inn. I hated myself for acting so crazy in front of Susie; I hated myself for running away and not trying to explain. It was too late now. No doubt I'd destroyed every spark of friendship she felt for me. She was probably already on the phone to Matt, telling him how mental I was.

I'd been so stupid. There was no way doing an Ouija board in the presence of my friend could ever have turned out well.

I wiped my eyes on my dress sleeve as I entered the driveway. I couldn't let Dad see me like this. It occurred to me that Ann might be waiting to attack me again, but even that fear paled in comparison to ruining things with my only friend. And when I crept indoors, all that met me was the comforting sound of Dad's piano-playing. I raced up the stairs to my room and flung myself onto my bed.

I curled onto my side and stared at the wall. My Normality List caught my eye.

'Get friends'.

I had to call Susie. I needed to make this right.

Sitting up, I upended my satchel, letting everything drop

out onto the duvet. I picked my phone out of the pile and scrolled through the address book. My finger hovered over Susie's name.

But what would I say? I couldn't just tell her about the Glimspes. And I wasn't about to beg her to act as if nothing had happened – that would only make things worse. I turned my phone off and let my hand fall into my lap. I might as well face it. 'Get friends' was doomed.

And so was I, if I were to believe Ann's threats. A black fog of unease thickened around me. Ann couldn't hurt me – her slap had been as insubstantial as a gust of air – but now Bess was gone, she'd clearly picked me as her latest object of jealousy.

It was so painfully ironic. As if I had any more chance with Zachary than she did! I'd heard of some weird relationships, but having a ghost as a boyfriend? Impossible.

I started to scoop my school things back into my satchel, then paused over my notepad. Beneath it lay a white-grey object, about the size of my thumb.

I knew instantly what it was, but I had to turn it over and over, examining the smooth exterior and the honeycombed inside, before I could believe what it was.

A piece of bone. Someone must have put it in my bag.

An hour after I heard Dad go to bed, I pulled on my coat and shoes, and tiptoed downstairs into the cool night.

'Elizabeth.' I heard Zachary's voice before I saw him. His steady footsteps crunched across the gravel towards me. The darkness took his shape at my side. 'What are you doing out here? Is something wrong?'

'We need to talk.' My voice was barely a whisper. 'Away from the inn, so no one hears.'

There was a solemn pause, then the darkness nodded. 'Follow me.'

He grabbed my hand, feeling stronger and more solid than ever, making my heart jolt. Before I could register what was happening, we were speeding off in the direction of the woods, as if we were being chased. Leaves crunched, damp grass swished, but all that existed was Zachary's hand in mine. I clutched his hand harder than I needed to. Dead or not, Zachary was my only real friend right now, and I needed him tonight.

The trees looked like holes cut in the dark fabric of night. Zachary slowed and moved to my side, guiding me in-between the trunks. It was like navigating an obstacle course. Twigs pulled my hair over my face, roots tangled round my ankles, making me stumble.

After a minute, Zachary stopped. 'This is far enough. Tell me what's the matter.' His voice was low and full of concern.

He let go of me. I put my hand in my coat pocket, trying to remember the feel of his fingers, smooth and warm in leather gloves, as long as possible. I needed the comfort.

'It's Ann,' I said.

He swore.

'She's been threatening me. Telling me to stay away from you and to stop looking for Bess. She said you were hers.'

'Damn her to hell.' Zachary swung out at the air, grunting with frustration. 'The girl's relentless. Plaguing Bess was evil enough, but you – what does she think you and I are going to do together?'

His question was so angrily rhetorical, that I couldn't help but flinch, though I knew he was right. I pushed my fists hard into my coat, hoping he couldn't see my face.

'How did she threaten you?'

'She . . . Look I know it sounds dramatic, but she pretty much threatened to kill me.'

'She is insane. You're certain she cannot touch you?'

'She tried to slap me. I felt it, but it didn't hurt.'

His hand rested on my shoulder, reassuringly solid and strong. His eyes glittered in the darkness, intent on me. 'I'm to blame. If I could force her to stop, then I would, but God knows how hard I tried when she plagued Bess. If you feel it's necessary to stop meeting me, I will understand.'

I hesitated. That was the last thing I wanted. 'But we still need to find Bess.'

'I have not forgotten. But if anyone knows the value of life, it's me, and I refuse to destroy yours.'

'No one's destroying my life.' I made my voice light. 'Least of all you. And Ann's not going to either. The worst she can do is scare me.'

He nodded, and lifted his hand from my shoulder. But he didn't step back.

'I have something else to tell you.' I paused. 'Zachary, Ann didn't threaten me here – it was across the village, in my friend Susie's bedroom. That's the third place in Hulbourn I've seen her. It's obvious that she's found a way to be more free in her movements than you can be. And I think I know her secret.' I fished in my coat pocket for the piece of pale grey bone, and held it up for Zachary to see.

He said nothing. His fingertips grazed mine as he tried, and failed, to touch it. 'Is that a bone?'

I nodded. 'I found it in my school bag, which I had with me at my friend's place today. I think it's how Ann managed to follow me there. The other place I saw her was at Meg's house,

222

the old lady psychic I told you about, and she has a bowl full of bones just like this in her living room.'

I waited for Zachary to say something. He remained silent. I continued. 'I think Ann's going where her bones are,' I said, hushing my voice though we were in the woods. 'That's the only reason I can think for why she's not confined to the graveyard. One of the bones at Meg's must be hers. There must be one at the inn. And this,' I said, twisting the cold bone I was holding up, 'must belong to Ann, too.'

I waited for his reaction. I could hear his breathing, steady but deep. Leaves rustled under my feet as I shifted from foot to foot.

It all made sense. And it fitted what Meg had told me – *Spirits can no more escape their bodies than you and I can escape gravity.*

The question of who had put Ann's bone into my satchel in the first place was another issue. Meg was the obvious answer. Scott was my other suspect. He had grabbed my bag that morning, and his warnings were unnervingly parallel with Ann's, but the thought of him being able to see Ann – and choosing to help her – was too wild, and too awful.

Zachary studied the bone, turning my fingers gently this way and that to see it from different angles. 'You believe this is Ann's?'

'Yes,' I said. 'I do. What do you think?'

'I believe it's very possible.' His voice held an undercurrent of excitement now. 'And horrific though that is, if it's true, the implications—'

'It means you could travel beyond the inn too.' I smiled. 'You could come with me to look for Bess.'

Zachary made a muffled noise. 'Elizabeth, I knew it. I

knew the moment I laid eyes on you that you would change everything.' He laughed. 'My prayers are being answered. I'll finally leave here. We'll find her. Together.' He grew sober. 'And if my brother remains in this world, I'll find him too. When shall we go?'

'The weekend? I have school for the next couple of days.' My stomach churned at the thought of facing Susie tomorrow. 'But that'll give you time to decide where you want to go first.'

'And to find one of my bones.' His voice grew even more serious. 'That will not be so easy. And it is something I cannot do.'

I tried to imagine myself going to the crossroads one night with a spade to unearth Zachary's skeleton. I tried to imagine holding his remains in my hand. It was too like a scene from a horror film to even seem a possibility, but there was no question; I would do it – I had to.

'I can handle it,' I said.

'Thank you.' He was quiet. 'I cannot express how much I loathe being so useless. I despise the fact you have to do so much for me. If I were alive, you wouldn't have to do so much as open a door when I was around.'

I smiled. 'That's okay. I like opening doors for myself.'

He tilted his head to the side. 'Bess would have liked you. You have so many traits in common.'

My smile grew a little sadder. 'She will like me,' I said. 'Because we're going to find her.'

'Indeed we are.'

There was a long pause. Then Zachary held out his hand. 'I rather think I'm ruining your sleep patterns.'

I grasped his gloved fingers, though I no longer needed to, my eyes had adjusted to the darkness. We headed back through

GLIMPSE

the woods together, stopping just before stepping out of the trees. The outline of the inn sprawled, squat and dark as a giant toad, beyond the stretch of grass.

I took Ann's bone out of my pocket, and threw it as hard as I could into the woods we'd just come from. I heard it plink against a branch, and a rustle as it dropped into the overgrowth.

'Do you know how it came to be in your bag?' Zachary asked, as though thinking of it for the first time.

I shifted and looked through the trees in the direction of the outbuildings. 'That, I'm not sure about.'

'You must be careful. Promise me.'

'I'm always careful.' I drew my coat tighter around me. 'So, shall I meet you here tomorrow night? I'll bring a spade, you bring the moonlight.' I tried to keep my voice bright.

He shook his head as though with wry laughter. 'I can barely wait. Goodnight, Elizabeth.'

He held my gaze for a long, smiling moment, then melted into the darkness of the woods and was gone.

Chapter Thirty-Two

I walked to the bus stop the next morning determined not to lose my first real friend in seven years; determined not to be known as 'Loony Liz' again.

I had come to the conclusion that, though it was stupid of me to do the Ouija board in front of Susie, it was even stupider to run away. I was ashamed. I was stronger than that now: if I had the courage to attack Glimpses, to help ghost boys, to have feelings for ghost boys, I had the guts to be myself with my only friend.

The crowd at the bus stop was still small (I'd left the inn early) and I saw Susie and Matt immediately. From a distance they looked like one mass. As I walked closer, the mass divided into two parts, like an amoeba, and Susie walked to meet me.

'Hey,' I called.

'Hey.' She stopped in front of me, her eyebrows slightly drawn.

'Susie, I'm—'

'If you say sorry one more time,' she interrupted, her voice stern, 'I'm going to force-feed you beetroot cake.'

226

That disarmed me. 'I am sorry though. For running off like that. It was totally crazy. I owe you an explanation.'

She glanced behind her, and said, 'Come on, let's walk a bit.' When we were a safe distance from prying ears, she said, 'Liz, what the hell was that in my room yesterday?'

I wasn't sure if she meant my behaviour or Ann. I pressed my lips together. Here goes. 'Would you believe me if I said it was a ghost?'

Susie stopped walking and stared at me. 'Well, yeah I'd believe you.' She sounded annoyed. 'The whole point was to summon a ghost.'

I exhaled with a relief so strong it was painful.

'So you can see them?'

I nodded.

'Was yesterday the first time?'

I thought for a moment. And made a choice. 'No,' I confessed. 'I've been able to see ghosts for as long as I can remember.'

'Why did you run off?'

'I guess I assumed you'd think I was crazy. I mean, my reaction and stuff . . . It doesn't usually make people want me around.' I looked at her. 'You really believe me then?'

'Liz, this is me we're talking about. I might not be able to see ghosts, but I've believed in them – just known they were real – for ever.' She hooked her arm with mine, grinned, and tugged me towards the bus stop. 'I have a lot of questions to ask you.'

The rest of Thursday passed in a daze. At school, Scott gave me evils when we passed in the corridor, but he kept his distance.

Susie alternated between excitement and awed delight, but

mercifully she said nothing when Matt or anyone else was in earshot. She now knew every one of my secrets, apart from Zachary – the Glimpses, my amnesia, my dead mother. And she still wanted to be my friend. I couldn't believe it. And I couldn't think about anything else.

So it came as a bit of a jolt when, on the way home, I remembered what I had to do later that night.

Dig up Zachary's grave.

That evening, I had English homework, but I couldn't settle to it. Instead, I sat on the sofa next to Dad, twisting my hair around my fingers and not paying any attention to what was happening on TV. After a while Dad went to the dining room to play his piano, and I started to formulate a plan.

I found a torch under the sink, and some fresh batteries in one of the kitchen drawers. I snuck outside and, without getting close enough to the outbuildings for Crowley or Scott to see me, checked their garden tools were still piled up against the outside wall.

Then I made myself a Thermos of coffee – I was already feeling blurry at the prospect of another late night – and went upstairs. I picked out my most suitable outfit for grave-digging – my baggiest pair of jeans, the trainers I'd worn for PE at secondary school and a ratty black wool sweater riddled with so many holes I'd long stopped wearing it.

I looked at myself in the mirror. I felt like a child preparing for a really macabre game of make-believe.

I looked at the Normality List and snorted. 'No more Glimpses'. What a joke that had turned out to be. If I'd known a few weeks ago even half the things I would be doing in my new home – visiting graveyards, Ouija boards, tying my heart in knots over a dead boy – I wouldn't have needed Derek to call me loony; I'd have done it for him.

I sat on my bed sipping coffee in the dusk. I needed to be extra-sure tonight that Dad wouldn't know I was gone. There could be no good explanation for being caught knee-deep in a hole at the crossroads in the middle of the night.

When my bedside clock read 1 a.m., I tucked my heart locket under my jumper, put my phone in my pocket, picked up my torch and my trainers, and snuck downstairs and into the darkness.

The moon was brighter tonight, the sky less cloudy, but the temperature had dropped. My breath misted in front of me as I scanned the line of trees for Zachary.

An arm lifted from the shadows in greeting. I smiled, despite the ball of nerves in my stomach, and waved back. But I didn't go straight over, and I didn't turn on my torch. Instead I crept towards the outbuildings to grab a spade. The second it was in my hand, I ran across the grass towards him.

He turned to watch me, his arms poised by his sides. 'Elizabeth.' His voice was low, with an undercurrent of energy that matched my own nervous excitement. 'Are you certain you wish to do this?'

'I am.'

He nodded, and took my hand like it had become the most natural thing in the world. It kind of had – his touch had become more solid to me every time we met, and was now almost as solid as a living person's. I held tight, and we raced into the woods. As soon as the inn was behind us, I flicked on the torch. Small creatures scuttled out of the torch's beam, ivy tugged at my trainers as we crashed through it, but the rest of the world felt deadly silent, frozen stiff in the night air.

The field on the other side was awash in moonlight. Furrows

in the soil striped the bare earth with shadow. Compared to the time I'd been here with Zachary in daylight, it felt eerie and exposed, a parallel universe where nothing could be trusted. We kept close to the deeper shadows by the line of trees like night creatures, as we headed towards the road.

I stole sideways glances at Zachary. Moonlight was his natural setting, and he looked so vibrant and alive tonight that it was hard to get my head around what I was about to do.

I wondered how I would feel when I held a piece of his real, human body in my fingers. I was painfully aware of the way I'd started to feel around him – the fluttering in my stomach, the electricity of his touch. I wondered if I'd still feel like that after tonight, after his other-ness was driven home.

A big part of me hoped so. I'd never felt this way before. And I liked it. It made me want things that were nothing to do with my messed-up past. It made me look forward to my days and nights in a way I never had before. And it felt so natural, so normal.

Which, of course, was just typical of me. Nothing about this was the slightest bit normal. Feeling anything for Zachary could only end in misery. Even if he wasn't a ghost, he was in love with someone else: that was the kind of line you couldn't cross.

Zachary ran to the hedge that marked the boundary between the field and the road. I watched him run, caught myself, cursed my idiocy.

Seriously. I should have been feeling something appropriate to a horror film, not to a drama about doomed, unrequited love.

I shoved through the gap in the hedge. When I emerged onto the road, I didn't look at Zachary, I just marched to the crossroads, my torchlight skittering over potholed concrete and long grass ahead.

'Where do I dig?'

Zachary jogged to a spot on the verge at the corner of the crossroads. I shone the torchlight on him. His jaw was tight.

'Here.' He pointed to his feet.

I nodded, and a tsunami of adrenaline crashed in on me. I propped the torch on a rock so it pointed at the grass at his feet. I shuddered, only partly with cold.

'Tell me if any cars come,' I said.

I checked around me one last time, then took a deep breath and stabbed at the earth with the spade. The hardness of the soil vibrated up through my hands, jarring my shoulders. The spade only went a couple of inches below the grass.

I groaned. I'd guessed this was going to be hard work, but I hadn't let myself consider how hard; it's not like there was any other way to do this.

'Lend me your muscles, Zachary.' I stabbed again at the ground, heaving up a lump of grass.

'I'd be doing this myself, if I could.'

'Just tell me you're not buried six feet under.'

'With that, luck is on your side.' He paced at the edge of the torchlight, his gaze on the road. 'And I am no longer in one piece. I was interred without a coffin. The soil has been disturbed by farm vehicles multiple times. If luck remains with us, there should be a piece of . . . of . . . a piece near the surface. I feel it.'

'What does it feel like?' I heaved up a chunk of earth and rocks and tossed it aside. I was sweating already, despite the chill.

'There's no easy way to explain. I can only liken it to being near a fire. I can feel the hottest parts and the cooler areas and where there's no heat at all. Yet it isn't heat. It resembles no feeling I knew when I was alive.'

He paused to watch me. 'Place your foot on the spade as you push it into the earth, then pull back on the handle to break it up.' He stood behind me, watching me dig, so close he could have reached around me and taken the spade handle. He obviously wanted to.

I was hyper-conscious of his proximity. I wanted to lean back into him. It would have been so nice to rest my back against his chest, or lean my head onto his shoulder. I was scared I might actually do it, the way you do things in dreams you'd never dare to in real life, so I held my body rigid as I dug, aware of my every movement, careful not to touch him even accidentally. The space between us had its own force field.

Zachary sighed, his breath stirring the wisps of hair by my ear, sending shivers down my spine. 'I hate that I can't help you.'

He moved away and crouched by the growing pile of soil at the edge of the torchlight. I inhaled deeply, finally able to breathe again. Zachary examined the pebbles and bits of broken pottery I dug up with the earth, but I was sure I felt his eyes on me just as much. My face burned like his gaze was hot. I hoped he'd think it was just from exertion.

I spotted something white and angular among the soil and rocks, and pulled it free. 'Look. Is it yours?'

Zachary leaned closer, eyes alert, but shook his head. 'I don't feel anything from it. Many criminals were buried here. We're near farmland, there might be animal bones too.'

I nodded, and returned to digging. I tried to put all my

focus into my hands on the spade handle, my feet sliding in the crumbling soil.

The night fell silent. The only sounds were the pant of my breath, the crunch of the spade in the stony soil and the occasional hoot or bark of a night animal. The hole grew, inch by slow inch. My face and hands felt both cold and too hot. Sweat stuck my plait to the back of my neck.

A couple of times, Zachary saw car lights in the distance, and I raced to turn off the torch and crouch in the bushes. Both times were false alarms – no cars passed us by, and I returned to digging.

Then . . .

'There,' Zachary half-shouted.

I dropped the spade. I followed where he pointed and grabbed the shard sticking out of the soil. I wiped the dirt off it. It wasn't a whole bone, but it was certainly bone. 'Is this yours?' I asked.

He brought his hand close to mine. 'It's mine,' he said.

Chapter Thirty-Three

I scraped the bulk of the soil back into the hole, after pocketing the bone. It was small, but it was a burning weight. I picked up the torch and turned away from the crossroads. Neither of us spoke until we made it back through the hedge.

'Are you all right?' Zachary asked when we got into the field, his voice low with concern.

I nodded, and flashed him a small smile. 'I'm fine. I should be asking you if you're okay. You're the one who just saw your . . .' I hesitated over the word 'grave'.

He shrugged. 'I've had enough years to get used to the idea of having a body that isn't this one.' He glanced down at himself.

He smiled at me in the moonlight.

The torchlight bounced through the furrows in the soil ahead of us.

After a minute, he said, 'I'd like to speak with you again about your mother.'

I looked up at him, surprised by the twist in the conversation.

He kicked at the clods of earth as he walked, though no soil sprayed from his feet like it did from mine. 'That was the deal we made,' he said, responding to my surprise. 'You help me, and I tell you what I know. I don't like being so in your debt.'

I pulled my locket from my sweater and held it, though my fingers were caked with grime. I wasn't prepared for this right now, but there was no way I'd say no. 'Okay,' I said.

'First, a question.' I felt his eyes on me. 'You said before that you have no memory of your mother. Why is that?'

I glanced up at the starry sky. 'I was in a car accident when I was ten, on the road outside the inn. A deer ran out in front of our car, and Dad swerved into a tree. My mum died. I sustained a trauma to my head, lost my memory and started to see things other people couldn't.'

'Elizabeth, I remember the accident.'

I stopped walking. Zachary kept going for a second, then stopped when he realized I had. He looked back at me.

'You remember?'

He walked back towards me. 'Yes. I came to the inn, and it was in chaos.' His eyes held mine, watching the effect his words were having on me. 'The innkeeper and the staff were in shock and deep in mourning. Their emotions struck me, because they reflected mine – I had already lost Bess.'

His lips formed a thin, sympathetic line. 'I deeply regret that you lost your mother, Elizabeth. Yet I am very glad you survived. I didn't know, at the time, if you had. I simply knew that the girl I had seen at the inn never returned.'

I nodded. 'Everyone tells me I'm nothing like how I was as a child. Do you think that's true?'

He tilted his head to one side. 'When I was seventeen, I'd been working the roads for a year and I'd killed my own brother. I was far removed from my childhood self too. You've lived through great trauma. You cannot escape its effects.'

I let the spade slip through my hand, and stabbed it into the hard soil by my foot. 'I wish I could.'

'No,' he said with a smile, 'you do not.' He took my elbow, and we started walking again towards the dark trees. He let go of me after a few paces.

'My life was a disaster,' he said, 'yet, Philip aside, I wouldn't change a moment of it, because it brought me to the Highwayman Inn and to Bess. The years since Bess disappeared have been the most trying of my existence, alive or dead. I didn't think any experience could be worse than losing Philip, but when Philip died, I at least had the small comfort of believing I would join him in death soon. When Bess went, I knew I was facing – perhaps am facing – an eternity without her. I wished many times my existence would end, but it didn't. And now I've met you, and the possibilities in the future are blinding.'

I glanced up at him. His face shone with the moonlight and a vibrancy that was purely Zachary.

'I believe it will be the same for you. You may not feel now that there's a purpose to what you've been through, but somewhere along the road, you'll reach a place you couldn't have travelled to by any other route, and you'll be grateful for it.'

'I hope so.'

'You don't need to hope. Because it will happen.'

I looked at my feet as they moved across the soil, and allowed myself a moment to feel the slow hope that ran in my veins like honey. Maybe he was right. I'd wished many times I could scrub out the last seven years from my life, but if I had, I'd never have met Susie, I'd never be forming the bond I was starting to with Dad. And I'd never have met Zachary.

Zachary who was perfect, who I could be my weird self with. Zachary who, for now, was all mine.

We continued through the woods in silence, Zachary staying by my side to take my hand when I had to pick my way through exposed roots or over a fallen branch. It wasn't necessary – I was getting just as good at clambering around at night as him – but he had a good excuse for being old-fashioned, and I wasn't going to turn down an opportunity to take his hand.

We stopped when the black outline of the inn loomed beyond the trees. I turned off the torch, and stifled a yawn. The caffeine was wearing off.

'Meet me here on Saturday morning?' I asked.

He nodded. Then he grinned, like he'd remembered all over again that a miracle was about to happen; that he was finally going to leave the inn.

'I can scarcely wait,' he said. He lifted my hand and kissed it, then he dipped his head to me and drew back into the darkness of the trees.

I turned to face the inn before he could see my silly grin. I headed across the grass towards the outbuildings, swinging the spade by my side as if it weighed nothing, as if I'd used it to make sandcastles, not dig up human bones.

I was so dreamily elated when I put the spade back on the pile of tools next to the door of the outbuildings, I barely winced at the scraping sound it made. When I stood up, I was just in time to see the net curtain at the window twitch.

I froze. I stared at the window. The curtain stayed still, but I hadn't imagined the movement. I pictured Crowley or Scott, watching me. Goosebumps prickled my skin. I stepped backwards, breath shallow, senses on red alert. I had to get inside the inn.

Before I could move, an angry growl vibrated through the air. I turned towards the inn. Ann hurtled towards me, a blur of textile and white teeth.

I gasped, and bolted – away from the inn, away from the outbuildings, back over the grass, sending chaotic bursts of torchlight towards the woods.

'Why do you never listen?' Ann screeched.

Panic pumped my legs faster. Then, abruptly, my panic fractured – I could not let her do this to me. I stopped so fast I stumbled in the damp grass. I turned to face Ann, arms raised to fend off her attack.

I had less than a second to take her in – the violence on her face, her ringlets flying out behind her head like Medusa's snakes – before I realized she wasn't going to stop. I flinched, bracing myself for the impact, forcing myself to stand firm.

It was like being hit full on by a solid block of wind. I dropped the torch. There was an overwhelming stench in my nostrils: mildewed fabric and mould. Then Ann snarled with anger – from behind me. I opened my eyes to see only the dark inn.

I spun to face her. Her eyes were hidden in malevolent shadows, her mouth a full display of tiny white bones.

'I told you to stay away from him.' She lunged for my coat pocket, as if she knew Zachary's bone was inside, tearing futilely at the fabric. I flinched away, though her touches were nothing but angry air. The darkness blurred with cold hair and corpse-white skin; Ann surrounded me like a whirlwind.

'You think you're so clever, don't you?' she demanded.

'Get off me.' My voice was strong. I twisted towards the

inn, trying to get away from her grip. 'Leave me alone. I'm nothing to do with you.'

But Ann didn't stop, and my nightmare slammed into my mind – an image of my mother tearing at me the same way Ann was. The strength I'd been holding together dissolved. I twisted faster, trying to get Ann behind me, away from me, but it was like trying to escape the wind.

I picked up the torch, shone it in her face, illuminating ice-blue eyes and thin lips.

'Leave me alone!' I said. I couldn't take this any more. Standing up to Ann was one thing, torturing myself was another. I ran, shaking my arms as if Ann was a wasp I could bat away.

I barely registered Zachary flying out of the woods before he was on Ann – a flash of his grim face, a blur of lithe body, then he and Ann were a tangle of limbs and brown fabric on the ground.

I stifled a yelp, skittering away from them. They only struggled for a moment before Ann leapt to her feet, lunging towards me. Zachary caught the bottom of her long dress, and she got no more than a step in my direction. In a second, Zachary was standing behind her, holding her wrists expertly behind her back. It was disturbing how easily he held her – a testament to his fighting abilities, not to her lack of strength. Ann was small, but agile and vicious as a terrier.

'You should never have come back,' she snarled at me.

'Stop it, Ann.' Zachary's voice was tired, like he'd said the same words a thousand times before. His eyes met mine over Ann's shoulder. 'This is what she was like with Bess, for over two hundred years.'

'I can hear you, you know.' Ann strained against Zachary's

grip. His face turned stony with the effort of holding her still. 'Let me go,' she snapped. 'I'll leave your girl be.'

My face flared, but Zachary didn't act like he'd registered the words. *Your girl.*

'If you attack her again—' he began.

'Let her go, Zachary,' I interrupted. 'She can't do anything to me.'

He gave me a surprised look, but he did as I said. Ann yanked her arms free, shooting an affronted look at Zachary. She stalked towards me. I forced myself forwards to meet her.

'You've ignored me too many times,' she said.

'No.' I made my voice sharp as hers. 'You've ignored me too many times. Give it up, Ann, and leave me alone.'

She stared at me for a long moment. I held her hard gaze. I could smell the mouldy fabric of her dress, cold and damp as rotting weeds.

Then Ann drew back, the left side of her mouth quirking up in a humourless smile. 'I'll see you again, Elizabeth,' she said, then she brushed past me and stalked away.

My heart pounded. My legs felt like all my bones had dissolved.

Zachary's face was pale and troubled. He looked like he wanted to talk to me, but instead he strode past me, following Ann, dipping his head to me. 'I'll make sure she doesn't come back.' He hesitated, holding my eyes for half a second, then broke into a run.

By the time I turned around, both of them were gone.

I stood for a minute in stunned silence. The night folded in around me. I turned and headed for the inn.

Too late, I remembered the twitching of the curtain. I looked over at the outbuildings . . . and froze.

The curtain wasn't just twitching this time. It was wide open. And framed in the window was Scott's pale face, staring straight at me.

Chapter Thirty-Four

In my nightmare, my mother tears at me, snarling, 'Get out, get out, get out!'

Ann leans in beside her. She shoves at my body with her delicate hands. She can't touch me. But I don't understand why she wants to.

I don't understand why either of them hates me so.

I'm sobbing, but I can't move. I'm terrified, but I can't make them stop.

I woke, my mind fuzzy, my body weak and sore as if I'd been through a spin cycle. I glanced at the clock and groaned – it was almost time for school. I'd only had a few hours' sleep.

I rolled over and grabbed my locket, too tired to open it to look at my mother's picture. I pressed the gold surface to my nightdress, over my heart.

I wanted nothing more than to stay in bed. I didn't want to think about Scott or Ann.

It bothered me that Scott had seen me last night. Either he'd seen me attacking thin air and talking to myself, or he could see Zachary and Ann – which by now, seemed pretty certain – and knew I'd ignored his threats. Both scenarios were unbearable.

I forced myself out of bed. I had to go to school. If Scott decided today was the day to blab to everyone that 'Liz sees things that aren't there', I was better off on the front line. I had no intentions of talking to the boy, but it made sense to keep him in my sights.

School also had the advantage of being one place I had never yet seen Ann. After her craziness last night, that was a big advantage.

I dragged myself to the shower to wash the soil from under my fingernails. Then I put on the first thing that came to hand, a long vintage dress with pink and blue paisley patterns – feeling comfortable today seemed more important than squeezing myself into skinny jeans.

I gave myself a pep talk in the mirror as I plaited my hair. Neither Ann nor Scott could hurt me at school. Tomorrow, I would have Zachary all to myself. We'd go where Ann couldn't, we'd look for Bess, and I'd get him to tell me the rest of what he knew about Mum.

I pulled my lips up in the mirror – my smile wasn't very convincing, but it would have to do – and went downstairs to Dad.

Chapter Thirty-Five

'What time's your interview again?'

I sat at the kitchen table on Saturday morning, sipping tea and watching Dad jitter around the room as if he was going on a first date. I was excited too, for different reasons. Today was the day I got to spend with Zachary, far from Ann and Scott. Luckily, Dad was too distracted to notice my distraction.

'Eleven. The taxi's picking me up any minute now. Are you sure what I'm wearing is all right?' Dad spread his arms and looked down at his outfit: pinstriped jeans, the 'Ripe Banana Studios' T-shirt I recognized from photos – now slightly too tight, but passable – and a grey blazer.

'You look great. Very hip.'

'Thanks, Liz.' He looked at his reflection in the microwave door and swiped at his hair, which he'd finally had cut into something more surf-dude than shaggy. He exhaled. 'You'll be all right while I'm gone?'

I nodded, and took another sip of tea. 'I'm meeting a friend in the village, so I might not be here when you get back. But I'll have your phone.'

Dad nodded and rushed from the room, muttering something about his wallet. A moment later, there was a knock on the door.

'Bye!' I called. 'Good luck!'

The door banged shut behind him. I waited five minutes to be sure the taxi was gone, then went upstairs to get my satchel. I wrapped Zachary's bone in a scarf, put it in my bag, took a deep breath and headed into the sunlight.

Today, we might find Bess. Today could be the day when everything changed.

When I stepped out of the inn's front door, my eyes darted first to the outbuildings – Scott's car was mercifully absent – then to the line of trees.

Zachary stepped out of the trunks and started to walk over to me. It only took one glance at him to make locking the front door become a complicated business. I'd never seen him in full daylight before, and it was . . . distracting.

Door successfully locked, I dropped my keys into my satchel and faced him as he walked across the grass towards me. It was like seeing the moon in the middle of the day.

I couldn't imagine how I'd ever thought he was alive. I wouldn't have, if I'd seen him in daylight. His colours were too coldly beautiful, bright and muted at the same time, like it wasn't the sun shining on him but the moon, enhanced.

I walked to meet him, and he fell into step with me. The knowledge that we were really about to leave the inn – together – made my heart leap. It was like I was walking with him for the first time.

I glanced sideways at him. 'Are you nervous?'

'Not nervous,' he said. 'Terrified.' But he grinned, like being scared was the greatest thing in the world. 'Let's do this.'

He held out his hand, and I took it. We raced the final metres to the end of the driveway. Zachary took a deep breath, like he was about to plunge into deep water. He exhaled it in a loud whoop! as we ran from the gravel onto the pavement by the road.

'It worked!' I said.

'Damn, yes, it worked.' Without slowing down, he scooped me up and spun me around three hundred and sixty degrees.

I shrieked with delight. Though my feet barely left the concrete, and I had to do some of the spinning myself, it was amazing that he could swing me at all. I stumbled back into a run, still holding on to his hand. His enthusiasm was infectious; I wanted to run and dance and shout.

But a car coming down the road towards us made me pull my hand from his. I didn't want to be seen shrieking and holding hands with thin air, like a bad mime artist. I slowed to a walk, the last of my laughter bubbling out of me, though I kept my smile.

'So where are we going?'

'Dalsham, if you have no objections to a walk. It's a few villages distant from here.'

I hadn't expected him to want to go so far. 'I could check the bus timetable,' I said, uncertain.

He looked pointedly at my satchel, indicating the bone within it. 'I don't know if even carrying that with you would allow me to enter a vehicle.'

'Then let's walk.' I shrugged.

Using a combination of Zachary's memory, road signs and the maps app on Dad's phone, we made our way out of the village, taking narrow roads that – to me, at least – looked exactly the same as the one Zachary had existed next to for centuries.

But it was obviously new enough to Zachary. When the initial excitement wore off, he fell quiet, gazing around him in wonder, head thrown back to take everything in. After a little while, public footpath signs directed us across the fields. I smiled to myself as the wonder played on his face.

Over the last couple of days, I'd pictured all the new things I'd show him – the shops in Hulbourn centre, the village war memorial, the sculpture of the highwayman at my school. I'd imagined being his tour guide, showing him the wonders of the modern world.

But somehow, this felt better. Zachary belonged in the countryside, as much as he belonged in the night. The further we walked, the more he relaxed, his smile losing its hard angles. He even took off his gloves, and rolled his sweater up to his elbows. His forearms were contoured with muscle, crossed with small scars like the one on his jaw, betraying the dangerous way he'd made a living. I found myself wondering what other hidden scars he had, and had to mentally slap myself.

'So what's it like?' I asked.

'Like being in a rainbow after centuries of monochrome. Those blackberries—' he gestured at the bushes we were passing '—bring to mind picking berries with Bess for her parents to ferment into wine. Those trees over there—' he pointed across the field '—you see the shape of them, like the canopy is formed of clouds? They remind me of the woodland I lay low in for a week when thief takers were searching for me. It was the coldest, most miserable seven days of my life. And that—' he pointed at a dirty white T-shirt strewn in a hedge '—makes me recall bathing in streams.'

I kicked my way through the long grass. 'It must be so strange to remember things like that after all this time.'

'It is overwhelming. Like dredging up parts of myself I'd forgotten were there. I've scarcely thought of half of these memories in centuries, yet here they are, in my skull.' He stretched his arms up to the sun as though easing a centuries-old tension from his muscles. 'You cannot know the gift you've given me.' He looked at me. 'Or maybe you can.' He sighed. 'We will find your trigger, Elizabeth. There must be something that will make you remember. If I can recall so much after over two hundred years, so can you.'

'I know.' I smiled, more at the kindness behind his words than because I believed them any more.

'What can I tell you that I haven't already,' he mused to himself. He bent to sweep his hands through the long grass, not seeming to care that he made no impression on the stalks.

I looked down at the ground, watching my feet move, as Zachary launched into a series of anecdotes about my mother. He talked about when she'd lived at the Highwayman with the innkeeper – my granddad – when she was young, about when she returned to the inn with first my father, and then me. He told me how Bess had taken an interest in my mother, since both she and Bess were innkeeper's daughters; he said that when we found Bess, she'd be able to tell me so much more.

I smiled when he said that, because I was meant to. But the hope it gave me was heavy as a wet rag; hardly hope at all.

I'd been so determined, when I came to Hulbourn, to remember my mother and my life before the accident. But nothing I'd tried had worked. It wasn't that I was ready to give up – I didn't know if I'd ever give up – but maybe it was time to give my hope-muscle a rest.

I played absently with my locket and checked the map on my phone. 'Almost there. We should hit the road again in a minute, then we'll be at Dalsham. Are you ready?'

'I've been prepared for two hundred years,' he said, but the relaxed tone had gone from his voice. He rolled his sleeves back down and pulled on his gloves.

We left the fields, and stepped onto the road that led into Dalsham. The road was narrow, like all the others we'd walked along, but unlike the others it was completely overhung with trees. After the open, sunny fields it was like stepping into a tunnel.

I shivered as we hit the cooler, darker air. What little light broke through the canopy dappled the concrete like ripples on water. I fell quiet, clamping my satchel to my side.

Zachary went quiet too. His pace slowed. Then, without warning, he stopped altogether.

I stopped too, alarmed. 'What is it?'

'This is the place.' His voice was low. 'I recognize it from my nightmares. This is where I killed Philip.'

Shivers prickled up my spine. I hadn't realized this journey was about Philip. I'd thought we were coming here to look for Bess. 'Are you sure?'

His mouth was a thin line. 'If a thousand years passed, I'd remember this place.'

He started walking again, more slowly than before, as if he didn't want to miss a single leaf on the trees around us, a single shadow between the trunks.

I followed him, my mouth dry. For the first time, I considered what would happen if Zachary didn't find what he was looking for, after all this build-up. My disappointment when I'd come to Hulbourn and not remembered my childhood had been the disappointment of only months of hoping; Zachary's would be the disappointment of centuries.

I monitored my skin for Glimpses as Zachary scrutinized the road. I didn't sense anything.

'Philip probably won't be here, you know,' I said, trying to prepare him.

'Good. I want him to be gone. It's tortured me for years, the idea that he could be stuck like me.' Zachary glanced at me, his face carved out of marble. 'Tell me if you sense anyone.'

I nodded, and turned my focus fully on my skin. I had goosebumps, but not from Glimpses. I couldn't help trying to imagine Zachary here, two and a quarter centuries ago, surrounded by four corpses.

'The soldiers took Philip's body this way.' He nodded further down the road. 'I hid in these trees—' he gestured to his right '—and watched them. The crossroads aren't far.'

He sped up. I followed. The crossroads came into view up ahead. The tree canopy had tried, but failed, to reach over all four roads, and the centre of the crossroads was lit up by a cross-shaped patch of light.

Zachary broke into a jog, as if he couldn't wait a moment more to get this over with. I picked up my pace to match his, but tingling skittered across my skin, making me stumble.

Oh no. My heart stuttered along with my feet. Please let me be imagining it.

I sprinted to catch up with Zachary. With every step, the tingling got worse. I opened my mouth to shout, to warn him. Philip or not, we were running towards a Glimpse.

But it was already too late. Zachary's steps faltered. A man-shaped Glimpse stepped from the trees up ahead.

Chapter Thirty-Six

Zachary jolted to a halt, as if his boots were fixed in the concrete. I caught up, looking first at him – his shoulders heaving – and then at the Glimpse.

Beyond the patch of light at the crossroads, the Glimpse-man wandered into the road, his pace bored and unhurried. He hadn't noticed us yet. His hair was the same as Zachary's – longer, but the same red gold, with the same gentle curl. His build was the same, slim yet strong. And when he turned his head towards us—

Zachary gasped and stopped breathing.

The Glimpse-man's face transformed from blank boredom to rigid attention. His mouth opened in a silent O as his eyes met Zachary's.

The universe narrowed to contain only them. I watched, an outsider, as Zachary's face went slack. Whatever was beating through his blood – happiness, distress – it had eclipsed his whole world.

Zachary took a step forwards, as if he was moving through treacle. The man mirrored him.

'Philip?'

The man's face crumpled. 'Zachary . . .?'

And then they lurched towards each other, running and stumbling. They collided in the patch of light, embracing violently, muffled shouts and cries and incoherent words.

It was too much to hold in. I yelped too, on the road on my own.

I pressed my fingers to my lips, holding in the tears that choked my throat. My vision blurred, and I blinked frantically to clear it. At the crossroads, the sun had got brighter, as if shining a spotlight on the brothers. I wanted to believe that it was; that two ghosts, who the natural world ignored, were, for a moment, the most important thing in it.

Philip and Zachary broke apart. It took all my self-will not to run towards them, to give them this moment alone. Philip's hand was on the back of Zachary's neck, keeping him close. They spoke in low, urgent voices, for a long time. Finally, Zachary looked at me, his eyes wide and shining wet. 'Elizabeth, come over here.'

I walked over to them, biting my lip with sudden nerves. Philip watched me with obvious fascination. I looked back with equal interest. I saw now that his eyes were the same green as Zachary's, though the whites were red with tears. His lips were thinner and framed with a rakish moustache that looked too old for his young face. His clothes were elaborate where Zachary's were simple – long boots, a red corduroy waistcoat, a long black velvet coat with huge lapels that framed his neck.

I had never felt like I was with a 200-year-old boy when I was with Zachary. But I could feel the weight of the years rolling off Philip.

'I'm so happy we found you,' I said. The words felt frivolous

– there were no words big enough for this moment – but I backed them up with a huge smile.

I had only to look at Zachary's face to know I was feeling a thousandth of what he was. I'd never seen so much elation, so much pain.

'Sweet girl—' Philip's voice was rocky '—you must be an angel. You have brought my heaven to me.'

My throat tightened. All I could do was maintain my smile.

Philip turned his gaze back to Zachary, his hand still wrapped around the back of his neck. 'My little brother. Whose life I ruined by my selfishness. Who I thought I would never see again. I believed I had been locked out of Heaven, separated from him forever as punishment—' Philip choked up and bent his head, unable to continue.

Tears rolled silently down Zachary's cheeks. He didn't even take his eyes off Philip to blink them away.

'I came with you by choice,' Zachary said, his voice both soothing and insistent. 'I am to blame. I attacked you—'

'God damn it, Zachary.' Philip dragged his velvet coat sleeve across his eyes. 'I refuse to hear another word. I caused that situation. I put a gun in your hands. I am the only one to blame.' He turned his swollen eyes to me. 'You are an angel, and you were sent here for my brother. I am elated that, although he is like me, he is not alone.'

I blushed. 'I'm not an angel. Zachary's my friend; I'll be there for him—' I thought of Bess '—for as long as he needs me.'

Zachary caught Philip's wrists. 'Come back with us. I know a way you can leave this place. We'll return – tonight, tomorrow, as soon as is possible, and take you with us.'

'All these years, I have desired nothing more—' Philip smiled '—than to know you had survived the life I doomed you to. In seeing you again, all my prayers have been granted; it seems impossible to desire more. But, of course, I will come with you.'

Zachary beamed, and looked at me. 'Let's go now. Philip, come with us towards the inn, as far as you can.'

Philip smiled, but for a moment didn't seem like he was going to. Then he nodded, and we walked together back down the road. His boot heels tapped firmly, slowly, on the concrete, as if there was all the time in the world.

He turned his face to Zachary's, and it shone, like he'd brought the sun from the crossroads with him. He placed an arm over Zachary's shoulder; an arm that seemed to have become more translucent.

'I love you, my brother,' he said. 'You have brought me more peace today than I dreamed was possible.'

Misgiving stirred inside me, because I could see the mossy shade of Zachary's clothes through Philip's almost-glowing body.

Philip smiled, and he was so bright, it was like looking directly at the sun. My vision glowed bright white and red and black. When the glowing shapes faded, Philip was gone.

Zachary stopped. He turned a slow circle, the ghost of a smile still on his face, as if by keeping it there he could force what had just happened to not be true. 'Philip?' he said.

My breath caught in my throat. I spun too, looking for his brother – I couldn't help myself, though my mind was a step ahead of my heart.

I knew already that Philip was gone. Really gone. The tingling had vanished from my skin like a candle being snuffed out. Glimpses didn't just disappear like that; they had to walk away.

I wanted to be wrong.

'Philip?'

'Zachary,' I said, through the lump in my throat. 'I don't think he's—'

'No, Elizabeth, don't say it.' His smile had gone now, his face whiter than bone. He sprinted back up the road to the patch of light at the crossroads. 'Philip!' he shouted.

I jogged after him. I didn't know what to do. I felt empty, as though I'd witnessed a miracle and then someone had turned off the light. I couldn't begin to imagine what this was going to do to Zachary.

I went straight up to him and caught his hand, holding it tight. His eyes searched every inch of the landscape around us. He even looked up at the sky, as though his brother might be there.

'I don't understand.' His voice was broken. He finally turned his eyes to me. 'Are you able to sense him? Can you tell where he's gone?'

I shook my head, knowing each shake was a jab to his chest. 'He's gone. Completely. I'm so sorry.'

Zachary's eyes widened, then he scrunched them shut.

I grabbed his other hand. I was trembling, but I forced myself to hold his fingers firmly.

'Philip thought he'd been denied Heaven for destroying your life,' I said. 'And you proved to him today that he hadn't. You showed him you were okay. Maybe that's all that was keeping him here – his guilt over you.'

I didn't know if what I was saying was true, but it felt right. I knew there was somewhere else that ghosts were meant to be, whether it was Heaven or Hell or somewhere, something, else entirely. Philip's fading had felt natural, like a beam of light disappearing when the sun goes behind a cloud.

Still, it was too terribly tragic. I imagined meeting my mum and then losing her again, and my eyes welled again.

Zachary kept his eyes closed for a long moment, but as the minutes passed, the heave of his chest grew shallower and more regular.

His eyes were damp when he opened them again, but I could see the storm had passed. 'Let's return home.'

I nodded, and gave his hands one final squeeze before letting go.

We walked back up the road and into the field. The sky had darkened as if it, too, was in mourning, and there was a new chill in the air. I thought vaguely that it might rain, and that I had no umbrella, though it was impossible to care.

Zachary only took a few steps into the field before he stopped walking and pressed his hand to his face, overcome with emotion again. Without thinking, I went to his side, and we wrapped our arms around each other. He was light in my arms, but solid enough for me to feel the tremble of every muscle.

We cried together for a long time. I thought of Philip's loneliness and of his release, of Dad's grief and his recovery, of not remembering Mum and how that might one day have to just be okay. I wanted all this heartache over, for me and for Zachary.

I didn't notice when we both stopped crying, I just realized that the pain had gone. In its place, I was filled with a bittersweet peace. It felt so right to hold Zachary like this, even though I wasn't the one meant to be in his arms. I wished, just for one moment, that I could be Bess, that this could be more than a snatched moment that was never meant to be mine.

Zachary had fallen still too. He unfolded his arms from around my shoulders, as though he'd hugged me in his sleep and had only just become aware of what he'd done. He gave my forehead a slow, deliberate kiss as he stepped back, and it felt like being brushed with a golden feather.

'Philip spoke the truth when he said you are an angel.' His eyes were clear of tears, but soft with emotion. 'You returned my brother to me; you gave Philip peace; you have given me the world again, literally.' He opened his hands and looked around him, as if to lay the existence of the trees, of the sky, at my feet.

I smiled. 'I dug up a bone, Zachary. That's all I did.'

'No. It's not.'

I looked down at the grass. I bit my lip, then looked back up at him. 'I can't imagine how hard today must have been for you. But I'm glad Philip's moved on. It feels like it was the right thing.' I sought for the courage to ask the question that had been floating around my mind. 'Don't you ever feel like . . . you'd want to follow him?'

Zachary inhaled, as though surprised. 'Why would I?'

'Because that's what spirits do. It seems to me that Philip stayed here because he felt so guilty over you, and when he found out you were okay, he was able to leave. You . . .' I sought my mind, not wanting to say the wrong thing. 'There must be some reason why you haven't moved on too. Maybe for you it was Philip too – you felt guilty about what happened, just like he did.'

'I have no desire to leave, Elizabeth.'

'Yes, because you still have to find Bess. But when you find her . . .' I trailed off. The lump returned to my throat.

'I can make no promises about what will happen to me. After what we saw—' he gestured back at the road, and I knew he was thinking of Philip's fading '—I cannot pretend to know how my existence works. Yet I can tell you that I am not done with this world. Look at it.' He gestured again at the trees and sky, and then he gestured at me. 'Look at you.' His voice softened. 'How could I want to leave any of this?'

There was a soft but frantic sensation in my chest, like flowers unfurling. 'But you might not get a choice,' I said.

'I've decided my own destiny thus far—' he held my gaze '—and I intend to continue.' He smiled then, wide, and held out his arm.

I took it, and we turned together into the fields. I tried to calm the fluttering in my chest – he was Bess's – but it was impossible.

I was wobbling over a precipice. I knew that if I fell for him, I really would fall; the end result could only be destruction. But it was too late. I was already mesmerized by the thrill of the free fall.

Chapter Thirty-Seven

We parted outside the inn. Neither one of us attempted to rush our goodbye. The sky hung heavy with late-afternoon dusk, giving his features a brooding edge I knew well from our night-time meetings.

We talked about all the places we'd go together, on days just like this; both places Bess might be and places that just sounded like fun. I could have planned every weekend for months. We parted, agreeing to meet again tonight if the rain held off.

I ran into the inn. I was met with a celebratory, muffled piano jingle from the end of the hallway.

'Dad!' I shrieked. I ran to the dining room without pausing to take off my shoes, and threw my arms around his neck.

Dad grinned, and ran his fingers from the top of the piano keys to the bottom. 'I got the job.'

'I knew it!' I felt giddy, as if I'd spent the day on a bouncy castle. 'Tell me what happened.'

'They acknowledged that the seven-year hole in my CV was not ideal—' he ran his fingers back up the piano keys '—but my overall experience far outweighed that of the other two people interviewing for the job. This helped.' He tugged at his

Ripe Banana Studios T-shirt. 'I worked with some big names in my time.'

I hugged tighter around his neck. 'I am so proud of you.' And I was. I barely had the words to tell him how much. 'When do you start?'

'Three weeks on Monday.'

'So you'll be getting the bus?'

'Yes, but not your one, don't worry.' He smiled. 'I thought I'd give it a few weeks, and then book some refresher driving lessons, just to see how I get on.' He didn't look at me, but his cheeks were pink with pride.

I stood up straight, and did a little dance behind Dad's back. Then I beamed upwards and said a silent thank you, as though it was the sun shining on me and not the dusty glow of the cobwebbed chandeliers.

'I think you deserve a celebratory coffee,' I said.

'That would be lovely, Liz.'

I took a hot chocolate up to my bedroom, which was dark with the impending storm outside. I turned on the light, dumped my satchel on the bed, and drifted to the window. The rain started just as I got there, small spatters streaking across the window, but I really didn't care. As far as I was concerned, the sky was sunshine and rainbows.

Dad was moving on with his life. He hadn't got over Mum, but he'd loosened his grip on his grief, and it had let him move forwards. It was all I'd ever wanted for him.

I'd seen a lot of that today. Philip had let go of his guilt, and he'd literally moved on. And Zachary seemed to be doing the same. He hadn't given up on Bess, but he was finding ways to move his life forwards.

And me . . .?

I turned and looked at my Normality List. 'No nightmares'. 'No Glimpses'. I hadn't achieved either, just like I hadn't remembered Mum or anything else about my past. And though I did have a friend now, though I wasn't bullied in school, I certainly hadn't become 'normal'.

But thinking about Dad and Philip and Zachary, the way they'd managed to move on without rewriting their pasts, made me wonder if it was time for me to do the same. To just...let my issues go. Accept I was always going to see Glimpses, and have amnesia, and then let my new life truly begin.

I folded my Normality List and slotted it into the bin. Then I lay back on my bed and removed my locket from the neck of my dress. I popped it open and looked at the photo of me and Mum. I imagined letting her go, like Philip had done with Zachary. I was never getting her back, not really, not even if I remembered her. Maybe it was time to set her memory free completely.

One more try, I promised. One more big push to replace the mother of my nightmares who hated me with some real memories of her loving me, and then, perhaps, I would let her go.

Chapter Thirty-Eight

'So what do you think?' Susie's mum watched me through eyes rimmed with glittery green eyeshadow. 'Do courgette cakes make the school menu or not?'

I rubbed cake crumbs off my fingers, careful not to drop them on Marmalade, who was perched on my lap. 'They're actually pretty good. They taste like carrot cake.'

She smiled, and narrowed her eyes at Susie. 'I told you they were nice.'

'Okay, okay, I surrender.' Susie held up her hands. 'Courgette cake is nice. But seriously – change the name, Mum. No one at school's going to eat a cake if they know it's been anywhere near a courgette.'

I smiled and shuffled to the edge of the sofa, forcing Marmalade to ooze off my lap. 'I should really be heading off. Thanks so much for the cake and hot chocolate, Ms Boyd.'

'You're very welcome.' Susie's mum bounced out of her chair. 'Give me a moment and I'll wrap some cakes for you to take with you.' She headed out of the living room.

I turned to Susie and exhaled some of my nerves. I'd been keeping them under control for the last hour since I'd got to her house, but now I was really about to head to Meg's, my jitters were resurfacing.

'Thanks,' I said, 'I needed this.'

'Hey, what are ghost-hunting sidekicks for? Hope Meg's less crazy with you this time.'

'Me too.' I widened my eyes to show how much I meant it. Susie didn't know the half of how weird Meg had been with me. 'If you hear screaming, come and rescue me, will you?' I joked.

'I'll grab Matt and we'll be over in a jiffy.'

I was hoping my visit with Meg today would be third time lucky. As far as remembering my mother was concerned, Meg really was the only one who could help me. I'd let her refuse to answer my questions last time; this time would be different.

I waved goodbye to Susie and her mum as I stepped out of their house, a foil package of warm cakes in my hand.

I arrived at Meg's and rapped on the door with authority, my head held high as I waited for her to answer.

'You again.' Meg sounded so surprised, she forgot to sound crabby. She made a quick recovery. 'I told you not to come back.'

'I know.' I held her narrow-eyed, watery gaze. 'And I promise, this is really the last time you'll see me.' I held out the foil package. 'Ms Boyd sent you some cakes. And I'd like to pay you for a final reading.'

Meg frowned at me. I stepped forwards anyway, pretending she'd already opened the door to me. If what I had planned was to work, I had to be decisive.

To my surprise, Meg stepped mutely aside to let me through. Keeping my steps confident, I pushed past her and headed down the now-familiar narrow hallway. 'I'll put the cakes in here.' I deposited the foil package on Meg's coffee table, then swallowed my nerves and grabbed the bowl of bones from the bookcase.

Meg appeared in the doorway just in time to see me turning around with the bowl. Her confusion shifted quickly to alarm. 'What are you doing? Put that down!'

'I'm sorry, Mrs Sanders—' I pushed gently past her, back into the hallway '—but I need to speak to you in private today. I'll put your bowl somewhere safe. I'll be back soon.'

Steeling myself, I marched towards the front door.

Meg's, 'But . . . but . . . wait!' followed me into the street.

I held the bowl in front of me, trying not to look at its contents, as I turned right out of Meg's front garden. Guilt pinched me – I wouldn't have dared to do this if Meg hadn't been so old and frail – but I ignored it. Removing Ann's bones from Meg's house was the only way I could think of getting Meg to speak openly with me.

I headed down the street away from Susie's house, away from the centre of the village. My heart beat like a kid throwing a tantrum.

I kept my focus on my skin as I speed-walked through residential street after residential street. It took only five minutes for me to feel the first prickling. I braced myself. Here we go . . .

'What do you think you're doing, Elizabeth?' Ann's voice next to my ear was cold, but the anger bubbling beneath it was just as scary as her screams on Thursday night.

Ann swerved out from behind me and danced in front of me, making me gasp, despite myself. She made a single, futile swipe at the bowl, as if she couldn't help but try. It felt like being attacked by dead leaves. She bared her teeth in frustration.

I didn't let myself swerve off my path. I kept my gaze straight ahead; I had no idea who could be watching me from their windows.

'You believe you're so clever, don't you,' Ann said, 'with your skin and your bones and your heartbeat.' She was a couple of inches shorter than me, and had to tilt her head back to snarl in my ear. 'So clever to be alive. So superior to me.'

'I don't think anything like that,' I said, trying not to move my lips too obviously in case anyone was watching. 'But since we're talking about it – yes, I think I'd be cleverer than to stay on earth for a boy who doesn't even like me.'

Ann laughed. 'You believe I stay for him? Zachary will be the jewel in my crown, true. But he is not the only reason I haunt here.'

'So what are you trying to prove? Why attack me? Why stop me talking to Meg?'

I turned a corner, not far now. Last night I'd marked the distance Zachary could move from his body and guessed that I needed to take Ann's bones the equivalent distance from Meg's house now, to make sure she wouldn't be able to follow me back.

Ann stayed by my side. 'I'll prove to you what I can do, Elizabeth. Oh, I will. You wait. I'm cleverer than you credit.'

I couldn't get a handle on her; she veered so quickly between displays of pure lunacy and apparent coherence. All I knew was that I'd be stupid to underestimate her power.

At the end of the street, I looked around for a place to hide the bones. I couldn't wait to get rid of them.

Ann regarded me with a deeply unimpressed expression. I ignored her. I found a tree on the street corner with a nettle patch at its base, and used the tip of my shoe to push the bowl between the nettles and out of sight.

Then I turned and ran, my long dress flapping around my legs.

Ann ran alongside me, screeching and careening. I couldn't tell if she was genuinely crazed or just trying to disturb me, but I was relieved when we reached the road before Meg's and Ann finally lagged behind me, unable to follow.

'I'll be waiting for you at the inn tonight, Elizabeth!' she called, her hands cupped around her mouth, her voice sweet as though she was inviting me to a party. 'Don't be late.'

On Meg's street, I slowed to catch my breath and wait for the tingling on my skin to fade. Ann's words made me uneasy, but I forced myself to push them to the back of my mind. I had more pressing concerns.

I knocked on Meg's door, for the second time in twenty minutes. For a moment, I thought she might not let me back in – that my theft had been a step too far – but then the door opened a fraction, and I saw Meg's eye at the gap. She seemed more concerned than angry.

'I'm sorry, Mrs Sanders,' I said, meaning it. 'I know that was bad of me. But I'm desperate. I need answers.'

The door creaked wider, then all the way open. 'Do you know the trouble you're going to get me into?' Meg demanded. But it wasn't a 'no'.

I took the open door as a good sign and stepped inside. Meg shut the door behind us.

'Ann knows I took the bones,' I said. 'She can't blame you.'

'I don't know about that.' Extra wrinkles formed around Meg's lips. She gestured down the hallway towards the living room. 'Well, hurry up. I'll give you a minute, no more. And as far as Ann's concerned, I haven't spoken to you at all – I sent you straight back to get the bowl, understood?'

I nodded enthusiastically, and took a seat on the sofa as Meg took her usual spot in her armchair. Her eyes darted to where the bowl of bones should be, and she sagged.

I leapt straight into my questions. 'Is Bess still haunting?'

Meg started. 'Good God, girl, you don't beat about the bush.'

'Is she?'

'Yes.'

Excitement, tempered by a touch of selfish disappointment that I couldn't suppress, flared through me. 'Where is she?'

'That—' Meg fixed me with her gaze, her expression grim '—you really will have to find out on your own. I absolutely cannot help you with that.'

'Because of Ann?'

Meg hesitated, then gave a single nod. 'Because of Ann.'

'But she doesn't have to know you told me.'

'Oh, she would know.' Meg raised her sparse eyebrows.

I changed tack. 'So, Ann knows where Bess is?'

Meg hesitated again, nodded again. 'She does, but you didn't learn that from me.'

I nodded. I tried to imagine telling Zachary.

'Is that it?' Meg asked. She cast a nervous glance at the door.

'No.' I shifted closer to the edge of the sofa. I'd done my part for Zachary, now I needed to focus on myself. 'I need to know about my mother.'

Meg sighed, and started to shake her head.

'Please Mrs Sanders. I remember nothing about her.' I fumbled with my locket, unclasped it and opened it, and thrust it into Meg's hand. 'Look. This is her. Just give me something.'

I hesitated, then: 'If you can't tell me anything else, at least tell me if she still loves me.'

Meg looked down at the locket for a long moment. Then she snapped it shut and slid to the edge of her chair. She handed the necklace back to me, and folded my fingers around it with hers. Her skin was dry and papery.

'Your mother loves you,' she said, her voice low and sympathetic.

Relief flooded through me. I focused on our linked hands. *My mother loves me.*

'But the woman in that photo,' Meg said, her voice even more sympathetic than before, 'doesn't.'

I jerked my hand away from Meg's. 'What?'

Meg shrugged. 'You asked me. I answered.'

I fastened my locket quickly around my neck. 'For a minute there, I thought you were actually going to help me. But you still can't give me a straight answer, can you?'

'Oh, you poor child. That woman—' she pointed at my locket '—that woman hates you. But it's not your fault. Ann is your enemy here, not me.'

With surprising speed, Meg grabbed my hand back between hers. I stiffened my fingers in hers, but she held tight anyway. 'Here's my final piece of advice. Take it and think about it, because it's the best I can give you.' Her gaze fixed on mine. 'I warned you about the boy, and you ignored me. It's too late now to ask you to give him up. But think long and hard about him, my dear. He's the reason Ann has it in for you. He's the answer to everything.'

She sat back in her chair, leaving me stunned.

'Now, go and get my bones.'

I barely noticed my run back to the street where I'd hidden

the bowl. Meg's words echoed like a gunshot in my mind, repeating over and over with my footsteps. *She hates you. She hates you, she hates you, she hates you.*

Get out, get out, get out.

It didn't help me to know my mother both loved me and hated me. I didn't want my mother to hate me at all. I needed to believe my nightmares were just that – dreams and nothing more substantial. Nothing to do with my real mum.

As for Zachary being the answer to everything, that made no sense either. Obviously he was the reason Ann hated me, but he had nothing to do with my mum or my amnesia or anything else in my life.

I reached the tree where I'd hidden the bones, and nudged the bowl out of the nettles with my shoe, stinging my ankles in the process. I returned the bowl to Meg without saying a word.

I headed back to the inn.

I'd made my final push to learn something about my mother, and it had failed.

Chapter Thirty-Nine

I flopped onto my bed. I had failed. I was tired of this – of getting my hopes dashed; tired of never learning anything new about my mum, of never remembering; tired of these fears that she didn't love me, these nightmares.

I unclasped my locket and dropped it on my bedside table. I could always put the locket back on, could always try again to remember my mother. But for now, I just needed some peace. My heart couldn't take any more.

With my bedroom door still open, I could hear Dad moving around, followed by a burst of melody from the piano. His music was becoming as pervasive as the blare of his TV had been, and I loved it. Tonight, the melody was melancholy and romantic.

I went to the window and looked out at the woods. Maybe it was the effect of Dad's music, but I couldn't help my thoughts turning to Zachary. Every time I pictured my life moving forwards – like Dad's had, like Philip's had, like Zachary's was starting to – Zachary was involved.

When I was being realistic, I imagined finding Bess for him, then remaining his friend. When I was being fanciful, I imagined much more. I imagined the impossible.

The impossible. A ghost and a living girl. A highwayman who loved Bess, yet ended up with me.

Scott and Crowley moved around on the gravel below me, loading Scott's car boot with tools, but I ignored them, thinking only of Zachary walking out of the woods later tonight. I knew the way he'd look, I knew the way he'd smile, I knew the way his arms would feel around me if my daydreams played out.

Around 10 p.m., Scott's car pulled out of the driveway, headlights bright in the fallen night. I was glad – I didn't want to have to think about Scott, I wanted Zachary to be the only thing on my mind tonight.

Zachary must have seen me at the window, because a few minutes after Scott left, gravel crunched lightly far below.

I looked over my shoulder at the door. Dad was still playing his piano. It was risky seeing Zachary this early, but I'd hear Dad if he started to come upstairs. I couldn't wait another three hours.

I closed my bedroom door and opened the window. Zachary looked up at me, his skin luminescent in the moonlight, his smile huge.

'Come up,' I whispered down to him.

I didn't move away from the window this time as he climbed. I watched every movement – the easy way he swung upwards, from branch to branch, reaching for his next handhold without needing to look. When he stood up on the branch that led to my window, the moonlight brightening his smile and contouring his body with shadow, my insides twisted, though not with the fear he'd fall.

He thudded into my bedroom, bringing the scent of trees and earth. 'Who's that playing the piano?' he asked, surprised. 'It's delightful.'

'My dad.' I smiled. 'He's still up. You're early.'

'I've arrived at the conclusion that life is too short to wait.'
He smiled too, not without irony. 'Your father cannot see me,
but if you'd rather I came back later—'

'No. This is fine.'

He nodded. He looked awkward suddenly, as though he
wasn't sure what to do with himself – a first for him. His gaze
swept the room, dismissing the bed, then he curled to the floor,
like he'd done on the night he'd told me his story.

He arranged his long legs. 'So how was your meeting with
the spirit-seer?'

I curled down next to him, crossing my legs, leaning back
on my hands, mirroring his posture. It would have been more
comfortable sitting on the bed – assuming he could sit on the
bed – but this felt just as intimate. Curled between the bed and
the wall, we were in our own private space.

'It was . . . interesting,' I said. I'd told Zachary my plans to
talk to Meg last night. 'The trick with the bones worked. It
got Ann out of the way, and Meg told me more than she did
last time. But I'm still not sure I can trust her. She did tell me
something interesting about Bess though.'

Zachary raised his eyebrows, looking more alert. 'What?'

I leaned forwards and spoke in a hushed voice. 'Meg told me
Bess is still here somewhere, that she hasn't moved on. She also
told me that Ann knows where she is.'

A cloud darkened Zachary's face. His posture, casual
before, grew stiff. 'I should have trusted my instincts.' He
sounded mad with himself. 'Ann denied any knowledge of
what happened.'

'Meg didn't say Ann caused it. Just that she knew where
Bess was.'

Zachary leaned forwards, matching me. 'Then I will ask her again. And this time I won't desist until she tells me. Thank you, Elizabeth, for the information. It'll be easier to talk to Ann now I know for certain she's been lying.'

I gave him a sympathetic smile. I was sure that nothing Zachary said could make Ann reveal something she didn't want to, short of him pledging his eternal love to her. Zachary's grim expression told me he knew it too.

'How about you?' He tapped the bottom of my foot with the toe of his boot. 'Did you find out what you wanted about your mother?'

I rolled my eyes, and explained what Meg had said about my mum both loving and hating me. 'Then she said something else that made even less sense. She told me—' I played with a ring on my finger '—she told me you were the answer to everything.'

Zachary's forehead creased. 'The answer to what?'

'She wasn't clear. I don't think she's capable of giving a straight answer. She just said to think harder about my connection with you.'

'You see me as if I'm alive,' he said. 'You help me, and I help you – as little as I'm able. We're—' he hesitated '—friends. What else is there to know?'

I shrugged. We held each other's gaze a long moment, each scrutinizing the other. I noticed little flecks of brown in the green of his eyes, the way the scar on his jaw was slightly indented, the dusty texture to his hair as though he'd been sprinkled with soil, but nothing that was the answer to everything. At least, not in the way Meg meant.

My cheeks started to feel too warm. I leaned back on my hands. 'I don't know how much I trust her. She might have just been trying to confuse me.' I licked my lips. 'So what are you going to do about Bess?'

Zachary sighed. 'Elizabeth, you know how much I love her.'

'I do.' I kept my voice neutral.

'She was my world for so long. And I am going to do everything possible to get her back.' He shifted, as though uncomfortable. 'But I have to say, since meeting you . . .'

He trailed off, and I held my breath.

'Since meeting you, I've remembered there's a world outside my own. I have no desire to be like my brother.' Pain flashed through his eyes. 'I don't want my sole existence to consist of waiting for something, searching for something.'

He could have been speaking of me and my mother, as much as about him and Bess. I didn't want to spend my life waiting to remember my mum.

'I wish Bess hadn't gone,' he said. 'Yet I also know that if she hadn't, nothing would have changed. Bess and I would be continuing the same routine, meeting every night, discussing events that occurred centuries ago, eavesdropping on the lives continuing without us.'

'I understand,' I said. And I meant it – completely. 'I want to move on from my past too. For the same reasons. I want a future and a life.'

'Then we understand each other.' He tapped my foot with his again. I tapped him back, making him smile. 'If Bess comes back, I won't return to my old ways. I'd like you to remain my friend. I'd like us to go to all those places we talked about.'

I smiled, though something clawed and wailed in the pit of my stomach at the mention of the word 'friend'. 'Glad to hear it,' I said.

'And you?' He brushed the hem of my dress, his fingers skating through the lace. 'What happens next, with your mother?'

'I think it's time to give her a break. Like you said, I don't want my existence to be taken up with searching for something that might be impossible to find.'

'Sounds a wise decision.'

I nodded, and played with my dress hem where he'd touched it. 'I'm ready for a future too. I have one good friend at school, but I want to make more. I want to get involved in some of the activities at school this year. I've always been too scared I'd make a fool of myself, and I'm tired of it. This is my last year at school, and maybe of being at home with my dad, and I want to make it as perfect as it can be.

'And I'm looking forward to being your friend too. In that future.' It wasn't what I wanted to say at all, but my cheeks flared anyway, as if I'd said what I really meant. *If we don't find Bess, I want to be more than your friend.*

He said nothing, but he smiled, more with his eyes than his mouth. Then he lifted my hand, his eyes on mine, and kissed the backs of my fingers. His lips were firm yet soft on my skin. It wasn't a promise, but it wasn't a 'no' either.

Dad chose that moment to creak past my bedroom door, both ruining and saving me from a moment almost unbearably intense.

'Are you going to bed soon, Liz?' His voice floated through the door. 'School in the morning.'

'Yes, Dad,' I called.

His footsteps creaked on, punctuated by the bang of his bedroom door.

'I should let you retire,' Zachary said. 'That was another

reason for coming here earlier. I've been keeping you up too late.'

I nodded, though I didn't want him to leave. Not ever. 'Stay a little longer?'

'It would be my pleasure.'

I got ready in the bathroom, changing into my longest nightdress. When I got back to my room, I turned off the light and climbed under the covers. My thudding heart calmed almost instantly. It should have been a big deal to have a boy in my room at night, but it didn't feel like it with Zachary. He was barely a shadow in the darkness next to my bed, but his calm breathing relaxed me. When he reached his hand under the covers to hold mine, I knew I wouldn't have nightmares tonight.

I drifted towards sleep. Images and music swirled through my mind as my dreams descended.

Zachary's whisper cut through them. 'Elizabeth, I have to go.' There was a sense of urgency to his voice that pulled me out of my sleep, but only for a moment. My dreams sucked me back down.

'I'll return tomorrow night,' he whispered.

I nodded into the pillow, and sleep reclaimed me. Zachary filled every dark velvet fold of my dreams, and I found Meg was right – he really was everything.

Chapter Forty

Someone grabbed my arms and yanked me upright in bed. It was like being tipped from sleep into a bath of icy water. I choked on a gasp. I only had a split second to register the bulky figure standing over me in the dark before something coarse plunged over my head, blinding me, scratching my skin, forcing a scream from my lungs.

Hands grabbed my ankles. I kicked out, too late. I squirmed, but more hands grabbed my arms. Pain shot through my shoulders, the bed dropping away, as the hands lifted me, swinging me blindly through the air.

I screamed again, my breath humid against the sack. My mind was fully awake now. Disorientated.

I tried to shout for Dad, but panic destroyed my words. All that came out was a wail.

'Shut up or you're dead,' Crowley's voice growled above me.

Suddenly, it was impossible to breathe. My thoughts fogged with panic.

The floorboards groaned like something in pain. Electric light seeped through the holes in the sacking. My head tipped downwards as they carried me down the stairs. I swung from side to side with their footsteps, my joints protesting.

I found my voice, though it shook. 'What are you doing?'

'Shut it. No one's going to help you.' Scott was with him.

I was too panicked to cry. I hyperventilated into the sack, inhaling dust and mildew. There wasn't enough air.

Crowley and Scott's footsteps shifted from creaking floorboards to the crunch of gravel. Cold air oozed through the holes in the sack and prickled over my skin. Their footsteps shifted again, from gravel to concrete. We were at the outbuildings.

I braced myself, expecting to be dropped, but instead Crowley grunted above me and my head tipped downwards. We were going down more stairs – some kind of a basement below the outbuildings?

Why this was happening, I had no clue. A thousand scenarios – kidnap, rape, murder – ran through my mind. But why would Crowley and Scott want to do me any harm?

The air grew colder as we moved downwards. Crowley swore whenever he stumbled, which was often. He almost dropped me more than once. Electric lights shone orange through the burlap. Scott's breathing was loud and violent.

After what felt a long while, the ground slammed into my back. My elbows saved my head from another whack. Pain ricocheted up my arms, but I couldn't think of that now. I struggled, fighting to find the opening of the sack.

When I got free, I took stock of my immediate surroundings. I was in an underground room. Propped upright against the wall like a rag doll was Dad.

Pins and needles spread through my body. In the corner stood the reason for all this. Ann.

Chapter Forty-One

In one glance, I took everything in. Small red-brick room, jagged walls, floor crumbling into brick dust, curved ceiling – and only one possible exit, guarded by Crowley and Scott. Ann danced from foot to foot, gleeful as a fool, watching me.

I ran to Dad, dropped to my knees and put my hands to his face. He was warm, his skin damp. His chest rose and fell, but his breaths were shallow.

I looked up at Ann. Anger boiled like acid through my veins, overriding my fear. 'What have you done to him?'

She clasped her hands behind her back and rocked on the soles of her shoes, like a proud child. 'Good morning to you too, Elizabeth.' Her voice was sweet. 'He's not hurt. Simply drugged. I brought him here to ensure you cooperate.'

I had never wanted to hit anyone before now, but I wanted to slap her, claw at her. I wanted to destroy her.

'He's nothing to do with you. You should never have brought him into this. All because you're jealous? You're crazy.'

I turned now to Crowley and Scott, appealing to them with my sheer outrage, certain that if they only saw how stupid this was they'd let me and Dad go.

But something was wrong. They stared at the wall in front of them, unseeing, eyes void. Terror gripped me. Ann was no longer an annoyance who couldn't hurt me. She had power. It was one thing controlling Meg, but these were two fully grown, strong men.

Scott's warnings . . . Too late, I realized what he'd been warning me against, I thought of the bone in my bag. Scott must have been under Ann's spell all this time.

I faced Ann, wary. 'Why am I here?'

'Because you refused to listen.' She took dainty steps towards me. Tap, tap, tap.

I stepped back, brick shards digging into my bare feet.

'Because I told you, multiple times, to stay away from Zachary. I gave you a chance. And you ignored me, every time.'

'So what now?' I glanced at Scott and Crowley, at their military stance. 'You're going to get them to hurt me?'

'Yes.' Ann smiled, showing her tiny white teeth.

'For talking to Zachary?'

'No, not for just talking to Zachary.' Ann's smile grew hard. 'For being you.' She spat the word. 'For refusing to stop being you.'

I reached instinctively for a locket that wasn't there.

'For always acting like you were better than me,' Ann said. 'For swanning around this inn like you're the best thing that ever happened to it. For bewitching Zachary. For coming back.'

'I don't know what you're talking about. I only just moved here. I was a child the last time I was—'

Ann laughed, a noise like breaking glass. 'You are so incredibly dumb. I know all about you. About your nightmares, your lost memories, your poor mother, and – oh dear – all these nasty spirits you see. You truly are witless.' Her smile was smug.

'I don't understand.'

Ann stopped her slow advance. She snapped her fingers at Scott. 'Fetch.'

I watched in fascinated horror as Scott scuttled from the room, returning a moment later with the painting of Bess. He propped it against the wall where Ann pointed, then retreated to his post by the door.

Ann moved next to the painting and crooked a finger conspiratorially to me. 'Let me tell you a story.'

I moved a few steps forward, uncertain, keeping my distance. Her words were calm, but she was like a ticking bomb.

'You see this girl?' Ann pointed at the painting. She didn't wait for a response. 'Elizabeth. Or Bess, as she is better known.' Ann's lips twitched. 'She worked alongside me, before we passed over, and the way she carried on, you'd have thought she was royalty round here. Oh, look at my dark curls,' Ann simpered, tugging at her hair, 'look at my dresses, see how intelligent I am. No one even noticed me, because I was a simple barmaid, and she – Queen Bess – was the innkeeper's daughter.

'Then along came Zachary. He saw me first, but one glance at Bess, and he was bewitched. It was sickening; they acted so in love. Bess flaunted herself with him. Each night I watched him climb up to her window. If it hadn't been for Bess, it would have been me he came to visit.'

I glanced at Dad. I needed to get him out of here. 'What has this story to do with me, Ann?'

'Patience,' she snarled. 'I was always underestimated. No

one saw what I was, who I could be, because Bess blocked out my light. And after we passed, it got worse.' She rolled her blue eyes. 'Can you imagine two hundred years of watching her with Zachary? Centuries of seeing paintings made of her, poems being written about her? Can you?' Her voice trembled.

I opened and closed my mouth. I shook my head. I didn't know what to say.

Ann cocked her head to the side and smiled. 'But you see, I'm smarter than Bess. I always was. I found a way to travel. I made deals with Meg, and our Mr Crowley here.' She nodded an acknowledgement to him. 'I procured information. I didn't languish, like Bess did. I discovered, for example, that souls can enter human bodies as they lie dying. When one soul comes out, then, smooth as you like, in we can slip, taking their place. Your Mr Crowley over there, that body is his second vessel. He has been with me a long time.' She smiled fondly in his direction.

My stomach churned. It couldn't be true. But Crowley didn't deny it. Scott didn't even blink.

'The only problem,' Ann continued, 'with a soul entering a new body, is that it's extremely traumatic. The soul tends to forget things, even their true identity. Luckily for Mr Crowley, I was there to remind him. If not—' she smiled at me '—well he'd be just like you, wouldn't he? All forgetful.'

Ann jigged in front of the painting, tiny skipping steps. 'The day the accident happened, right in front of my inn, I saw an opportunity. I'm clever like that.' She swivelled and looked at me. 'I knew dear Bess would come running, all worried and tender and wanting to help the poor, mangled family, and then with one little push,' Ann shoved her hands through the air between us, 'Poof! Bess would be gone, Zachary forgotten.'

I choked on my own breath. 'What are you trying to say – you crazy, crazy—'

'And it worked.' Ann beamed. 'You don't remember a thing. Seven whole years, you were gone.' Her smile hardened. 'Then you returned, like a curse. You bewitched Zachary. Again. I warned you, but you didn't listen. Again.'

I backed away until I hit the wall. I pressed my hands against it, bricks crumbling to dust. 'You're even crazier than I thought.' My voice shook. 'Are you trying to tell me that – that I'm Bess?'

Ann sighed.

She had this all wrong. In her delusion, she had made a huge mistake. She was going to hurt me over something that wasn't even true.

'Scott,' I called across the room. 'There's no way you can believe this.'

'I tried to warn you.' Scott shrugged, not meeting my eye. 'It's not my fault what happens to you now.'

I gaped between Scott, Crowley and Ann. They were mad. All of them. Not remembering my past proved nothing.

'Zachary behaves like you're Bess,' Ann said. 'Meg tried to tell you – I intend to make her suffer for it. I thought I'd disposed of you once, but back you came. So now I need to dispose of you again. For good this time.'

She snapped her fingers at Scott. He walked towards me, still not meeting my eye.

I wanted to back away. I wanted to run. But there was nowhere for me to go. 'Scott, don't be stupid.' I looked at Ann. 'What are you going to do?'

'Well. I'm going to have you killed. And then Mr Crowley is going to take your bones – both sets – and throw them in the sea, far away from Zachary. Which is what I should have had him do in the first place.' She sighed. 'Ah, well, we all learn.'

Scott went to the corner of the room and picked something out of the dust.

A hunting rifle.

I could do nothing but gasp for air.

Scott stopped a metre away from me. The gun shook in his hands.

'Seriously,' I garbled, 'please. You can't . . .'

'Walk out of this room and back to the inn.' His voice jumped as much as mine.

Ann sighed. 'Scott darling, be a man about it.'

Scott flinched. Then he squared his jaw and bridged the gap between us.

I stumbled sideways away from him. Something jabbed my ribs and I froze.

Hard, cold metal.

'Up to your room,' Scott repeated, more firmly.

I held my hands out to the side. Then I walked forwards – past Dad, past Ann, past Crowley, who opened the door. Scott followed, a single pace behind me, so close I could smell his aftershave and sweat.

We entered a long, low-ceilinged corridor, dark but for the dim light coming from a staircase at the end.

The moment Ann was behind us, I shifted against the gun at my back, trying to twist to see Scott. He was my link to the real world and my only hope – he had to let me go.

But he just prodded me with the gun barrel. 'Keep moving.'

The metal was cold through my nightdress, the jab to my spine strong enough to bruise.

My eyes filled with tears. I thought of Lucy, the drowned girl, and realized Scott really might intend to kill me. I hadn't even said bye to Dad.

Scott's heavy breathing and the constant pressure of the gun in my back forced me to walk fast. I wanted to slow to a crawl, give the world time to make sense, but there was no time. I forced my quaking legs up the staircase at the end of the corridor, Scott still my shadow.

We emerged into Crowley's office. The rug had been thrown back, revealing the trapdoor. All this time, while Dad had been playing piano and I'd been in my room thinking of Zachary, Scott and Crowley could have been underground with Ann.

'Don't do this, Scott,' I said, struggling to keep my voice calm. I had to bring some reason back to this situation. 'I know you. You don't want to do this. Just let me go.'

'Too late. I gave you enough chances.' His voice jumped with nerves. 'Don't think about running when we get outside. I'll shoot you the second you move.'

My hand shook almost too much to open the door, but I managed it. The driveway was bathed in grey light and early morning dew. I hobbled out onto it, gravel sticking into my bare feet.

'Were you spying on me this whole time? For her?'

'Open the inn door.'

The inn was cool and dark and silent inside. Scott jabbed me towards the stairs.

'Not this whole time.' His voice was resentful. 'My dad wanted me to help right from the start, right from when you

285

moved here, but you know what, Liz? I wanted to help you.'
He jabbed me again, making me wince.

We were almost at my bedroom now. And after that – there
was nowhere else, unless I jumped out of the window.

'I warned you, so many times, not to get involved with that
highwayman. I even wanted to be your friend. If you'd just
listened, none of this would be happening. But you threw it all
back in my face.'

I stumbled into my room, then turned to face him, my
hands up. Scott's face was twisted and blotched. Sweat stuck
his hair to his forehead in wet spikes. Dark patches stained the
underarms of his shirt.

'I didn't know,' I pleaded. I had to make him hear me. I had
to make him want to stop. 'Please, Scott, I thought you were
just being mean. I didn't know you were trying to help.'

'You never gave me a chance.' Spit flecked the corners of
his mouth. He let the gun drop to his side, gesticulating at me
with his other hand. 'You knew nothing about me, but you
judged me just like everyone else. I didn't kill Lucy, you know
that? She was my friend, my friend who died. It was a terrible
accident, but everyone just assumed it was me. Even you, and
you don't know me. Can you even begin to imagine what
that's like?'

I shook my head. 'I'm sorry. You're right. But if you . . .' I
gestured at the gun. It was hard to even say the words. 'If you
. . . shoot me, then you will be guilty. Why would you do that?
Why would you do that for Ann?'

'Because she appreciates me.'

He stepped into my bedroom, forcing me to retreat until the
bed hit the back of my legs. But the gun stayed by his side, and
that was all I cared about – that gun not pointing back at me.

'And my dad appreciates me. They both think I'm worth something. Unlike you. Unlike everyone else in this village.' He looked down at the gun.

Panic choked in my throat. 'But what about your friends?'

He snorted. 'They're not real friends. They're just the only ones who'll talk to me. And they'd betray me in a flash.'

'But you can't believe Ann's telling the truth? She's mad, Scott. I'm not Bess. I'm not!'

He gave a one-shouldered shrug. 'I saw Bess . . . you, whatever . . . and that highwayman around the inn when I was a kid. You don't seem that much different now. Hanging around in the woods together. Hanging around this room. My dad's gone into another body. Ann says she'll help me do the same when I get old. Kinda like being immortal. So, yeah.' He met my gaze, and this time his eyes were cold. 'I believe that you're Bess.'

The cold space around my heart hardened and froze. I tried to swallow, but my throat was too tight. I backed around the edge of the bed away from him, hands still raised. I thought of dying. Of how it would feel if he shot me. Of being like Zachary, or worse – of just being gone from this world, like my mum.

Observing with eerie detachment, Scott lifted the gun and pointed it at me. His eyes looked into mine, empty as a shark's. 'Don't be afraid. It's not like you haven't died before. You even shot yourself before. I've read the poem. You're meant to be dead.'

I was out of time. There would be no more talking. I threw myself at him, no plan, except I had to get that gun. Scott shoved me with his whole body, spinning me around, and—

BOOM

I opened my mouth to gasp. Nothing came out. My ears rang with the echo of the gunshot. My vision tunnelled, till I could see only the window.

Hot wet blood trickled down my back.

Only then did the pain splinter my body. I tried to scream, but I couldn't. Inky blackness ate my vision. I sank to my knees, and fell onto my side.

Chapter Forty-Two

'Elizabeth! Elizabeth!'

Zachary's face appeared over mine, out of nowhere. I clutched for him, but my body wouldn't work. My fingers groped uselessly on the wooden floor.

His face was white with terror. Blood streaked his skin. I tried to speak but my tongue wouldn't work. Nothing existed but my pain and Zachary's face—

Then, as easily as taking a breath, the pain fell away. Just like that.

'Zachary.' His name burst from my lips like I'd been holding it back for centuries. I reached for him, and this time it worked.

He scrabbled back from me, taking me with him. His eyes were pure white, the green almost eclipsed in his panic. 'No,' he choked.

And I froze. I looked down at my hands, which were grabbing his arms. Long brown sleeves covered my arms, lace at my cuffs. A black plait, longer than my own, swung over my shoulder and into the space between us.

I let go of him. I felt my own body. I stumbled upright, almost tripping on my long skirts. I put my hands to my hair.

I stared at Zachary and then at Scott, who stood rigid in the doorway, white as a corpse, his mouth open. I looked at the gun hanging limply in his hand.

Then I turned very slowly, and looked down at . . . at me . . . lying unconscious on the floorboards, blood oozing from my back.

'Bess?' Zachary said.

And the whole world tumbled in.

Scott made a strangled sound and ran from the doorway, dropping the gun with a clatter. Zachary's arms, more solid than they'd ever been, were a vice around my waist, stopping me from falling.

'Bess.' Zachary was embracing me and I clung to him, the right shape for him. I knew every part of him, though we hadn't touched like this before. He leaned back from me, holding my face. Tears ran down his cheeks. Questions spilled from him, barely coherent. 'What were you doing? Where have you been?'

I had no answer. I didn't understand anything. But I felt like I was starting to. My dress fitted better than skin. Zachary's arms were the structure the world had been missing.

But the girl on the floor . . .

I looked back at her.

'Ann told me. She told me I was Bess.' I frowned. 'She told me—' I pointed at the girl, at me '—she told me . . . in the car accident, I . . . went in someone else's body . . . she shoved me into that body.' I shook my head. My thoughts were so confusing, they were painful.

Zachary put his lips to my forehead.

I put my hand to my mouth. The shape was unfamiliar and familiar at the same time, like the worst case of déjà vu.

'She's dying.' My voice hitched. My eyes blurred, turning the girl on the floor into a kaleidoscope of white and red.

Zachary gasped for a breath. 'Don't go anywhere,' he said. And he ran from the room.

I didn't know what to do. I ran to the doorway, then stopped and ran back. I stooped to the girl, tried to put my hand over the hole oozing blood, but pushed right through her body. I staggered back, careening through the bed, gasping as the mattress floated around my knees.

A shout from outside turned my head to the window. I staggered there so fast I almost fell, but when I looked outside, everything inside me went still.

Below me, Scott raced down the driveway towards the road, kicking gravel, stumbling, arms flailing, crying like an animal that knows it's caught.

Zachary ran behind him, straight and solid as a bullet. Scott turned back and saw him, yelped again, ran faster.

The two of them stumbled through the open inn gates, out into the road. Zachary flew around Scott, a vicious whirlwind. He couldn't touch Scott, but Scott ducked and spun and cried out in terror all the same.

Brakes squealed. A car ploughed into view. On the pavement, a woman shrieked. Zachary backed away, hands raised. But I wasn't looking at him. I was looking at Scott's body, a crumpled heap in front of the car.

The woman stumbled from her position by the inn's gates. Meg! She called out to Zachary.

My grip on the windowsill loosened. I grabbed for a handhold – the bed frame, the wardrobe – but my hands slipped through everything. I tipped backwards, landing on the body on the floor.

And suddenly, there was pain again. My body exploded with it. I screamed for Zachary, screamed for the pain, screamed until everything went black.

Chapter Forty-Three

The lights were too bright, even through my eyelids. I kept my eyes closed until I was forced to open them.

'Elizabeth? Liz?' a woman called softly. I opened my eyes to see a kind face looking down at me, but even that movement sparked pain. I moaned and closed my eyes again. There was an odd, tugging sensation at the back of my hand, and the pain flowed away with my consciousness.

The touch on my arm woke me. The room was darker now, the only light yellow and unnatural. Dad's face was haggard and lined. I smiled at him as best as I could, my muscles working hard to locate themselves.

Thank God. He was okay.

Dad smiled, and patted my arm with his fingertips, as though I was glass that might shatter. Behind a veil in my mind a hundred dim shapes took form – a gun, a girl on the floor, Zachary, blood, Scott, a car. And pain. So much pain.

I let myself sink back into oblivion.

A few times, the fog lifted. I felt around in my consciousness, probing for something to hold on to. And I found it. Instead of a meagre trace of memory, a thousand rushed in. Zachary and the inn and my dad and another dad, and a mother – a mother with a soft stomach and a dimpled smile who was not the woman in my locket—

A cool cloth touched my forehead, wiped tears from my eyes. I was in a hospital, and I was hurt, and Dad was by my side.

All the rest of it – Zachary, and . . . Bess – could wait. It was too immense. An unintelligible puzzle. I couldn't look at it now.

Awareness flicked in and out. Daylight came and went. When I opened my eyes tubes would be gone, replaced by smooth, plastic-sheened bandages. My lucidity grew longer and stronger. I tried to keep it under control. I knew understanding was there but I tried not to look at it.

The knowledge of Zachary. The knowledge of Bess.

There was a soft cough by my bed. A doctor squinted down at me, a clipboard tucked against his chest.

'How are you feeling, Elizabeth?'

I struggled to focus my vision. It was hard, like staying awake after being disturbed from a deep sleep. My eyes kept slipping from his face; it was uncomfortable to keep them steady. When I succeeded I saw a balding head and glasses, and an expression of detached concern.

'I've felt better.' The crisp syllables I'd formed in my head came out slurred, but the doctor smiled, some of his worry lifting.

'You've been very lucky. I'm sure your father will tell you everything when you feel up to it.' He looked towards the foot of the bed, to Dad, arms rigid across his chest.

Guilt tugged at me. I'd made Dad worry, again.

The doctor continued, his voice quiet and professional as though he said this kind of thing every day. 'You have sustained a gunshot wound in your back. Fortunately, the bullet missed your spinal cord and didn't hit any organs, but it shattered a couple of ribs and you lost a lot of blood. It was lucky the ambulance was able to get to you as fast as it did.'

The doctor pretended to look at his clipboard, but his eyes stayed on me. I looked back as steadily as I could.

'We've got you stable, and your temperature's down so we're not worried about infection. We'll be moving you to the main ward within a few days. The nurse will be round to see you later, and maybe we'll try solid food in a couple of hours. It's looking good, Elizabeth.' He flashed me a smile, like the final act in a much-practised routine. 'I'll tell the nurses you can receive visitors now.' He replaced the clipboard at the foot of the bed and headed for the door.

Dad walked over and made a show of plumping my pillows. I winced as the small movement shot pain through my torso. Dad froze.

'I'm okay,' I whispered.

He sank into the chair next to my bed, his shoulders hunched. His hair was unbrushed and flat on one side as if he'd just woken up. 'Oh, Liz. I'm so sorry you're here again.'

'It's not the same as last time.'

'No. You remember who I am.'

I didn't say anything. If what Ann said was true, if I was really someone else – if I wasn't Liz – it explained why I hadn't known my own dad after the car crash.

And it explained a lot more than that. My amnesia, my nightmares, the way I was so different from the little girl in

295

Dad's photos, the reason I didn't remember my mother, my feelings for Zachary, my connection with him that made him so alive to me . . .

But just because it made sense, didn't mean it felt real. I was less disorientated than the last time I'd woken in hospital, but the life I'd woken into – the one where I might be someone else – still didn't seem quite my own.

I moved my hand across the blanket towards Dad. All I knew was that, whatever the truth, he would always be my father.

'I'm okay,' I said. 'Really.'

He squeezed my hand. 'I know. You're going to be fine. I'm just so happy to still have you.' His face crumpled, but he held himself together. 'And I'm not the only one. Look at all these.'

He wiped his eyes, and picked up a pile of already-open cards lying flat on the bedside table. He held a few up for me. There was a card from 12G, group cards from my History, English and Geography classes, one from Miss Mahoney, and one from Susie that read 'Thanks for making me do the presentation on my own. Come back soon. Miss you.'

I smiled. I missed Susie too. I wondered what she'd say if she knew what had really happened to me.

I thought of the last time I'd seen Dad, slumped on the floor. 'Dad, tell me what happened. There's too much I don't understand.'

He shifted in his chair. 'Now? I want you to rest, Liz. We can talk about it when you've recovered more.'

'No, Dad.' I made my voice firm, though it hurt to work my lungs harder. 'Please. I need to know now.'

He sighed and made a show of propping up my cards. 'There was an attack on the inn,' he said. 'I'll tell you the basics, but I don't want you to worry. It's all being sorted out by the police.'

'Just tell me. All of it. I can handle it.'

There was a long pause. Finally, he spoke. 'The police think the inn was raided by burglars looking for your granddad's antiques.'

Instantly, a weight lifted. Dad had no idea of the truth. But I, in turn, had no clue where the burglary idea had come from.

'They didn't take anything,' he said. 'The police think they scarpered when things went wrong.' His voice slowed, each word dragging from his lips. 'They drugged me, and left me in a cellar under Crowley's office. The police found me down there. I didn't come to till they got me to hospital.

'As for what happened to you . . . The police aren't sure, but they think the attackers panicked when they saw you. Maybe they didn't realize you were in the house. Either way, you ended up . . .' His voice trembled.

I gripped his hand and squeezed it as hard as I could without pain.

'Crowley's been arrested.' Dad had to pause again. 'The police think it was an inside job, that Crowley set it all up. They found the drugs that were used on me in his office.'

'I told you he was bad news,' I said.

'I know. I should have listened. But I just can't believe it. He worked for your granddad for years, ever since his last caretaker died. He knew your mum.' Dad shook his head.

I moistened my dry lips. 'What about Scott?'

Dad held my gaze, more steadily now. 'Scott, now. He, Liz, is the hero in this.'

I did my best to keep my face blank. So Scott was still alive. But . . . hero?

'It seems that Crowley tried to get Scott out of the way

while he was doing the burglary. But Scott came to the inn anyway, and thank goodness he did, Liz. He was just in time to hear the gunshot. From what I understand, he ran into the inn, saw you, and ran into the street to get help. He was so frantic he ran straight into the path of a car—' Dad's eyes narrowed in pain '—but he managed to tell the driver about you before he blacked out. The ambulance mustn't have known what was going on when they got a call about a shooting and a car accident all at the same address. Scott saved your life, Liz.'

Dad smiled but his lips wobbled. I squeezed out a smile. Scott hadn't saved my life, he'd tried to end it. And he was alive; he could still come for me.

'Poor boy's been waiting outside for days. The doctors wouldn't let anyone else in here but me. He'll be overjoyed to know he can see you now.'

No. He couldn't be here.

'It must be tough for him, knowing his father's caused all this,' Dad carried on. 'But he doesn't seem to care. Says he's glad his father's been arrested, that he deserves it for what he tried to do. All he seems to care about is whether you're okay.'

There was a funny look in Dad's eyes now, as if at some private joke. If this was a joke, it was a sick one. I stared at him. I didn't know what he was talking about, but it didn't matter.

Dad let go of my hand and lifted his jacket from the back of the chair.

'Where are you going?' I clutched at the blanket where his hand had been.

'To get a coffee. Give you a chance to absorb what I've said.' He seemed almost in a rush now to get out of the room, or maybe my mind was speeding things up as my final moments of safety ebbed away. 'I'll be back soon.' He patted my hand, left the room without looking back.

'Dad!' I squeaked.

He was already gone. It was too late. My ribs hurt with panic.

The door swung open. A familiar blond head bounded towards me. I struggled, ignoring the pain that screamed through me. I grappled with the wires attaching me to the bed. I had to get free!

Scott's hand clamped down on my arm, pinning it to the bed and covering the tube I'd been trying to tear from my inside elbow.

For a second, I thought my heart would break. It had all been for nothing. I'd survived just to die again.

'Be calm, Elizabeth.'

I looked up at him. His hair was ruffled. His face was soft, a total mismatch with the twist of terror and blank hatred in my last memory of him.

'You shot me,' I said.

Scott's grip relaxed at that and I snatched my arm free. I made a grab for the alarm button by my bed, but he was too quick for me. He caught my hand clumsily, and for the first time I registered the plaster cast on his arm. He folded my fingers in his own so I couldn't press the button.

'All is well,' he said, his voice weirdly soft. He leaned down over me, his face alive with emotion. I watched him like he was a hissing snake.

'Elizabeth . . . Bess . . . it's me!'

Scott lifted his un-bandaged hand to touch my face. I flinched and he let his hand drop.

'Look at me. Look at me, properly.' He leaned over me, the movement sending a familiar scent towards me.

Something earthy, like the night.

I stared at him. There were flecks of green in his blue eyes.

'I stopped Scott. I pursued him into the road and a vehicle hit him. His soul came out of his body. Meg was there – she told me how to take his place.'

I was seeing Scott, but hearing Zachary.

'Crowley and Scott exhumed my remains. That's why I had to leave you on Sunday night. I was so disorientated, I was almost out of my mind. I raced to follow them, until I realized it must be a trap. I managed to return to the inn because you had a part of me that they didn't – in more ways than you know. I arrived just in time to see you . . . to see you injured.' His voice filled with emotion. 'It was then that I realized who you are. I saw you again.'

His hand caressed mine. Hope radiated inside me, molten and nuclear and too, too hot.

But still, I shook my head. 'You shot me.'

His eyes widened. 'Bess, Meg explained this. Ann tricked you into taking another body, and that's how you left me the first time. That's why we didn't recognize each other when you returned. Though I did recognize you – I knew I loved you, I felt our connection, I simply couldn't tell you. I believed you were . . . a different Elizabeth. I believed you were someone else. I felt so guilty.'

I closed my eyes, scrunching them tight. I wanted to erase the whole world. I wanted to open my eyes again, and see only Zachary.

But I didn't. It was impossible. When I opened my eyes, he was still Scott.

I reached up and touched his cheek, despite the ache that splintered through my side at the movement. His skin was soft, but his face was the wrong shape under my palm. 'Prove it then,' I said.

He fixed me to the bed with his gaze, steady and calm, the way Zachary used to. 'We spent every day, every night, together, for lifetimes. When you came to the inn, I thought you were Bess, that very first night; I recognized something in you, but you didn't know me. Mere nights ago, I kissed your hand and told you I wanted you in my future . . .' He trailed off.

Silent tears rolled down my cheeks. My heart expanded with so much hope and fear and joy, I thought it was going to kill me. 'It's really you?' I whispered.

He nodded, and though his lips were the wrong shape, his smile was bright as the moon.

With all my strength I pulled him towards me. He sank over me, his cast across my stomach, his face burying in my curls. I twined my fingers into his too-short hair. He was Zachary, and I would never, ever let him go.

'Is this it? Is this really happening? Can we be together now, for good?'

Zachary pulled back till I could see his face. His expression was solemn but radiant, like he was lit inside by candles. 'Ann's gone. Meg told me she was tired of working with Ann, that she came to the inn that morning to stop Ann's plans. She was devastated she was too late to stop you being hurt. She helped me locate Ann's bones at the inn and we took them all back to the cemetery. Ann can't come near us.'

'And Scott's really gone?'

He nodded, but not happily.

My breathing hitched around a sob, absurd though it was. 'He wasn't bad,' I whispered. 'It was Ann and Crowley. They corrupted him. He tried to warn me, but I rejected and rejected him . . .' I bit my lip to stop myself from crying.

Zachary stroked my hair. 'He put a bullet in you. That was still his choice.'

He glanced at the door, then climbed up onto the edge of the bed next to me. He wrapped his uninjured arm around me, taking care to avoid my bandages, and kissed my lips, so gently. I closed my eyes, blocking out the sight of Scott's face, and just let myself feel his love. It swelled in every part of me, filling the seven-year hole inside me.

I didn't know if I was Bess, or a girl from a poem, or Liz, but I knew I was me. And that was more than I'd had before. It was all I needed.

I reached for my locket, and was surprised to find its familiar heart-shape at my neck. Dad must have put it on me. I stroked its surface, with a bittersweet smile. I knew now why Liz's mother hated me. I knew now why I felt no connection to her. But it was all right. Liz's mother loved Liz – and, it turned out, that wasn't quite who I was.

A finger pressed to mine, over the locket. 'Your mother loved you.' Zachary's voice was soft. 'Do you remember that?'

I nodded. And smiled. Because I did.

The bang of the door reached me through the warm cloud in my head. Zachary scrambled off the bed, awkward with his cast. 'Sir,' he said.

I shifted my head to watch Dad as he walked towards us, polystyrene cup in hand and an embarrassed look on his face. 'I don't know why you've started calling me that, Scott,' he said, 'but you've really got to stop.'

Dad smiled at me, a little too brightly. He drew his chair discreetly back from the bed and slotted himself into it. He kept his eyes averted from Zachary and me, as he peeled the lid from his cup. Instant coffee aroma competed with the scent of the woods in the small room.

'I always thought there was something between you two,' he said into his cup. 'Lifts to school, hanging around outside your window.'

I gave him a sharp look.

'Don't think I didn't notice,' he said, sipping his coffee. 'You pretended to hate each other, but I knew.' He grinned at his drink, but I knew the grin was for me and Zachary.

Zachary's fingers smoothed my hair, stroking each of my curls to the ends as though there was no one in the room but him and me. Dad coughed and shuffled back out of the room, muttering something about sandwiches.

I closed my eyes, letting my imagination fill. The Zachary I knew – all strength and moonlit beauty – loving the girl I'd just learnt I could be.

Who was that girl? Bess? Liz? Or Elizabeth – a fusion of the two?

It didn't really matter. I saw ghosts, I had nightmares, I worried my dad, but I had friends and a boy who loved me. I'd wanted a future, and now I had the prospect of one so bright, it was blinding.

I opened my eyes and watched the love play on Zachary's face. I had my highwayman. And, for the first time in my life, I knew who I was.